CAPTURED!

Hard to write.

They got me this morning.

It grabs your mind. Like before. Squeezing in your head.

But after a while it is better. Feels good. But a buzzing all the time, you can't think.

Picked me up while I was crossing an arroyo. Didn't have any idea they were around. A platform.

Took me to some others. All Egyptians. Been caught like me.

Marched us to the Nile.

All around are the bird-headed ones . . .

> —from Gregory Benford's
> "Of Space-Time and the River"

ISAAC ASIMOV'S
ALIENS

**EDITED BY
GARDNER DOZOIS**

ACE BOOKS, NEW YORK

ISAAC ASIMOV'S ALIENS

An Ace Book/published by arrangement with
Davis Publications, Inc.

PRINTING HISTORY
Ace edition/January 1991

ISBN: 0-441-01672-3

Ace Books are published by The Berkley Publishing Group,
200 Madison Avenue, New York, New York 10016.
The name ''ACE'' and the ''A'' logo are
trademarks belonging to Charter Communications, Inc.
PRINTED IN THE UNITED STATES OF AMERICA

10 9 8 7 6 5 4 3 2 1

CONTENTS

ANGEL *by Pat Cadigan*   1

CRYPTIC *By Jack McDevitt*   21

THE BISHOP'S DECISION
  by Phillip C. Jennings   41

IRIDESCENCE *by Dean Whitlock*   57

THE ALIEN IN THE LAKE *by Andrew Weiner*   75

A MIDWINTER'S TALE *by Michael Swanwick*   85

DINOSAURS *by Walter Jon Williams*   103

TRUE COLORS *by Kathe Koja*   133

TRADING POST *by Neal Barrett, Jr.*   151

PEOPLE LIKE US *by Nancy Kress*   177

THE ROSE GARDEN *by Steven Popkes*   187

OF SPACE-TIME AND THE RIVER
  by Gregory Benford   207

ACKNOWLEDGMENTS

The editor would like to thank the following people for their help and support:

Shawna McCarthy, who purchased some of this material; Sheila Williams, who has labored behind the scenes on *IAsfm* for many years and who played a part in the decision-making process involved in the buying of some of these stories; Susan Casper, who helped me with much of the word-crunching and lent me the use of her computer; Ian Randal Strock and Charles Ardai, who did much of the other thankless scut work involved in preparing the manuscript; Florence B. Eichin, who cleared the permissions; Cynthia Manson, who set up this deal; and especially to my own editor on this project, Susan Allison.

ISAAC ASIMOV'S
ALIENS

"ANGEL"

Pat Cadigan

"Angel" was purchased by Gardner Dozois, and appeared in the May 1987 issue of IAsfm, with a double-page illustration by J.K. Potter. "Angel" was an important story for the magazine, and went on to be a finalist that year for the Hugo Award, the Nebula Award, and the World Fantasy Award—one of the few stories ever to earn that rather unusual distinction. Cadigan is one of the mainstays of IAsfm, and has been so under two different editors, since her first sale to the magazine, under Shawna McCarthy, in 1982. Her IAsfm story "Pretty Boy Crossover" has recently appeared on several critics' lists as among the best science fiction stories of the 1980s.

Pat Cadigan was born in Schenectady, New York, and now lives in Overland Park, Kansas. She made her first professional sale in 1980, and has subsequently come to be regarded as one of the best new writers in SF. She was the co-editor, along with husband Arnie Fenner, of Shayol, perhaps the best of the semiprozines of the late 1970s;

it was honored with a World Fantasy Award in the "Special Achievement, Non-Professional" category in 1981. She has also served as Chairman of the Nebula Award Jury and as a World Fantasy Award Judge. Her first novel, Mindplayers, *was released in 1987 to excellent critical response, and she has just completed her second novel,* Synners. *Her most recent book is the collection* Patterns, *widely recognized as one of the most important collections of 1989.*

Stand with me awhile, Angel, I said, and Angel said he'd do that. Angel was good to me that way, good to have with you on a cold night and nowhere to go. We stood on the street corner together and watched the cars going by and the people and all. The streets were lit up like Christmas, streetlights, store lights, marquees over the all-night movie houses and bookstores blinking and flashing; shank of the evening in east midtown. Angel was getting used to things here and getting used to how I did nights. Standing outside, because what else are you going to do. He was *my* Angel now, had been since that other cold night when I'd been going home, because where are you going to go, and I'd found him and took him with me. It's good to have someone to take with you, someone to look after. Angel knew that. He started looking after me, too.

Like now. We were standing there awhile and I was looking around at nothing and everything, the cars cruising past, some of them stopping now and again for the hookers posing by the curb, and then I saw it, out of the corner of my eye. Stuff coming out of the Angel, shiny like sparks but flowing like liquid. Silver fireworks. I turned and looked all the way at him and it was gone. And he turned and gave a little grin like he was embarrassed I'd seen. Nobody else saw it, though; not the short guy who paused next to the

Angel before crossing the street against the light, not the skinny hype looking to sell the boom-box he was carrying on his shoulder, not the homeboy strutting past us with both his girlfriends on his arms, nobody but me.

The Angel said, Hungry?

Sure, I said. I'm hungry.

Angel looked past me. Okay, he said. I looked, too, and here they came, three leather boys, visor caps, belts, boots, keyrings. On the cruise together. Scary stuff, even though you know it's not looking for you.

I said, them? *Them?*

Angel didn't answer. One went by, then the second, and the Angel stopped the third by taking hold of his arm.

Hi.

The guy nodded. His head was shaved. I could see a little grey-black stubble under his cap. No eyebrows, disinterested eyes. The eyes were because of the Angel.

I could use a little money, the Angel said. My friend and I are hungry.

The guy put his hand in his pocket and wiggled out some bills, offering them to the Angel. The Angel selected a twenty and closed the guy's hand around the rest.

This will be enough, thank you.

The guy put his money away and waited.

I hope you have a good night, said the Angel.

The guy nodded and walked on, going across the street to where his two friends were waiting on the next corner. Nobody found anything weird about it.

Angel was grinning at me. Sometimes he was *the* Angel, when he was doing something, sometimes he was Angel, when he was just with me. Now he was Angel again. We went up the street to the luncheonette and got a seat by the front window so we could still watch the street while we ate.

Cheeseburger and fries, I said without bothering to look at the plastic-covered menus lying on top of the napkin holder. The Angel nodded.

Thought so, he said. I'll have the same, then.

The waitress came over with a little tiny pad to take our

order. I cleared my throat. It seemed like I hadn't used my voice in a hundred years. "Two cheeseburgers and two fries," I said, "and two cups of—" I looked up at her and froze. She had no face. Like, *nothing*, blank from hairline to chin, soft little dents where the eyes and nose and mouth would have been. Under the table, the Angel kicked me, but gentle.

"And two cups of coffee," I said.

She didn't say anything—how could she?—as she wrote down the order and then walked away again. All shaken up, I looked at the Angel, but he was calm like always.

She's a new arrival, Angel told me and leaned back in his chair. Not enough time to grow a face.

But how can she breathe? I said.

Through her pores. She doesn't need much air yet.

Yah, but what about—like, I mean, don't other people *notice* that she's got nothing there?

No. It's not such an extraordinary condition. The only reason you notice is because you're with me. Certain things have rubbed off on you. But no one else notices. When they look at her, they see whatever face they expect someone like her to have. And eventually, she'll have it.

But you have a face, I said. You've always had a face.

I'm different, said the Angel.

You sure are, I thought, looking at him. Angel had a beautiful face. That wasn't why I took him home that night, just because he had a beautiful face—I left all that behind a long time ago—but it was there, his beauty. The way you think of a man being beautiful, good clean lines, deep-set eyes, ageless. About the only way you could describe him—look away and you'd forget everything except that he was beautiful. But he did have a face. He *did*.

Angel shifted in the chair—these were like somebody's old kitchen chairs, you couldn't get too comfortable in them—and shook his head, because he knew I was thinking troubled thoughts. Sometimes you could think something and it wouldn't be troubled and later you'd think the same thing and it would be troubled. The Angel didn't like me to be troubled about him.

Do you have a cigarette? he asked.

I think so.

I patted my jacket and came up with most of a pack that I handed over to him. The Angel lit up and amused us both by having the smoke come out his ears and trickle out of his eyes like ghostly tears. I felt my own eyes watering for his; I wiped them and there was that *stuff* again, but from me now. I was crying silver fireworks. I flicked them on the table and watched them puff out and vanish.

Does this mean I'm getting to *be* you, now? I asked.

Angel shook his head. Smoke wafted out of his hair. Just things rubbing off on you. Because we've been together and you're—susceptible. But they're different for you.

Then the waitress brought our food and we went on to another sequence, as the Angel would say. She still had no face but I guess she could see well enough because she put all the plates down just where you'd think they were supposed to go and left the tiny little check in the middle of the table.

Is she—I mean, did you know her, from where you—

Angel gave his head a brief little shake. No. She's from somewhere else. Not one of my—people. He pushed the cheeseburger and fries in front of him over to my side of the table. That was the way it was done; I did all the eating and somehow it worked out.

I picked up my cheeseburger and I was bringing it up to my mouth when my eyes got all funny and I saw it coming up like a whole *series* of cheeseburgers, whoom-whoom-whoom, trick photography, only for real. I closed my eyes and jammed the cheeseburger into my mouth, holding it there, waiting for all the other cheeseburgers to catch up with it.

You'll be okay, said the Angel. Steady, now.

I said with my mouth full, That was—that was *weird*. Will I ever get used to this?

I doubt it. But I'll do what I can to help you.

Yah, well, the Angel *would* know. Stuff rubbing off on me, he could feel it better than I could. He was the one it was rubbing off *from*.

I had put away my cheeseburger and half of Angel's and was working on the french fries for both of us when I noticed he was looking out the window with this hard, tight expression on his face.

Something? I asked him.

Keep eating, he said.

I kept eating, but I kept watching, too. The Angel was staring at a big blue car parked at the curb right outside the diner. It was silvery blue, one of those lots-of-money models and there was a woman kind of leaning across from the driver's side to look out the passenger window. She was beautiful in that lots-of-money way, tawny hair swept back from her face, and even from here I could see she had turquoise eyes. Really beautiful woman. I almost felt like crying. I mean, jeez, how did people get that way and me too harmless to live.

But the Angel wasn't one bit glad to see her. I knew he didn't want me to say anything, but I couldn't help it.

Who is she?

Keep eating, Angel said. We need the protein, what little there is.

I ate and watched the woman and the Angel watch each other and it was getting very—I don't know, very *something* between them, even through the glass. Then a cop car pulled up next to her and I knew they were telling her to move it along. She moved it along.

Angel sagged against the back of his chair and lit another cigarette, smoking it in the regular, unremarkable way.

What are we going to do tonight? I asked the Angel as we left the restaurant.

Keep out of harm's way, Angel said, which was a new answer. Most nights we spent just kind of going around soaking everything up. The Angel soaked it up, mostly. I got some of it along with him, but not the same way he did. It was different for him. Sometimes he would use me like a kind of filter. Other times he took it direct. There'd been the big car accident one night, right at my usual corner, a big old Buick running a red light smack into somebody's nice Lincoln. The Angel had had to take it direct because I couldn't handle that kind of stuff. I didn't know how the Angel could take it, but he could. It carried him for days afterwards, too. I only had to eat for myself.

It's the intensity, little friend, he'd told me, as though that were supposed to explain it.

It's the intensity, not whether it's good or bad. The universe doesn't know good or bad, only less or more. Most of you have a bad time reconciling this. *You* have a bad time with it, little friend, but you get through better than other people. Maybe because of the way you are. You got squeezed out of a lot, you haven't had much of a chance at life. You're as much an exile as I am, only in your own land.

That may have been true, but at least I *belonged* here, so that part was easier for me. But I didn't say that to the Angel. I think he liked to think he could do as well or better than me at living—I mean, I couldn't just look at some leather boy and get him to cough up a twenty dollar bill. Cough up a fist in the face or worse, was more like it.

Tonight, though, he wasn't doing so good, and it was that woman in the car. She'd thrown him out of step, kind of.

Don't think about her, the Angel said, just out of nowhere. Don't think about her any more.

Okay, I said, feeling creepy because it was creepy when the Angel got a glimpse of my head. And then, of course, I couldn't think about anything else hardly.

Do you want to go home? I asked him.

No. I can't stay in now. We'll do the best we can tonight, but I'll have to be very careful about the tricks. They take so much out of me, and if we're keeping out of harm's way, I might not be able to make up for a lot of it.

It's okay, I said. I ate. I don't need anything else tonight, you don't have to do any more.

Angel got that look on his face, the one where I knew he wanted to give me things, like feelings I couldn't have any more. Generous, the Angel was. But I didn't need those feelings, not like other people seem to. For awhile, it was like the Angel didn't understand that, but he let me be.

Little friend, he said, and almost touched me. The Angel didn't touch a lot. I could touch him and that would be okay, but if *he* touched somebody, he couldn't help *doing* something to them, like the trade that had given us the money. That had been deliberate. If the trade had touched the Angel first, it would have been different, nothing would have happened unless the Angel touched him back. All touch meant something to the Angel that I didn't understand. There was touching without touching, too. Like things rubbing off on me. And sometimes, when I did touch the Angel, I'd get the feeling that it was maybe more his idea than mine, but I didn't mind that. How many people were going their whole lives never being able to touch an Angel?

We walked together and all around us the street was really coming to life. It was getting colder, too. I tried to make my jacket cover more. The Angel wasn't feeling it. Most of the time hot and cold didn't mean much to him. We saw the three rough trade guys again. The one Angel had gotten the money from was getting into a car. The other two watched it drive away and then walked on. I looked over at the Angel.

Because we took his twenty, I said.

Even if we hadn't, Angel said.

So we went along, the Angel and me, and I could feel how different it was tonight than it was all the other nights we'd walked or stood together. The Angel was kind of pulled back into himself and seemed to be keeping a check on me, pushing us closer together. I was getting more of those fireworks out of the corners of my eyes, but when I'd turn my head to look, they'd vanish. It reminded me of the night I'd found the Angel standing on my corner all by himself in pain. The Angel told me later that was real talent, knowing he was in pain. I never thought of myself as any too talented, but the way everyone else had been just ignoring him, I guess I must have had something to see him after all.

The Angel stopped us several feet down from an all-night bookstore. Don't look, he said. Watch the traffic or stare at your feet, but don't look or it won't happen.

There wasn't anything to see right then, but I didn't look anyway. That was the way it was sometimes, the Angel telling me it made a difference whether I was watching something or not, something about the other people being conscious of me being conscious of them. I didn't understand, but I knew Angel was usually right. So I was watching traffic when the guy came out of the bookstore and got his head punched.

I could almost see it out of the corner of my eye. A lot of movement, arms and legs flying and grunty noises. Other people stopped to look but I kept my eyes on the traffic, some of which was slowing up so they could check out the fight. Next to me, the Angel was stiff all over. Taking it in, what he called the expenditure of emotional kinetic energy. No right, no wrong, little friend, he'd told me. Just energy, like the rest of the universe.

So he took it in and I *felt* him taking it in, and while I was feeling it, a kind of silver fog started creeping around my eyeballs and I was in two places at once. I was watching the traffic and I was in the Angel watching the fight and feeling him charge up like a big battery.

It felt like nothing I'd ever felt before. These two guys slugging it out—well, one guy doing all the slugging and the other skittering around trying to get out from under the fists and having his head punched but good, and the Angel drinking it like he was sipping at an empty cup and somehow getting it to have something in it after all. Deep inside him, whatever made the Angel go was getting a little stronger.

I kind of swung back and forth between him and me, or swayed might be more like it was. I wondered about it, because the Angel wasn't touching me. I really was getting to *be* him, I thought; Angel picked that up and put the thought away to answer later. It was like I was traveling by the fog, being one of us and then the other, for a long time, it seemed, and then after awhile I was more me than him again, and some of the fog cleared away.

And there was that car, pointed the other way this time, and the woman was climbing out of it with this big weird smile on her face, as though she'd won something. She waved at the Angel to come to her.

Bang went the connection between us dead and the Angel shot past me, running away from the car. I went after him. I caught a glimpse of her jumping back into the car and yanking at the gear shift.

Angel wasn't much of a runner. Something funny about his knees. We'd gone maybe a hundred feet when he started wobbling and I could hear him pant. He cut across a Park & Lock that was dark and mostly empty. It was back-to-back with some kind of private parking lot and the fences for each one tried to mark off the same narrow strip of lumpy pavement. They were easy to climb but Angel was too panicked. He just *went* through them before he even thought about it; I knew that because if he'd been thinking, he'd have wanted to save what he'd just charged up with for when he really needed it bad enough.

I had to haul myself over the fences in the usual way, and when he heard me rattling on the saggy chainlink, he stopped and looked back.

Go, I told him. Don't wait on me!

He shook his head sadly. Little friend, I'm a fool. I could stand to learn from you a little more.

Don't stand, run! I got over the fences and caught up with him. Let's go! I yanked his sleeve as I slogged past and he followed at a clumsy trot.

Have to hide somewhere, he said, camouflage ourselves with people.

I shook my head, thinking we could just run maybe four more blocks and we'd be at the freeway overpass. Below it were the butt-ends of old roads closed off when the freeway had been built. You could hide there the rest of your life and no one would find you. But Angel made me turn right and go down a block to this rundown crack-in-the-wall called Stan's Jigger. I'd never been in there—I'd never made it a practice to go into bars—but the Angel was pushing too hard to argue.

Inside it was smelly and dark and not too happy. The Angel and I went down to the end of the bar and stood under a blood-red light while he searched his pockets for money.

Enough for one drink apiece, he said.

I don't want anything.

You can have soda or something.

The Angel ordered from the bartender, who was suspicious. This was a place for regulars and nobody else, and certainly nobody else like me or the Angel. The Angel knew that even stronger than I did but he just stood and pretended to sip his drink without looking at me. He was all pulled into himself and I was hovering around the edges. I knew he was still pretty panicked and trying to figure out what he could do next. As close as I was, if he had to get real far away, he was going to have a problem and so was I. He'd have to tow me along with him and that wasn't the most practical thing to do.

Maybe he was sorry now he'd let me take him home. But he'd been so weak then, and now with all the filtering and stuff I'd done for him, he couldn't just cut me off without a lot of pain.

I was trying to figure out what I could do for him now when the bartender came back and gave us a look that meant order or get out, and he'd have liked it better if we got out. So would everyone else there. The few other people standing at the bar weren't looking at us, but they knew right where we were, like a sore spot. It wasn't hard to figure out what they thought about us, either, maybe because of me or because of the Angel's beautiful face.

We got to leave, I said to the Angel but he had it in his head this was good camouflage. There wasn't enough money for two more drinks so he smiled at the bartender and slid his hand across the bar and put it on top of the bartender's. It was tricky doing it this way; bartenders and waitresses took more persuading because it wasn't normal for them just to give you something.

The bartender looked at the Angel with his eyes half closed. He seemed to be thinking it over. But the Angel had just blown a lot going through the fence instead of climbing over it and the fear was scuttling his concentration and I just knew that it wouldn't work. And maybe my knowing that didn't help, either.

The bartender's free hand dipped down below the bar and came up with a small club. "Faggot!" he roared and caught Angel just over the ear. Angel slammed into me and we both crashed to the floor. Plenty of emotional kinetic energy in here, I thought dimly as the guys standing at the bar fell on us, and then I didn't think anything more as I curled up into a ball under their fists and boots.

We were lucky they didn't much feel like killing anyone. Angel went out the door first and they tossed me out on top of him. As soon as I landed on him, I knew we were both in trouble; something was broken inside him. So much for keeping out of harm's way. I rolled off him and lay on the pavement, staring at the sky and trying to catch my breath. There was blood in my mouth and my nose, and my back was on fire.

Angel? I said, after a bit.

He didn't answer. I felt my mind get kind of all loose and runny, like my brains were leaking out my ears. I thought about the trade we'd taken the money from and how I'd been scared of him and his friends and how silly that had been. But then, I was too harmless to live.

The stars were raining silver fireworks down on me. It didn't help.

Angel? I said again.

I rolled over onto my side to reach for him, and there she was. The car was parked at the curb and she had Angel under the armpits, dragging him toward the open passenger door. I couldn't tell if he was conscious or not and that scared me. I sat up.

She paused, still holding the Angel. We looked into each other's eyes, and I started to understand.

"Help me get him into the car," she said at last. Her voice sounded hard and flat and unnatural. "Then you can get in, too. In the *back* seat."

I was in no shape to take her out. It couldn't have been better for her if she'd set it up herself. I got up, the pain flaring in me so bad that I almost fell down again, and took the Angel's ankles. His ankles were so delicate, almost like a woman's, like *hers*. I didn't really help much, except to guide his feet in as she sat him on the seat and strapped him in with the shoulder harness. I got in the back as she ran around to the other side of the car, her steps all real light and peppy, like she'd found a million dollars lying there on the sidewalk.

We were out on the freeway before the Angel stirred in the shoulder harness. His head lolled from side to side on the back of the seat. I reached up and touched his hair lightly, hoping she couldn't see me do it.

Where are you taking me, the Angel said.

"For a ride," said the woman. "For the moment."

Why does she talk out loud like that? I asked the Angel.

Because she knows it bothers me.

"You know I can focus my thoughts better if I say things out loud," she said. "I'm not like one of your little push-overs." She glanced at me in the rear view mirror. "Just *what* have you gotten yourself into since you left, darling? Is that a boy or a girl?"

I pretended I didn't care about what she said or that I was too harmless to live or any of that stuff, but the way she said it, she meant it to sting.

Friends can be either, Angel said. It doesn't matter which. Where are you taking us?

Now it was *us*. In spite of everything, I almost could have smiled.

"Us? You mean, you and me? Or are you really referring to your little pet back there?"

My friend and I are together. You and I are *not*.

The way the Angel said it made me think he meant more than not together; like he'd been with her once the way he was with me now. The Angel let me know I was right. Silver fireworks started flowing slowly off his head down the back of the seat and I knew there was something wrong about it. There was too much all at once.

"Why can't you talk out loud to me, darling?" the woman said with fakey-sounding petulance. "Just say a few words

and make me happy. You have a lovely voice when you
use it.''

That was true, but the Angel never spoke out loud unless
he couldn't get out of it, like when he'd ordered from the
bartender. Which had probably helped the bartender decide
about what he thought we were, but it was useless to think
about that.

"All right," said Angel, and I knew the strain was awful
for him. "I've said a few words. Are you happy?" He
sagged in the shoulder harness.

"Ecstatic. But it won't make me let you go. I'll drop
your pet at the nearest hospital and then we'll go home."
She glanced at the Angel as she drove. "I've missed you
so much. I can't *stand* it without you, without you making
things happen. Doing your little miracles. You knew I'd
get addicted to it, all the things you could do to people.
And then you just took off, I didn't know what had happened
to you. And it *hurt*." Her voice turned kind of pitiful, like
a little kid's. "I was in real *pain*. You must have been, too.
Weren't you? Well, *weren't you*?"

Yes, the Angel said. I was in pain, too.

I remembered him standing on my corner, where I'd hung
out all that time by myself until he came. Standing there in
pain. I didn't know why or from what then, I just took him
home, and after a little while, the pain went away. When
he decided we were together, I guess.

The silvery flow over the back of the car seat thickened.
I cupped my hands under it and it was like my brain was
lighting up with pictures. I saw the Angel before he was
my Angel, in this really nice house, the woman's house,
and how she'd take him places, restaurants or stores or
parties, thinking at him real hard so that he was all filled
up with her and had to do what she wanted him to. Steal
sometimes; other times, weird stuff, make people do silly
things like suddenly start singing or taking their clothes off.
That was mostly at the parties, though she made a waiter
she didn't like burn himself with a pot of coffee. She'd get
men, too, through the Angel, and they'd think it was the
greatest idea in the world to go to bed with her. Then she'd

make the Angel show her the others, the ones that had been sent here the way he had for crimes nobody could have understood, like the waitress with no face. She'd look at them, sometimes try to do things to them to make them uncomfortable or unhappy. But mostly she'd just stare.

It wasn't like that in the very beginning, the Angel said weakly and I knew he was ashamed.

It's okay, I told him. People can be nice at first, I know that. Then they find out about you.

The woman laughed. "You two are *so* sweet and pathetic. Like a couple of little children. I guess that's what you were looking for, wasn't it, darling? Except children can be cruel, too, can't they? So you got this—*creature* for yourself." She looked at me in the rear view mirror again as she slowed down a little, and for a moment I was afraid she'd seen what I was doing with the silvery stuff that was still pouring out of the Angel. It was starting to slow now. There wasn't much time left. I wanted to scream, but the Angel was calming me for what was coming next. "What happened to you, anyway?"

Tell her, said the Angel. To stall for time, I knew, keep her occupied.

I was born funny, I said. I had both sexes.

"A hermaphrodite!" she exclaimed with real delight.

She loves freaks, the Angel said, but she didn't pay any attention.

There was an operation, but things went wrong. They kept trying to fix it as I got older but my body didn't have the right kind of chemistry or something. My parents were ashamed. I left after awhile.

"You poor thing," she said, not meaning anything like that. "You were *just* what darling, here, needed, weren't you? Just a little nothing, no demands, no desires. For anything." Her voice got all hard. "They could probably fix you up now, you know."

I don't want it. I left all that behind a long time ago, I don't need it.

"*Just* the sort of little pet that would be perfect for you," she said to the Angel. "Sorry I have to tear you away. But

I can't get along without you now. Life is so boring. And empty. And—" She sounded puzzled. "And like there's nothing more to live for since you left me."

That's not me, said the Angel. That's you.

"No, it's a lot of you, and you know it. You know you're addictive to human beings, you knew that when you came here—when they *sent* you here. Hey, you, *pet*, do you know what his crime was, why they sent him to this little backwater penal colony of a planet?"

Yeah, I know, I said. I really didn't, but I wasn't going to tell her that.

"What do you think about *that*, little pet neuter?" she said gleefully, hitting the accelerator pedal and speeding up. "What do you think of the crime of refusing to mate?"

The Angel made a sort of an out-loud groan and lunged at the steering wheel. The car swerved wildly and I fell backwards, the silvery stuff from the Angel going all over me. I tried to keep scooping it into my mouth the way I'd been doing, but it was flying all over the place now. I heard the crunch as the tires left the road and went onto the shoulder. Something struck the side of the car, probably the guard rail, and made it fishtail, throwing me down on the floor. Up front the woman was screaming and cursing and the Angel wasn't making a sound, but, in my head, I could hear him sort of keening. Whatever happened, this would be it. The Angel had told me all that time ago, after I'd taken him home, that they didn't last long after they got here, the exiles from his world and other worlds. Things tended to *happen* to them, even if they latched on to someone like me or the woman. They'd be in accidents or the people here would kill them. Like antibodies in a human body rejecting something or fighting a disease. At least I belonged here, but it looked like I was going to die in a car accident with the Angel and the woman both. I didn't care.

The car swerved back onto the highway for a few seconds and then pitched to the right again. Suddenly there was nothing under us and then we thumped down on something, not road but dirt or grass or something, bombing madly up and down. I pulled myself up on the back of the seat just

in time to see the sign coming at us at an angle. The corner
of it started to go through the windshield on the woman's
side and then all I saw for a long time was the biggest
display of silver fireworks ever.

It was hard to be gentle with him. Every move hurt but
I didn't want to leave him sitting in the car next to her,
even if she was dead. Being in the back seat had kept most
of the glass from flying into me but I was still shaking some
out of my hair and the impact hadn't done much for my
back.

I laid the Angel out on the lumpy grass a little ways from
the car and looked around. We were maybe a hundred yards
from the highway, near a road that ran parallel to it. It was
dark but I could still read the sign that had come through
the windshield and split the woman's head in half. It said,
Construction Ahead, Reduce Speed. Far off on the other
road, I could see a flashing yellow light and at first I was
afraid it was the police or something but it stayed where it
was and I realized that must be the construction.

"Friend," whispered the Angel, startling me. He'd never
spoken aloud to me, not directly.

Don't talk, I said, bending over him, trying to figure out
some way I could touch him, just for comfort. There wasn't
anything else I could do now.

"I have to," he said, still whispering. "It's almost all
gone. Did you get it?"

Mostly, I said. Not all.

"I meant for you to have it."

I know.

"I don't know that it will really do you any good." His
breath kind of bubbled in his throat. I could see something
wet and shiny on his mouth but it wasn't silver fireworks.
"But it's yours. You can do as you like with it. Live on it
the way I did. Get what you need when you need it. But
you can live as a human, too. Eat. Work. However, whatever."

I'm not human, I said. I'm not any more human than
you, even if I do belong here.

"Yes, you are, little friend. I haven't made you any less human," he said, and coughed some. "I'm not sorry I wouldn't mate. I couldn't mate with my own. It was too . . . I don't know, too little of me, too much of them, something. I couldn't bond, it would have been nothing but emptiness. The Great Sin, to be unable to give, because the universe knows only less or more and I insisted that it would be good or bad. So they sent me here. But in the end, you know, they got their way, little friend." I felt his hand on me for a moment before it fell away. "I did it after all. Even if it wasn't with my own."

The bubbling in his throat stopped. I sat next to him for awhile in the dark. Finally I felt it, the Angel stuff. It was kind of fluttery-churny, like too much coffee on an empty stomach. I closed my eyes and lay down on the grass, shivering. Maybe some of it was shock but I don't think so. The silver fireworks started, in my head this time, and with them came a lot of pictures I couldn't understand. Stuff about the Angel and where he'd come from and the way they mated. It was a lot like how we'd been together, the Angel and me. They looked a lot like us but there were a lot of differences, too, things I couldn't make out. I couldn't make out how they'd sent him here, either—by *light*, in, like, little bundles or something. It didn't make any sense to me, but I guessed an Angel could be light. Silver fireworks.

I must have passed out, because when I opened my eyes, it felt like I'd been laying there a long time. It was still dark, though. I sat up and reached for the Angel, thinking I ought to hide his body.

He was gone. There was just a sort of wet sandy stuff where he'd been.

I looked at the car and her. All that was still there. Somebody was going to see it soon. I didn't want to be around for that.

Everything still hurt but I managed to get to the other road and start walking back toward the city. It was like I could *feel* it now, the way the Angel must have, as though it were vibrating like a drum or ringing like a bell with all

kinds of stuff, people laughing and crying and loving and
hating and being afraid and everything else that happens to
people. The stuff that the Angel took in, energy, that I could
take in now if I wanted.

And I knew that taking it in that way, it would be bigger
than anything all those people had, bigger than anything I
could have had if things hadn't gone wrong with me all
those years ago.

I wasn't so sure I wanted it. Like the Angel, refusing to
mate back where he'd come from. He wouldn't, there, and
I couldn't, here. Except now I could do something else.

I wasn't so sure I wanted it. But I didn't think I'd be
able to stop it, either, any more than I could stop my heart
from beating. Maybe it wasn't really such a good thing or
a right thing. But it was like the Angel said: the universe
doesn't know good or bad, only less or more.

Yeah. I heard *that*.

I thought about the waitress with no face. I could find
them all now, all the ones from the other places, other worlds
that sent them away for some kind of alien crimes nobody
would have understood. I could find them all. They threw
away their outcasts, I'd tell them, but here, we *kept* ours.
And here's how. Here's how you live in a universe that
only knows less or more.

I kept walking toward the city.

"CRYPTIC"

Jack McDevitt

*"Cryptic" was purchased by Shawna McCarthy,
and appeared in the April 1983 issue of* IAsfm,
*with an illustration by Richard Crist. It was a Ne-
bula Award finalist that year, was picked up by a
"Best of the Year" anthology, and remains, in my
estimation, one of the finest and most thought-
provoking First Contact stories ever written.*

*Jack McDevitt went on to contribute a number
of important stories to* IAsfm, *under both Mc-
Carthy and Dozois. His well-received first novel,*
The Hercules Text, *published as an Ace Special,
was followed in 1989 by the critically acclaimed
novel* A Talent for War. *An ex-naval officer, ex-
English teacher, and former customs inspector, he
now lives with his family in Brunswick, Georgia.*

It was at the bottom of the safe in a bulky manila envelope. I nearly tossed it into the trash along with the stacks of other documents, tapes, and assorted flotsam left over from the Project.

Had it been catalogued, indexed in some way, I'm sure I would have. But the envelope was blank, save for an eighteen-year-old date scrawled in the lower right hand corner, and, beneath it, the notation "40 gh."

Out on the desert, lights were moving. That would be Brackett fine-tuning the Array for Orrin Hopkins, who was then beginning the observations that would lead, several years later, to new departures in pulsar theory. I envied Hopkins: he was short, round, bald, a man unsure of himself, whose occasionally brilliant insights were explained with giggles. He was a ridiculous figure; yet he bore the stamp of genius. And people would remember his ideas long after the residence hall named for me at Carrollton had crumbled.

If I had not long since recognized my own perimeters and conceded any hope of all immortality (at least of this sort), I certainly did so when I accepted the director's position at Sandage. Administration pays better than being an active physicist, but it is death to ambition.

And a Jesuit doesn't even get that advantage.

In those days, the Array was still modest: forty parabolic antennas, each 36 meters across. They were on tracks, of course, independently movable, forming a truncated cross. They had, for two decades, been the heart of SETI, the Search for Extra-Terrestrial Intelligence. Now, with the Project abandoned, they were being employed for more useful, if mundane, purposes.

Even that relatively unsophisticated system was good: as Hutching Chaney once remarked, the Array could pick up the cough of an automobile ignition on the moon.

I circled the desk and fell into the uncomfortable wooden chair we'd inherited from the outgoing regime. The packet was sealed down with tape that had become brittle and loose around the edges. I tore it open.

It was a quarter past ten. I'd worked through my dinner and the evening hours, bored, drinking coffee, debating the wisdom in coming out here from JPL. The increase in responsibility was a good career move; but I knew now that Harry Cooke would never lay his hands on a new particle.

I was committed for two years at Sandage: two years of working out schedules and worrying about insurance; two years of dividing meals between the installation's sterile cafeteria, and Jimmy's Amoco on Route 85. Then, if it all went well, I could expect another move up, perhaps to Georgetown.

I'd have traded it all for Hopkins's future.

I shook out six magnetic discs onto the desk. They were in individual sleeves, of the type that many installations had once used to record electromagnetic radiation. The discs were numbered and dated over a three-year period in 1991, two years earlier than the date on the envelope.

Each was marked "Procyon."

In back, Hopkins and two associates were hunched over monitors. Brackett, having finished his job, was at his desk reading.

I was pleased to discover that the discs were compatible to the Mark VIs. I inserted one, tied in a vocorder to get a hard copy, and went over to join the Hopkins group while the thing ran. They were talking about plasma. I listened for a time, got lost, noted that everyone around me (save the grinning little round man) also got lost, and strolled back to my computer.

The trace drew its green-and-white pictures smoothly on the Mark VI display, and pages of hard copy clicked out of the vocorder. Something in the needle geometry scattered across the recording paper drew my attention. Like an elusive name, it drifted just beyond my reach.

Beneath a plate of the Andromeda Galaxy, a coffee pot simmered. I could hear the distant drone of a plane, probably out of Luke Air Force Base. Behind me, Hopkins and his men were laughing at something.

There were patterns in the recording.

They materialized slowly, identical clusters of impulses: the signals were artificial.

Procyon.

The laughter, the plane, the coffee pot, a radio that had been left on somewhere: everything ratcheted down to a possibility.

More likely Phoenix, I thought.

Frank Myers had been SETI Director since Ed Dickinson's death twelve years before. I reached him next morning in San Francisco.

"No," he said without hesitation. "Someone's idea of a joke, Harry."

"It was in your safe, Frank."

"That damned safe's been there forty years. Might be anything in it. Except messages from Mars. . . ."

I thanked him and hung up.

It had been a long night: I'd taken the hard copy to bed with me and, by 5 AM, had identified more than forty distinct pulse patterns. The signal appeared to be continuous: that is, it had been an ongoing transmission with no indication of beginning or end, but only irregular breaches of the type that would result from atmospherics and, of course, the long periods during which the target would have been below the horizon.

It was clearly a reflected terrestrial transmission: radio waves bounce around considerably. But why seal the error two years later and put it in the safe?

Procyon is a yellow-white class F3 binary, absolute magnitude 2.8, once worshipped in Babylonia and Egypt. (What hasn't been worshipped in Egypt?) Distance from Earth: 11.3 light-years.

In the outer office, Beth Cooper typed, closed cabinet drawers, spoke with visitors.

The obvious course of action was to use the Array. Listen to Procyon at 40 gigahertz, or all across the spectrum for that matter, and find out if it was, indeed, saying something.

On the intercom, I asked Beth when we had open time

on the System. "Nothing for seventeen months," she said
crisply.

That was no surprise. The facility had booked quickly
when its resources were made available to the astronomical
community on more than the limited basis that had prevailed
for twenty years. Anyone wishing to use the radiotelescope
had to plan far in advance. How could I get hold of the
Array for a couple hours?

"Beth, would you come in a moment, please?"

Beth Cooper had come to Sandage from San Augustin
with SETI during the big move twenty years before. She'd
been secretary to three directors: Hutching Chaney, who
had built Sandage; his longtime friend Ed Dickinson; and
finally, after Dickinson's death, Frank Myers, a young man
on the move, who'd stayed too long with the Project, and
who'd been reportedly happy to see it strangled. In any
case, Myers had contributed to its demise by his failure to
defend it.

I'd felt he was right, of course, though for the wrong
reason. It had been painful to see the magnificent telescope
at Sandage denied, by and large, to the scientific community
while its grotesque hunt for the Little Green Man signal
went on. I think there were few of us not happy to see it
end.

Beth had expected to lose her job. But she knew her way
around the facility, had a talent for massaging egos, and
could spell. A devout Lutheran, she had adapted cautiously
to working for a priest and, oddly, seemed to have taken
offense that I did not routinely walk around with a Roman
collar.

I asked one or two questions about the billing methods
of the local utilities, and then commented, as casually as I
could manage, that it was unfortunate the Project had not
succeeded.

Beth looked more like a New York librarian than a secretary at a desert installation. Her hair was silver-gray. She
wore steel-rimmed glasses on a long, silver chain. She was
moderately heavy; but her carriage and her diction were

impeccable, imbuing her with the quality that stage people call presence.

Her eyes narrowed to hard black beads at my remark. "Dr. Dickinson said any number of times that none of us would live to see results. Everyone attached to the program, even the janitors, knew that." She wasn't a woman given to shrugs, but the sudden flick in those dark eyes matched the effect. "I'm glad he didn't live to see it terminated."

That was followed by an uncomfortable silence. "I don't blame you, Doctor," she said at length, referring to my public position that the facility was being under-utilized.

I dropped my eyes, and tried to smile reassuringly. It must have been ludicrous: her severe features softened. I showed her the envelope.

"Do you recognize the writing?"

She barely glanced at it. "It's Dr. Dickinson's."

"Are you sure? I didn't think Dickinson came to the Project until Hutch Chaney's retirement. That was '93, wasn't it?"

"He took over as Director then. But he was an operating technician under Dr. Chaney for, oh, ten or twelve years before that." Her eyes glowed when she spoke of Dickinson.

"I never met him," I said.

"He was a fine man." She looked past me, over my shoulder, her features pale. "If we hadn't lost him, we might not have lost the Project."

"If it matters," I added gently.

"If it matters," she confirmed.

She was right about Dickinson: he was articulate, a persuasive speaker, author of books on various subjects, and utterly dedicated to SETI. He might well have kept the Project afloat despite the cessation of federal funds and an increasing clamor among his colleagues for more time at the facility. But Dickinson was twelve years dead now: he'd returned to Massachusetts at Christmas, as was his custom. After a snowstorm, he'd gone out to help shovel a neighbor's driveway and his heart had failed.

I'd been in the East myself at the time, at Georgetown.

And I can still recall my sense of a genius who had died too soon. He had possessed a vast talent, but no discipline; he had churned through his career hurling sparks in all directions. But somehow everything he touched, like SETI, had come to no fulfillment.

"Beth, was there ever a time they thought they had an LGM?"

"The Little Green Man Signal?" She shook her head. "No, I don't think so. They were always picking up echoes and things. But nothing ever came close. Either it was KCOX in Phoenix, or some Japanese trawler in the middle of the Pacific."

"Never anything that didn't fit those categories?"

One eyebrow rose slightly. "Never anything they could prove. If they couldn't pin it down, they went back later and tried to find it again. One way or another, they eliminated everything." Or, she was thinking, we wouldn't be standing here having this conversation.

Beth's comments implied that suspect signals had been automatically stored. Grateful that I had not yet got around to purging obsolete data, I discovered that was indeed the case, and ran a search covering the entire time period back to the Procyon reception in 1991, looking for a similar signal.

I got a surprise.

There was no match. There was also no record of the Procyon reception itself.

That meant, presumably, it had been accounted for, and discarded.

Then why, two years later, had the recordings been sealed and placed in the safe? Surely no explanation would have taken that long.

SETI had assumed that any LGM signal would be a deliberate attempt to communicate, that an effort would therefore be made by the originator to create intelligibility, and that the logical way to do that was to employ a set of symbols representing universal constants: the atomic weight of hydrogen, perhaps, or the value of pi.

But the move to Sandage had also been a move to more sophisticated, and considerably more sensitive, equipment. The possibility developed that the Project would pick up a slopover signal, a transmission of alien origin, but intended only for local receivers. Traffic of that nature could be immeasurably difficult to interpret.

If the packet in the safe was anything at all, it was surely of this latter type. Forty gigahertz is not an ideal frequency for interstellar communication. Moreover, it was ongoing, formless, no numbered parts, nothing to assist translation.

I set the computer working on the text, using SETI's own language analysis program. Then I instructed Brackett to call me if anything developed, had dinner at Jimmy's, and went home. I was left undisturbed.

There was no evidence of structure in the text. In English, one can expect to find a "U" after a "Q," or a vowel after a cluster of consonants. The aspirate is seldom doubled, nothing is ever tripled, and so on. But in the Procyon transmission, everything seemed utterly random.

The computer counted sixty-one distinct pulse patterns, which was to say, sixty-one characters. None recurred at sufficient intervals to be a space. And the frequency count was flat: there was no quantitative difference in use from one character to another. All appeared approximately the same number of times. If it was a language, it was a language with no vowels.

And certainly too many letters.

I called Wes Phillips, who was then the only linguist I knew.

Was it possible for a language to be structured in such a way?

"Oh, I don't think so. Unless you're talking about some sort of construct. Even then . . ." He paused. "How many characters did you say?"

"Sixty-one."

"Harry, I can give you a whole series of reasons in maybe six different disciplines why languages need high and low frequency letters. To have a flat 'curve,' a language would have to be deliberately designed that way, and it would have to be non-oral. But what practical value would it have? Why bother?

"One more thing," he said. "Sixty-one letters seems a trifle much. If these people actually require that many characters to communicate, I suspect they're going to be doing it with drums."

Ed Dickinson had been an enigma. During the series of superpower confrontations near the close of the century, he'd earned an international reputation as a diplomat, and as an eloquent defender of reason and restraint. Everyone agreed that he had a mind of the first rank. Yet, in his chosen field, he accomplished little. And he'd gone to work for the Project, historically only a stepping-stone to serious effort. But he'd stayed.

Why?

Hutching Chaney was a different matter. A retired naval officer, he'd indulged in physics almost as a sideline. His political connections had been instrumental in getting Sandage built; and his assignment to head it was rumored to have been a reward for his services during the undeclared Soviet naval war of '87–'88.

He possessed a plodding sort of competence. He was fully capable of grasping, and visualizing, extreme complexity. But he lacked insight and imagination, the ability to draw the subtle inference.

After his retirement from Sandage, Chaney had gone to an emeritus position at MIT, which he'd held for five years.

He was a big man, more truck driver than physicist. Despite advancing age—he was then in his 70s—and his bulk, he spoke and moved with energy. His hair was full and black. His light gray eyes suggested the shrewdness of a professional politician; and he possessed the confident congeniality of a man who had never failed at anything.

We were in his home in Somerville, Massachusetts, a stone and glass house atop sweeping lawns. It was not an establishment that a retired physicist would be expected to inhabit: Chaney's moneyed background was evident.

He clapped a big hand on my shoulder and pulled me

through one of those stiff, expensive living rooms that no one ever wants to sit in, into a paneled leather-upholstered compartment at the rear of the house. "Martha," he said to someone I couldn't see, "would you bring us some port?" He looked at me for acquiescence.

"Fine," I said. "It's been a long time, Hutch."

Books lined the walls: mostly technical, some on naval engineering, a few military and naval histories. An articulated steel gray model of the Lance dominated the fireplace shelf. That was the deadly hydrofoil which, built at Chaney's urging, had been launched against the Soviets in vast numbers, and had swept them from the seas.

"The Church is infiltrating everywhere," he said. "How are things at Sandage, Harry?"

I described some of the work then in progress. He listened with interest.

A young woman arrived with a bottle, two glasses, and a plate of cheese. "Martha comes in three times a week," Chaney said after she'd left. He smiled, winked, dipped a stick of cheese in some mustard, and bit it neatly in half. "You needn't worry, Harry. I'm not capable of getting into trouble anymore. What brings you to Massachusetts?"

I extracted the vocordings from my briefcase and handed them across to him. I watched patiently as he leafed through the thick sheaf of paper, and saw with satisfaction his change of expression.

"You're kidding, Harry," he said. "Somebody really found one? When'd it happen?"

"Twenty years ago," I said, passing him the envelope and the original discs.

He turned them over in his hands. "Then there's a mistake somewhere."

"It was in the safe," I said.

He shook his head. "Doesn't much matter where it was. Nothing like this ever happened."

"Then what is it?"

"Damned if I have any idea."

We sat not talking while Chaney continued to flip pages,

grunting. He seemed to have forgotten his wine. "You run this yourself?" he asked.

I nodded.

"Hell of a lot of trouble for somebody to go to for a joke. Were the computers able to read any of it? No? That's because it's gibberish." He stared at the envelope. "But it *is* Ed's handwriting."

"Would Dickinson have any reason to keep such a thing quiet?"

"Ed? No: Dickinson least of all. No one worked harder for a success. He wanted it so badly he invested his life in the Project."

"But could he, physically, have done this? Could he have picked up the LGM? Was he good enough with the computers to cover his tracks?"

"This is pointless. Yes, he could have done it. And you could walk through Braintree without your pants."

A light breeze was coming through a side window, billowing the curtains. It was cool and pleasant, unusual for Massachusetts in August. Some kids were playing halfball out on the street.

"Forty megahertz," he said. "Sounds like a satellite transmission."

"That wouldn't have taken two years to figure out, would it? Why keep the discs?"

"Why not?" he said. "I expect if you go down into the storeroom you'll find all kinds of relics."

Outside, there was a sound like distant thunder, exploding suddenly into an earsplitting screech. A strippcd-down T-Bolt skidded by, scattering the ballplayers, and then accelerated. It took the corner stop sign at about 45. The game resumed, as though nothing had happened.

"All the time," Chaney said. His back to the window, he hadn't bothered to look around. "Cops can't keep up with them anymore."

"Why was Dickinson so interested in the Project?"

"Ed was a great man." His face clouded somewhat, and I wondered if the port hadn't drawn his emotions close to the surface. "You'd have had to know him. You and he would have got along fine. He had a taste for the meta-physical, and I guess the Project was about as close as he could get.''

"How do you mean?''

"Did you know he spent two years in a seminary? Yes, somewhere outside Philadelphia. He was an altar boy who eventually wound up in Harvard. And that was that.''

"You mean he lost his faith?''

"Yes. But he always retained that fine mystical sense of purpose that you drill into your best kids, a notion that things are somehow ordered. When I knew him, he wouldn't have presumed to pray to anyone. But he had all the drive of a missionary, and the same conviction of—'' He dropped his head back on the leather upholstery and tried to seize a word from the ceiling.—"destiny.

"Ed wasn't like most physicists. He was competent in a wide range of areas. He wrote on foreign affairs for *Commentary* and *Harper's*; he published books on ornithology, systems analysis, Malcolm Muggeridge, and Edward Gibbon.''

He swung easily out of his chair and reached for a pair of fat matched volumes in mud-brown covers. It was *The Decline and Fall of the Roman Empire*, the old Modern Library edition. "He's the only person I've ever known who's actually read the thing.'' He turned the cover so that I could see the inscription:

For Hutch,
   In the fond hope that we can hold off the potherbs and the pigs.

                                            Ed

"He gave it to me when I left SETI.''

"Seems like an odd gift. Have you read it?''

He laughed off the question. "You'd need a year.''

"What's the business about the potherbs and pigs?''

He rose and walked casually to the far wall. There were photos of naval vessels and aircraft, of Chaney and President Fine, of the Sandage complex. He seemed to screw his vision into the latter. "I don't remember. It's a phrase from the book. He explained it to me at the time. But . . ." He held his hands outward, palms up.

"Hutch," I said, "thanks." I got up to go.

"There's nothing to it," he said. "I don't know where that thing came from, but Ed Dickinson would have given anything for a contact."

"Hutch, is it possible that Dickinson might have been able to translate the text?"

"Not if you couldn't. He had the same program."

I don't like cities.

Dickinson's books were all out of print, and the used bookstores were clustered in Cambridge. Even then, the outskirts of Boston, like the city proper, were littered with glass and newspapers. Surly crowds milled outside bars. Windows everywhere were smashed or boarded. I went through a red light at one intersection rather than learn the intentions of an approaching band of ragged children with hard eyes. (One could scarcely call them children, though I doubt there was one over 12.) Profanity covered the crumbling brick walls as high as an arm could reach. Much of it was misspelled.

Boston had been Dickinson's city. I wondered what the great humanist thought when he drove through these streets.

. I found only one of his books: *Malcolm Muggeridge: Faith and Despair*. The store also had a copy of *The Decline and Fall*. On impulse, I bought it.

I was glad to get back to the desert.

We were entering a period of extraordinary progress, during which we finally began to understand the mechanics of galactic structure. McCue mapped the core of the Milky Way. Osterberger developed his unified field concepts, and Schauer constructed his celebrated revolutionary hypothesis on the nature of time. Then, on a cool morning in October, a team from Cal Tech announced an electrifying discovery: objects on the fringe of visibility were *not* receding; were, in fact, resisting expansion and moving slowly in our direction, against the tide. It seemed then, as it does now, that they are fragments of another universe.

In the midst of all this activity, we had an emergency one night in late September. Earl Barlow, who was directing the Cal Tech group, suffered a mild heart attack. I arrived just before the EMTs, at about 2 AM.

After the ambulance left with him, Barlow's men wandered about listlessly, drinking coffee, too upset to work. The opportunity didn't catch me entirely unprepared. I gave Brackett his new target, and the numbers. The ululating shriek of the emergency vehicle had barely subsided before the parabolas swung round and fastened on the bright dog-star Procyon.

There was only the disjointed crackle of interstellar static.

I took long walks on the desert at night. The parabolas are lovely in the moonlight. Occasionally, the stillness is broken by the whine of an electric motor, and the antennas slide gracefully along their tracks. It was, I thought, a new Stonehenge of softly curving shapes and fluid motion.

The Muggeridge book was a slim volume. It was not biographical, but rather an analysis of the philosopher's conviction that the West has a death wish. It was the old argument that God had been replaced by science, that man had gained knowledge of a trivial sort, and lost purpose.

It was, on the whole, depressing reading. In his conclusion, Dickinson took issue, arguing that truth will not wait on human convenience, that if man cannot adapt to a neutral universe, then that universe will indeed seem hostile. We must make do with what we have and accept truth wherever it leads. The modern cathedral is the radiotelescope.

Sandage was involved in the verification procedure for McCue's work, and for the "enigmatic Cal Tech" objects. All of that is another story: what is significant is that it got me thinking about verifications, and I realized I'd overlooked something: there'd been no match for the Procyon recordings anywhere in the data banks since the original reception. But the Procyon recordings might themselves have been the confirmation of an earlier signal!

It took five minutes to run the search: there were two hits.

Both were fragments, neither more than 15 minutes, but there was enough of each to reduce the probability of error to less than one percent.

The first occurred just three weeks prior to the Procyon reception.

The second went back to 1987, a San Augustin observation. Both were at 40 gigahertz. Both had identical pulse patterns. But there was an explosive difference, sedately concealed in the target information line: the 1987 transmission had come while the radiotelescope was locked on Sirius!

When I got back to my office, I was trembling.

Sirius and Procyon were only a few light years apart. My God, I kept thinking, they exist! And they have star travel!

I spent the balance of the day stumbling around, trying to immerse myself in fuel usage reports and budget projections. But mostly what I did was watch the desert light grow hard in the curtains, and then fade. The two volumes of Edward Gibbon were propped between a Webster's and some black binders. The books were thirty years old, identical to the set in Chaney's den. Some of the pages, improperly cut, were still joined at the edges.

I opened the first volume, approximately in the middle, and began to read. Or tried to. But Ed Dickinson kept crowding out the Romans. Finally I gave it up, took the book, and went home.

There was duplicate bridge in town, and I lost myself in that for five hours. Then, in bed, still somewhat dazed, I attempted *The Decline and Fall* again.

It was not the dusty rollcall of long-dead emperors that I had expected. The emperors are there, stabbing and throttling and blundering. And occasionally trying to improve things. But the fish-hawkers are there too. And the bureaucrats and the bishops.

It's a world filled with wine and legionaries' sweat, mismanagement, arguments over Jesus, and the inability to transfer power, all played out to the ruthless drumbeat of dissolution. An undefined historical tide, stemmed occasionally by a hero, or a sage, rolls over men and events, washing them toward the sea. (During the latter years, I wondered, did Roman kids run down matrons in flashy imported chariots? Were the walls of Damascus defiled by profanity?)

In the end, when the barbarians push at the outer rim of empire, it is only a hollow wreck that crashes down.

Muggeridge must have been there.

And Dickinson, the altar boy, amid the fire and waste of the imperial city, must have suffered a second loss of faith.

We had an electrical failure one night. It has nothing to do with this story except that it resulted in my being called at 4 AM (not to restore the power, which required a good electrician; but to pacify some angry people from New York; and to be able to say, in my report, that I had been on the spot).

These things attended to, I went outside.

At night, the desert is undisturbed by color or motion. It's a composition of sand, rock, and star; a frieze, a Monet, uncomplicated, unchanging. It's reassuring, in an age when little else seems stable: the orderly universe of the twentieth century had long since disintegrated into a plethora of neutron galaxies, "colliding" black holes, time reversals, and God knows what.

The desert is solid underfoot. Predictable. A reproach to the quantum mechanics that reflect a quicksand cosmos in which physics merges with Plato.

Close on the rim of the sky, guarding their mysteries, Sirius and Procyon, the bright pair, sparkled. The arroyos are dry at that time of year, shadowy ripples in the landscape. The moon was in its second quarter. Beyond the administration building, the parabolas were limned in silver.

My cathedral.

My Stonehenge.

And while I sat, sipping a Coors, and thinking of lost cities and altar boys and frequency counts, I suddenly understood the significance of Chaney's last remark! Of course Dickinson had not read the text: that was the point!

I needed Chaney.

I called him in the morning, and flew out in the afternoon. He met me at Logan, and we drove out toward Gloucester. "There's an excellent Italian restaurant," he said. And then, without taking his eyes off the road: "What's this all about?"

I'd brought the second volume with me, and I held it up for him to see. He blinked in apparent confusion.

It was early evening, cold, wet, with the smell of approaching winter. Freezing rain pelted the windshield. The sky was gray, heavy, sagging into the city.

"Before I answer any questions, Hutch, I'd like to ask a couple. What can you tell me about military cryptography?"

He grinned. "Not much. The little I do know is probably classified." A tractor trailer lumbered past, straining, spraying water across the windows. "What, specifically, are you interested in?"

"How complex are the Navy's codes? I know they're nothing like cryptograms, but what sort of general structure do they have?"

"First off, Harry, they're not codes. Monoalphabetic systems are codes. Like the cryptograms you mentioned. The letter 'G' always turns up, say, as an 'M.' But in military and diplomatic cryptography, the 'G' will be a different character every time it appears. And the encryption alphabet isn't usually limited to letters: we can use numbers, dollar signs, ampersands, even spaces." We splashed onto a ramp and joined the Interstate. It was sufficiently raised that we looked across rows of bleak rooftops. "Even the shape of individual words is concealed."

"How?"

"By encrypting the spaces."

I knew the answer to the next question before I asked it. "If the encryption alphabet is absolutely random, which I assume it would have to be, the frequency count would be flat. Right?"

"Yes. Given sufficient traffic, it would have to be."

"One more thing, Hutch: a sudden increase in traffic will alert anyone listening that something is happening even if he can't read the text. How do you hide that?"

"Easy. We transmit a continuous signal, twenty-four hours a day. Sometimes it's traffic, sometimes it's garbage. But you can't tell the difference."

God have mercy on us, I thought. Poor Ed Dickinson.

We sat at a small corner table well away from the main dining area. I shivered in wet shoes and a damp sweater. A small candle guttered cheerfully in front of us.

"Are we still talking about Procyon?" he asked.

I nodded. "The same pattern was received twice, three years apart, prior to the Procyon reception."

"But that's not possible." Chaney leaned forward intently. "The computer would have matched them automatically. We'd have known."

"I don't think so." Half-a-dozen prosperous, overweight men in topcoats had pushed in and were jostling one another in the small entry. "The two hits were on different targets: they would have looked like an echo."

Chaney reached across the table and gripped my wrist, knocking over a cup. He ignored it. "Son of a bitch," he said. "Are you suggesting there's an empire out there?"

"I don't think Ed Dickinson had any doubts."

"Why would he keep it secret?"

I'd placed the book on the table at my left hand. It rested there, its plastic cover reflecting the glittering red light of the candle. "Because they're at war," I said.

Understanding broke across Chaney's features. The color drained from his face, and it took on a pallor that was almost ghastly in the lurid light.

"He believed," I continued, "he really believed that

mind equates to morality, intelligence to compassion. And what did he find after a lifetime? A civilization that had conquered the stars, but not its own passions and stupidities."

A tall young waiter presented himself. We ordered port and pasta.

"You don't really know there's a war going on out there," Chaney objected.

"Hostility then. Secrecy on a massive scale, as this must be, has unhappy implications. Dickinson would have saved us all with a vision of order and reason. . . ."

The gray eyes met mine. They were filled with pain. Two adolescent girls in the next booth were giggling. The wine came.

"What has *The Decline and Fall* to do with it?"

"It became his Bible. He was chilled to the bone by it. You should read it, but with caution. It's quite capable of strangling the soul. Dickinson was a rationalist; he recognized the ultimate truth in the Roman tragedy: that once expansion has stopped, decay is constant and irreversible. Every failure of reason or virtue loses more ground."

"I haven't been able to find his book on Gibbon, but I know what he'll say: that Gibbon was not writing only of the Romans, nor of the British of his own time. He was writing of us. . . .

"To anyone who thinks in those terms, who looks around him, this world is fast sliding toward a dark age."

We drank silently for a few minutes. I had the sense that time had locked in place, that we sat unmoving, the world frozen around us.

"Did I tell you," I said at last, "that I found the reference for his inscription? He must have had great respect for you, Hutch." I opened the book to the conclusion, and turned it for him to read:

The forum of the Roman people, where they assembled to enact their laws and elect their magistrates, is now enclosed for the cultivation of pot-herbs, or thrown open for the reception of swine and buffaloes.

Chaney stared disconsolately at me. "It's all so hard to believe. He always seemed so optimistic."

"Maybe," I said. "But I think the reverse is true. A man can survive a loss of faith in the Almighty, provided he does not also lose faith in himself. That was Dickinson's real tragedy: he came to believe exclusively in radiotelescopes, the way some people do in religions."

The food, when it came, went untasted. "What are you going to do, Harry?"

"About the Procyon text? About the probability that we have quarrelsome neighbors? I'm not afraid of that kind of information; all it means is that where you find intelligence, you will probably find stupidity. Anyway, it's time Dickinson got credit for his discovery." And I thought, maybe it'll even mean a footnote for me.

I lifted my glass in a mock toast, but Chaney did not respond. We faced each other in an uncomfortable tableau. "What's wrong?" I asked. "Thinking about Dickinson?"

"That too." The candle glinted in his eyes. "Harry, do you think *they* have a SETI project too?"

"Possibly. Why?"

"I was wondering if your aliens know we're here. This restaurant isn't much further from Sirius than Procyon is. Maybe you better eat up."

"THE BISHOP'S DECISION"

Phillip C. Jennings

"The Bishop's Decision" was purchased by Gardner Dozois, and appeared in the March 1988 issue of IAsfm, with a playful illustration by the late Hank Jankus. A madly inventive new writer, Jennings' work is always clever, sometimes intensively complicated, and occasionally downright bizarre. Here, in a story that's as styly funny us it is powerfully strange, he gives us a look at the startling implications and consequences of a decision that must be made by a reluctant and hapless bishop in a far corner of medieval Europe.

One of the most prolific as well as one of the most popular of today's crop of new writers, Phillip C. Jennings has appeared in most of the major SF magazines and anthologies, in addition to publishing a number of stories in IAsfm. His first novel, Tower to the Sky, *was published in 1988. His most recent book was the fat and eccentric collection* The Bug Life Chronicles. *Jennings lives in Saint Cloud, Minnesota.*

All men envied King Louis XIV. Lesser princes aped his
splendor from Portugal to Muscovy. Least among them,
spiritual and temporal ruler of a patchwork episcopate in
the south of Germany, Bishop Von Zweitel was unable to
convert Schloss Mutlorn into a Versailles. Yet as he was
only five feet four inches tall he was happy to adopt the
sun-king's wig and high heels.

Brown curls tumbled from the heap atop his head. "Magnificent," he thought, admiring his stylish elevation in the
mirror. He strode back and forth for practice. What a fool
he'd make if he stumbled in front of his guests!

Not much chance of that. He flounced out his lace cuffs,
took a preliminary pinch of snuff, and instructed Father
Klosterman to carry the box as he followed in train.

They passed along an open gallery. In the bailey below
firewood lay stacked up to the eaves. What a vulgarity!
Would a guest at the French court be obliged to dismount
among cords of winter fuel?

The bishop shook his head sadly and hurried on. Trailed
by his tall, saturnine secretary, he entered the salon, where
buoyant saints drifted among pastel cloudbanks. Huddled
below this fanciful ceiling, the abbots and scholars, agents
and visitors of his petty court fell into a gratifying silence.
Only one voice continued to speak.

"—FLAT. ALL STUFFS OF YOUR LOCAL STAR IS-
LAND PRESSED INTO A DISK CIRCLING THIS EN-
ERGY. YOUR SUN WILL BE A COLUMN OF LIGHT—"

"I don't understand 'star island,'" remarked the bishop,
ignoring the derbwe's breach of etiquette.

The muscles that reared the derbwe's neck drew its caudal
knout up and over. It took energy to do that, to shatter and
shed the condensate ice that sheeted its all-covering suit;
perhaps the creature was in the throes of a violent passion.
Either that or its new stance was the equivalent of a bow.

Von Zweitel turned to peer through the cold fog that
veiled the derbwe's face. The muscles of the thing's eating
tendrils contracted. The sight unnerved him.

The scholarly Sister Casilda bent to whisper into her
bishop's ear. "Your Grace, the sun and all the fixed stars

are part of an island in the heavens, separated by vast distances from other clouds of stars.''

''Excuse me.'' Von Zweitel lifted the locks that muffled his right ear. ''Try that again. The sun and all the fixed stars—''

''You've seen the Milky Way. That's the heart of our island, and certainly most everything we view at night is part of it. Yet our island is merely one among thousands equally as large.''

''I've not read of this in De Fontenelle's new book,'' Von Zweitel complained, ''—notwithstanding I perused it just last night.''

''Our astronomers never knew what they were looking at. Their instruments couldn't distinguish one kind of nebula from another or judge their distances. We have the derbwem to thank for this new knowledge.''

Normally the creature on whom they nervously smiled their gratitude resembled a gondola balanced between the legs of an ostrich. In its present pose it looked more like a biped lyre. Its dorsal limbs rose stiffly like four miniature shipmasts, yet when it gestured with the foremost the motion was as supple as the writhing of an eel.

It had their attention. ''THOSE BRIGHT ISLANDS ARE UNDEVELOPED. ONCE WE MAKE OVER YOUR ISLAND ALL RADIATIONS NOW THROWN TO SPACE WILL SHOWER ONTO THIS FLAT DISK, MAKING IT DIM EXCEPT FOR EYES WHO SEE HEAT.''

Bishop Von Zweitel shook his head in nervous indulgence. These derbwem said strange things. At last night's private meeting their ambassador beached on a divan and spent twenty minutes describing how certain stars ''fell in'' to make holes in the universe. They could compel stars to collapse this way, punching through the fabric of creation. An extravagant way to send messages to God!

Von Zweitel ventured another remark. ''Excellency, in your evening visit you spoke of the speed of light. Is this your assertion? Does light take time to move across the ether?''

''EIGHT MINUTES FROM SUN TO EYES. FOUR

MILLION YEARS FROM OUR STAR ISLAND TO THIS
WORLD. YET WE NOT BE FOUR MILLION OLD. THE
EXPLANATION OF THIS I TELL YOU. TIME
CHANGES FOR US WHO TRAVEL—''

The derbwe launched into a lecture. Truly these beings
were uncouth, preaching at a moment's notice like some
anabaptist ranter!

Bishop Von Zweitel's attention wandered. He had trouble
conceding that light had speed. If light needed time to move
it was inadequate as a symbol of the Godhead. Yet the
derbwe insisted that light moved instantaneously *to itself*.
Time was a phenomenon apparent only to beings of more
material substance!

Too lazy to provide a mental refuge for a mass of crabbed
theological formulas, the bishop considered himself a friend
of science. He'd never suspected that science could impose
its own burden on the intellect, or that its revelations would
use language reminiscent of the wisdom of the Church.

What of it? Trust Sister Casilda to master that end of
things. His responsibility was to determine whether these
derbwem were creatures of a good God or mischiefs
spawned by Lucifer!

The derbwe finished its disquisition. The bishop nodded.
"Perhaps we can enlarge upon these topics at this afternoon's audience in the solarium."

He bowed. Clumsy in its all-covering costume, the
derbwe dipped in imitation. Ice tinkled to the floor. "WE
WILL TRADE BIG ANSWERS AT THAT TIME," it re-
sponded. "I DESCRIBED WHAT WE DO TO SISTER
CASILDA SO YOU CAN THINK OVER YOUR QUES-
TIONS BEFORE WE TALK."

Easing back into boat-shape, the derbwe waddled off,
trailing a cloud of frigid fog. At last the other occupants of
the salon felt free to speak. Amid a volley of nervous wit-
ticisms Sister Casilda probed the bishop's arm with her
lorgnette. "We must talk alone," she whispered.

Bishop Von Zweitel waved, nodded, and winked, taking
part in three conversations at once. He was a master in the
salon, able to hint and flatter, hinder and promise; all with

the affable elegance of a born aristocrat. He acknowledged Casilda's request with a brief pat. Half an hour later she was ushered into his study.

"I doubt it would do Father Klosterman any harm to stay and listen."

Sister Casilda ignored his pleasantry. Without invitation she moved to a gilded chair, spread her robes and sat. Though as formidable in education as in bulk, she'd never behaved in such a cavalier manner before. The bishop shrugged off her presumption. Clearly she was distraught. Thoughtful as ever, Father Klosterman poured her a glass of wine.

She swallowed and spoke. "The derbwem say two hundred intelligent races dwell in our region of heaven, and they must negotiate with each. They hope to take all the Earth and the planets of this system, even the sun itself. This and more, and more yet, until the very stars are gone!"

She fell back, pressing her hand to her heart. "Earth and heaven will be consumed in making a disk. They forswear themselves in calling it flat, for on both sides it will bear mountains and seas, rivers and forests. They measure the disk by zones, each fifty million leagues wide, and all encompassing what they call a 'Keffa,' a whirl of energy beaming forth as pillars of light—"

"Easy, easy!"

Sister Casilda shook her head. "Think of a plate with a hole at the center. Etch a circle about the Keffa-hole as large as you will, drawn as finely as to be invisible to the eye. If the width of your stylus is fifty million leagues, conceive the other dimensions!"

"I am outdone by numbers," admitted the bishop. "Our natural philosophers suggest the world might be older than six thousand years, yet none have been bold to prate of millions! The derbwem spent four million years in transit from their home. What then is all human history? A bagatelle, a mere nothing?"

"We are to have three zones as our own," the nun continued. "An inconceivable amount of territory!"

"If they can do such things why ask our permission?"

Von Zweitel shook his head. Mysteriously God had willed that these creatures select him to act for Christendom, nay, the whole world! The derbwem's spaceship might as easily have descended elsewhere. In the absence of a globe-encompassing government they'd have undertaken negotiations with Doge or Caliph, King, Bey, Maharajah, or Sachem.

Sister Casilda's eyes darted nervously. "If I could know! Consider the fearful danger! How important that we decide aright! I've prayed for a sign that these derbwem are leagued with the divine, for tales have it that the Devil too is a respecter of contracts!"

"Those stories are superstitions, nor do they represent Satan as deceptive. Nonetheless younger derbwem may be liars capable of manufacturing false signs to mislead our piety."

Father Klosterman spoke. "Your Grace, the derbwem must respect some entity or why would they speak of contracts and negotiations?"

"Yes!" Sister Casilda cried. "We must most certainly find out Who they obey!"

"The true name of God!" the bishop mused. His eyes focused. "We are to have three circles. Hell is composed of circles, is it not?"

"Circles are the most perfect of forms," Sister Casilda answered. "God is known to have taken form as a pillar of light, and angels dance in circles around him. The highest order of spirits are innermost. Our own position would be intermediate. As the derbwem require frigid cold they apportion the outermost dozens of circles to themselves. This is what they've done in other star islands."

"As angels they'd be of less rank than ourselves."

"Can that be doubted? They are powerful but by no means as beautiful as we, nor as gracious."

"Suppose I say no?" Bishop Von Zweitel asked. "Why shouldn't they take themselves elsewhere? Perhaps they'd find Sultan Suleiman more cooperative."

Father Klosterman spoke a second time. "If they're to

hear the word yes, let it be from us. We'd be the beneficiaries of their gratitude."

The bishop of Schloss Mutlorn was quite capable of such reasoning; what he sought was a higher wisdom, something to enable him to exercise a responsibility he barely understood. He looked from face to face and saw none forthcoming. Indeed, his two ministers seemed to be imploring him for solace!

What to do? "—I will take all these concerns into account. Thank you." The bishop led his advisers to the door and they made their exits. He tossed his peruke into the corner and kicked off his heels. A shrunken Von Zweitel began to pace the carpet.

Earth was to be riven at the end of time. The sun and stars would fall and the seas turn to blood—Perhaps the derbwem's proposal conformed to St. John's revelation!

Yet where was the Second Coming of Christ? And why should these things require a bishop's assent to be set in motion?

"Nor a real bishop, either!" he muttered. Von Zweitel was under no illusions that he was a worthy spiritual shepherd. The Elector had fulfilled a family obligation by appointing him to the Benefice of Zweitel. Gray-haired venerables kneeled before his staff while he was yet a lad of sixteen! He'd spent as many years learning to be a good ruler, yet he lacked the fire of true devotion. He loved life too much to be strict in his vows.

He moved to the windows. Schloss Mutlorn beetled from a pivot of rock almost surrounded by river. The hills of the south shore were covered by dark forest. Below lay a Brueghelesque village whose quays and nets might have belonged to a maritime port. Russet cupolas marked the local church, a baroque structure nestled among rude neighbors.

A depressingly German landscape. The bishop winced and turned away. This was no time to ponder aesthetics, not when he'd been singled out to ring in the Apocalypse. It was time to rally his thoughts, to pray and study.

If only he knew how! Were his Latin good he'd be paging

through the Vulgate. Instead he was obliged to fall back on memory, nor was the Book of Revelations one of his favorites.

There'd certainly be decimations if the numbers of faithful were reduced to 144,000. He'd insist on a greater number of survivors, nor only among humanity. Consider animals and birds and fish! Life would be intolerable without parks and gardens, flowers and hunts. Yes, he'd take a firm stand . . .

Firm? What *was* his position? Why should the derbwem make concessions?

The bishop returned to his desk, sharpened a quill and began to scribble notes for the afternoon meeting. He had lunch brought in. Toward the end of the meal he rang for his servant. "Fetch Father Klosterman," he ordered.

The tall, barepated priest entered the study so promptly he must have been waiting in the antechamber. "We used to try witches hereabouts, not so?" Von Zweitel asked.

Klosterman nodded. "During the wars."

The wars! Von Zweitel shuddered. Thirty years of strife and misery had killed seven out of ten of his subjects. The survivors' heirs were so disinclined to bloodshed that fog-trailing derbwem moved among them without fear of attack.

He mustered himself. "What of the clergy from those years? Do any survive? I'd have you speak to them and discover how deviltry might be confounded."

Klosterman frowned. "Your Grace—"

"We have repudiated superstition, nor are witches persecuted in my prebend. Still, those grim old torturers might have a word of advice for their spiritual lord."

"As might the witches they failed to catch."

"Are there any? We are forbidden to consult witches, but if there were one no longer active she might recollect something of advantage."

Father Klosterman showed distress by plucking imaginary lint from his cassock. "Do not pursue this course, Your Grace. Only by accident will they say anything useful."

The bishop opened his snuff-box, then paused. "Why?"

"The human soul has many powers. Among these is

reason, which sets us apart from the brutes. The derbwem possess a rational intellect and so we are brothers of a special sort, favored by God."

"Yes?"

"Witchcraft deals with facets of the mind which we prefer to ignore. We hardly have names for those mysterious faculties invoked during times of heroic challenge. Perhaps we share nameless attributes with the derbwem, but I doubt it. In all but reason itself, we and the derbwem are different. Those who map the human soul will only mislead you."

"I see. We need the advice of a derbwe witch!" The bishop leaned back and stroked his chin thoughtfully. "Yes, yes," he mumbled. "An interesting approach. That's the way to do it. Get inside their minds and soon enough we'll know why they act as they do."

The audience began an hour later. The derbwe ambassador was ushered into the solarium, a windowed excrescence built atop Mutlorn's most elevated artillery platform. Though the sun was their ally the bishop and his advisers wore thick robes against the chill emanating from the creature. As always, thin sheets of ice formed on the ambassador's suit, then slivered and fell to the carpet.

A servant distributed glasses of himbeergeist and retired to his corner. Von Zweitel sipped to kindle a fire in his belly. "You are beings of power and wisdom," he began. "You come to treat with all humanity. May I ask your title?"

"I AM AMBASSADOR FROM STAR ISLAND FAR AWAY."

The bishop shook his head. "This word, 'ambassador.' What is its literal translation?"

"WE LIKE ME ARE 'LONELY ONES.' "

"Why is that?"

"BECAUSE WE GO FROM THE MANY."

Von Zweitel frowned. "Are you of a special class by birth? A special breed?"

"NO. WE ARE TAKEN FROM THE MANY BY OTHER LONELY ONES, SO THAT WORK CAN BE DONE."

The bishop turned to Father Klosterman. "Isn't this method extolled in one of our utopias, where a wise aristocracy selects and trains their successors? The practice of the Church is rather similar."

Sister Casilda spoke. "Are you tested before being taken from the Many? Do you keep vows?"

"THIS WE TALK ABOUT SOME OTHER TIME," the derbwe responded.

"But you have us spellbound," Sister Casilda remarked. "If you represent the Church Celestial, as it seems you might . . ."

"WE NEVER TESTED," the derbwe conceded. "IT IS STUPID TO TEST. IF SMARTEST TAKEN TO BE LONELY ONES, THEN THE MANY BREEDS LESS SMART DERBWEM. YOUR CHURCH VOWS DO HARM. ALWAYS SMART ONES GO INTO CHURCH AND NOT HAVE CHILDREN. IN TIME HUMANS GET DUMBER AND DUMBER."

"So this 'Many' is the source of offspring?"

"THIS IS NOT IMPORTANT," the derbwe insisted.

Bishop Von Zweitel bent forward. "I have one or two more questions. First, your word for 'negotiation'; what does it signify?"

"WE ASK MANY QUESTIONS. YOU ANSWER. WE MEASURE WHAT WE DO TO FIT YOUR ANSWERS. THAT IS NEGOTIATION."

"When we negotiate with each other both parties give as well as gain. I don't think that word fits what we're doing today. Can you think of another?"

Sister Casilda inhaled sharply. The bishop turned. "Have you something to say?"

"It is the method of natural science to observe and make generalizations. The derbwem are scientific, so they boast. Can they pass judgments on all the world based on what we say today?"

"YES," the derbwe responded. "THAT WE DO."

"One of you, making a judgment about a whole word based on our answers," the bishop repeated. "Forgive me, Excellency, but the fact that you work this way tells me something about the other creatures of the universe. In the heavens there must be no great diversity; no kings, aristocrats, nor peasants.

"As for us, from the days of the Tower of Babel we've been sundered by religion, birth, and wealth. On other worlds your practice might be justified, but—"

"WE ALWAYS DO THIS," the derbwe interrupted. "WHY ASK BEFORE MAKING YOUR ISLAND BETTER? WE WERE MADE FOR THE WORK WE DO, AND IT IS SAD WHEN IGNORANT NATIVES SAY NO. TOO BAD. WE HAVE TO ASK ANYWAY."

"Why?"

"THE KEFFA AT THE CENTER OF THE GREAT DISK WE MAKE IS THE SOURCE OF ALL LIGHT AND HEAT. BEINGS OF STRONG ENERGY DWELL IN THE AXIAL BEAMS FLOWING FROM THE KEFFA. THEY CAN BEND LIGHT AND CHANGE DANGEROUS RADIATIONS. WE WORK WITH THEM FOR ALL HISTORY.

"THESE BEINGS NEVER FAIL US. YOU WANT DAYTIME AND NIGHT, SUMMER AND WINTER? THEY BEND THE RAYS OF THE KEFFA TO MAKE BRIGHTNESS OF SUN AND MOON JUST RIGHT FOR YOU. SAME FOR US, TOO."

"Yes?" Von Zweitel persisted.

"THEY MAKE US ASK PERMISSION. NO STAR ISLAND CAN BE REWORKED LIKE WE WANT UNLESS ALL WHO DWELL THERE SAY YES."

"You're not just an agent of the derbwem, but of other races as well?" Father Klosterman asked.

"MANY RACES FROM OTHER STAR ISLANDS COME TO LIVE HERE, BUT YOU NATIVES HAVE FIRST CHOICE, BIGGEST AND BEST PLACES. HUMANS COME TOO WHEN WE GO TO NEXT WILD ISLAND TO REWORK IT INTO DISK, BUT THEN YOU SHARE JUST ONE ZONE WITH MANY OTHERS."

The bishop raised an eyebrow. "You derbwem are more generous with yourselves. You hope to occupy dozens of circles."

"WE LIKE COLD. IF WE DID NOT LIVE IN COLD ZONES THEY WOULD BE WASTED. THERE ARE NONE OTHERS LIKE US, SO THE MAKING OF DISKS IS ADVANTAGE TO US DERBWEM. THEREFORE WE ARE EAGER TO TRAVEL THROUGH SPACE AND BUILD MORE. IT IS OUR SPECIAL WORK."

"Yet you're acquainted with other races. They might be better than you in dealing with humanity. How inept you derbwem are in the art of persuasion! You lack patience. I've yet to hear you tell a joke or indulge in flattery. Though you know something of the Church you've made no attempt to paint yourselves as creatures of God."

The derbwe stood silent for several seconds. "THE KEFFA-DWELLERS LIKE IT SO. YES, IN SOME WAYS WE ARE STUPID. WHY NOT, SINCE WE NEVER USE PERSUASION AMONG OUR OWN KIND?"

"Never use persuasion? What? No demagogues, no courtiers, no merchants? Are there any folk so artless among our human kind; magistrates, vintners, husbandmen?— Even the plowman coaxes his ox!"

As the perplexed bishop buried his face in his hands Sister Casilda began to expostulate. "Your Grace, these Keffa-dwellers are angels! The Keffa is a hole in the universe, so they're closest to God of the things of creation. Is it any wonder they're good, insisting we natives approve or deny the derbwem's proposals?

"As for their procedure, remember the words of Saint Paul? 'As through one man sin came into the world, so also by one man we are saved!' "

"Blasphemy!" Father Klosterman rebuked.

"I do not compare His Grace to Jesus Christ. I merely point out that God makes one person stand for many."

Von Zweitel raised his head. "How can any race exist without persuasion? What is language for? Before we are weaned, nurses cajole us, humor us, tempt us. Now we deal with a creature for whom none of this comes naturally?"

The derbwe stepped back. The humans in the solarium were enmeshed in yet another verbal frenzy. Their minds were nimble enough to dart from blasphemy to linguistics; its was not.

Sister Casilda tapped her lorgnette for attention. "Perhaps this derbwe is less than us, as its place is outermost from the Keffa. To us it lacks charm. Yet the good God has found a role for it. Does not the Lord use that which is foolish to confound the wise?"

The bishop waved for silence. Murky as his mental processes were, he could usually tell when he was on the verge of a brainstorm. Something of the sort was happening now. As the seconds passed he took a pinch of snuff and leaned back in his chair.

"If we assent to this proposal," he began. "—If we assent, I say, it would be out of no personal interest. We'd be better served if our subjects stayed close at hand. Transplanted to a celestial zone they'd be free to disperse over a region a thousand times the size of Asia."

Father Klosterman frowned. "We'd revert to savagery!" "Right now we're concerned with God's will. Should this derbwe be an agent of the Devil it would tempt us with wealth, pleasures, and power. In point of fact its proposals are by no means so venal.

"On the other hand, if we deny it the opportunity to rework our star island we should do so out of mistrust and because its manners are crude. As Sister Casilda mentioned, God uses the humble to bring down the great. If this event be a test of our spiritual maturity we'd be wise to accede to our strange visitors' proposals."

"Yes, yes!" exclaimed Sister Casilda.

The bishop felt perilously close to decision. He cast about for rescue. "Father Klosterman, what do you think?"

The tall priest scratched his pate. "The prophets tell us that creatures of light have visited our world. Like the derbwem's Keffa-angels, they work to promote righteousness."

"So you agree with Sister—"

"Your Grace, I find it difficult to bring all the facts into a single frame. Remember, the Keffa-angels use the derbwem for negotiation because yon creatures are direct and artless. It's easy to conclude that they disapprove of subtlety.

"If so, their earthly visitations could not have been meant to prepare us for the derbwem, although by their efforts we know of pillars of fire and dancing circles of Seraphs and Cherubs."

Father Klosterman fell silent. The bishop rapped the table. "Go on."

"Are there factions among the angelic host? Do our angels support or oppose the redevelopment of our star island? Our angels inspired Sacred Scripture. It has to be the policy of the Church to take their side. As they've come to Earth and brought us the consolations of religion, I'm inclined to believe they have other designs for humanity than those proposed by the derbwe ambassador."

"The Second Coming—"

"Exactly. The derbwem promise an apocalypse, but what about the dead? Will they be brought to life? Will there be a Last Judgment?"

Human eyes trained on the derbwe. "NO," the creature responded, rearing back into lyre-posture. Shingles of ice crashed to the floor. "WE NOT MAKE THE LONG DEAD ALIVE AGAIN. ONLY THE SHORT DEAD. THAT BE LESS DIFFICULT. YOU HUMANS LEARN HOW PRETTY SOON."

The bishop rubbed his chill hands. "You've heard our speculations. God has an agenda for humanity. What you offer is only part of the agenda, not all. Were we greedy on behalf of our race we'd say yes to you, but God's angels inspire us with dreams beyond such greed.

"As for the other items on the agenda, such as immortality; do you feel we might achieve these things within, say, a few centuries? Might we nurse such spectacular hopes?"

"PERHAPS. IF YOUR HISTORY GOES RIGHT—"

"We'll trust our angels to guide us."

The derbwe's tendrils contracted. "DOES THIS MEAN YOU SAY NO?"

"If the human race is distributed over three celestial zones we'd spread and scatter. Civilization would suffer. We'd be in no position to learn how to raise the dead nor judge the living. It's in our interest to delay you until we've bettered ourselves. Give us a thousand years, then come and ask again.''

''THREE HUNDRED,'' the derbwe responded. ''I VISIT TWO OTHER RACES IN THIS SECTOR, THEN COME BACK. ANYTHING MORE WASTES TOO MUCH TIME.''

''Three hundred, then!'' Bishop Von Zweitel leaned back in relief. ''I'll leave notes for my successor. Never fear: as long as the Holy Roman Empire survives your race will be welcomed in peace and amity!''

The ambassador altered postures, turned, and stalked off. With trembling hands the bishop signaled a second round of himbeergeist. As the room warmed he stood to propose a toast. ''When the tread of an ox fails to crush an ant, is there triumph? When the ant is killed is there tragedy? No. The forces were unequal, nor did the ant use wisdom in her ramblings.

''Likewise for us. If I knew why we were granted three hundred years I might say something to posterity. To what do we owe the preservation of our present status? Have I done well or not?

''Perhaps it does not matter. I have shifted the responsibility from my own shoulders, a personal victory and one not entirely selfish, since surely I'm not the wisest of men. Therefore I drink to the future, when death is overcome and magistrates of prudence rule all the Earth. They must do better than I! Here's to 1988!''

The derbwe returned to its spaceship. The vessel rose aloft. Once beyond this world's torrid atmosphere the ambassador removed its environment suit. It flipped a switch to open the main communication channel. ''WHAT DID THEY SAY?'' the navigator inquired.

''WHAT DO THEY ALWAYS SAY? 'WAIT! GIVE US A FEW GENERATIONS TO MAKE THE DECISION.' ''

''YOU ANSWERED NO, OF COURSE.''

''I ANSWERED YES. THERE'S SOMETHING PE-CULIAR ABOUT THIS PLANET. THEY CLAIM TO

HAVE HAD VISITATIONS; STRANGE ENTITIES, BEINGS OF LIGHT—''

''WE'D BETTER TREAT THEM GINGERLY. THE KEFFA-DWELLERS MAY BE MONITORING US AGAIN.''

''THEY WERE ABOUT TO AGREE TO OUR PLANS FOR REASONS I COULD NOT UNDERSTAND. A SHORT WHILE LATER THEY WERE READY TO SAY NO FOR EQUALLY MYSTERIOUS REASONS. I CONFESS I WAS RELIEVED WHEN THEY ASKED FOR A DELAY. IT MADE THEM NORMAL. I HOPE THE NEXT TIME I TALK TO THEM THEY'LL MAKE MORE SENSE!''

"IRIDESCENCE"

Dean Whitlock

"Iridescence" was purchased by Gardner Dozois, and appeared in the January 1989 issue of IAsfm, with an illustration by Richard Crist. A deceptively quiet writer, Whitlock's stories often pack a solid punch, as does this eloquent and suspenseful story of friendship and faith—and the price you sometimes have to be willing to pay for them.

New writer Dean Whitlock made his first sale in 1987, and has subsequently become a frequent contributor to IAsfm, The Magazine of Fantasy and Science Fiction, and other markets. Whitlock lives in Post Mills, Vermont.

It was a soap bubble, simple as that. It hovered for a minute over the heads of the crowd, lifted, and then popped in a tiny rain of shiny drops. Someone laughed, a sudden, happy sound. I went closer.

Another bubble rose over their heads. I watched colors swirl over the surface, a rainbow, mostly green, iridescent in the workday glow of the ceiling. Then it popped, too. I heard water plop on the sidewalk. And more laughter. I had spent the day wandering from level to level, up and down the lifts and the lanes of the city, with no more purpose than a vague sense of looking. I saw little and remembered less. Only the bubbles reached me.

I looked between the gathered heads to see the magician who turned soap and water into laughter. I saw a Lyrin, strange enough sight on a crowded street, stranger still making magic at the center of the crowd. He was thin and graceful, taut in his fine white fur. He dipped the end of a clear tube into liquid, lifted it to his broad lips, and blew out another bubble, big as my fist. It rested briefly over his other palm. Then, quickly, gently, he put down the tube, dipped the end of one long finger into a dish of dye, and spotted the bubble with color.

A light touch, here and here, and blue swirled across the curve. He drew away his lower hand, and the bubble rose. Lines of blue washed around the sphere, drawing out the swirling lines of film that made it whole. Drawing out my breath. The pattern changed, shifted. And the bubble popped. Tiny drops splashed my forehead. I laughed with the others.

The crowd was mostly human, mostly young, clerks and techs on their way home at the end of the day shift. They made a tight ring at the outer edge of the sidewalk, three deep, with the Lyrin in the center. A small group of Darniers stood to his left, chittering quietly as he picked up his tube and dipped it into the pan of soapy water. Yesterday, I would have had to break it up. Today, I craned for a better look.

Walkers pushed by behind me, forced to skirt the center rail. In the well, local shuttles glided past, crowded with tired faces. Expresses skimmed along the ceiling. People came and went from the shops and offices in the outer wall. The tunnel echoed with footsteps, tapping claws, and mumbled voices. Only our circle was still.

He blew the bubble and caught it on—no, *above* his palm. It hung there, turning slowly. He dipped more color, touched it to the surface. Green and blue. They swirled, melded. He drew his hand away, and the bubble hung before his face. I watched his eyes as he watched the colors swirl. He smiled at what he had crafted, a wide smile. I had never seen a Lyrin smile. Then his eyes brightened. I looked at the bubble as the swirls came to equilibrium. A moment of balance. Perfection? No. But the best I had seen that day and longer.

The crowd was silent, awed, and the Lyrin with them. That was when I first thought him an artist. When he shared our awe.

Then the bubble popped, and half of us gasped. The Darniers clicked in dismay. But the Lyrin laughed, laughed at the sheer joy of that moment, and I laughed with him. I had gone a little mad that morning. There was an edge to my laughter. The Lyrin looked past the others and found my eyes. He smiled again and made a little bow. Maybe he was mad, too. I bowed back. He dotted the next one red and blue and sent it over my head.

The crowd shifted as people joined and left the circle. Painted bubbles rose and popped above them. I stayed as the light faded to evenglow, slowly moving inward till I stood before the Lyrin across the ring.

Dots of color spotted his smooth fur. The six fingertips of his right hand were stained, each a different color. The long guard hairs there were carefully plucked and shaped to fine brushes. His other hand was dry and white. I watched as he held the bubbles a small space above his palm and wondered. He studied each one as it came off the tube, his wide, thin eyes all pupil, jet against the fur. He frowned, grimaced, smiled that wide smile, laughed with delight as he chose his colors and his points on the curve. He said nothing. He asked nothing. People dropped coins on the sidewalk before him, but he didn't seem to notice.

There was a stir to my left, but I ignored it, caught in his spell. The Lyrin was lifting his finger to paint, and I was watching closely. His fingertip brushed the sphere. And suddenly the bubble shattered. Red dye streaked his palm. For a moment, I thought it was blood. Then I remembered the crack and the dark coil that had whipped above his palm just as he touched the bubble. The Lyrin met my eyes again, then glanced left. I looked.

A Shivite stood at the edge of the ring. Its tool arms were crossed on its broad thorax. Its whip arms spiraled back above its head to curve along the gloss-black plates of its carapace. It seemed at ease, head cocked, leg arms spread in a balanced stance, towering black above the watchers. Its sighted eyes were blank, chelae still. Only the third eye seemed to watch. The crowd gave it room.

The Lyrin nodded to it slightly, then lifted his tube and blew another bubble.

Crack! A whip arm struck across the ring, the right arm. Water sprayed the people standing near the Lyrin. They moved back. The littler Darniers faded into the crowd. The Lyrin stood still a minute, smile frozen on his broad lips. Then he dipped his tube, blew another bubble.

The right whip struck out. The bubble disintegrated. The Lyrin blew another. The Shivite broke it. And again. And again. And again.

The crowd thinned. The circle shifted as people drew away from the Shivite and its whip. The Lyrin blew another bubble. The Shivite whip scattered rain across his face. No one seemed to move, but the circle was suddenly wider. Only three figures held their places—the Lyrin, the Shivite, and me.

The Lyrin was quick and lithe. He wore a knife, sheathed on his right thigh. But he was a Lyrin, for all his art and magic. He smiled patiently and blew another bubble. The Shivite had its own patience. It broke it as it left the tube. I had lost my patience long before. I stepped between them and turned to face the Shivite.

And in that moment, I remembered who I was. Or who I no longer was. I had no uniform. No badge, no weapon, no authority. No longer. I faced the Shivite boldly and felt naked.

"Human," the Lyrin said behind me. "Please . . ."

But the Shivite turned its sighted eyes on me. The facets bent light and shone with dark rainbows. The third eye hung between them, red and seeking, iridescent.

"Human . . . ," the Lyrin said again.

Then the Shivite struck.

There is a way to fight them barehanded. I've seen it done. But I had trained with a stick. A nightstick, a crop, even a cane would do. Something to catch the curling tip of the left whip. Something to deflect the sting.

I beat the blunt right whip aside with the edge of my hand and turned sideways. The left whip flicked the air where my shoulder had been. I glimpsed the hollow point of the stinger, sliding in its sheath below the tip. Then the arms coiled back, to hang like dark wings above its head. It stood silently, balanced.

Then it struck again. I ducked right, under the sting. But the other whip hit my arm. I staggered, crouching. The whips coiled, and struck again. I rolled back and came up with both arms swinging out. The right whip glanced aside. The other slid along my sleeve, parting threads, then drew back. I shifted my stance, centering, ready.

Then I felt the burning, saw the tiny welt on the back of my hand. Pain shot up my arm as the poison spread. The joints locked, then went limp. I stumbled, vision blurring. The Shivite stood over me, whips coiled, eyes glowing as the light faded in mine. My entire body began to burn. I fell forward, but hands caught me from behind.

The last thing I heard was "Human."

I came awake once in a dark place. Two eyes shone above me, and I struggled. But they were black, not green. Smooth, not jeweled.

A voice I knew said, "He wakes."

Another voice spoke and something hard pressed my lips. "Drink," he said.

I did, and choked, my throat tight and burning. But I drank again, and fell asleep.

The next time I woke, there was light. Dim light in a small, low room. I lay on a padded bench under a thin blanket. I looked around at two chairs and a table, a bed, a doorway. The Lyrin stood at a counter, slicing vegetables with his long knife.

He heard me move and looked up.

"He wakes," he said, and I recognized the voice. No one answered him this time. We were alone. He rinsed his knife, wiped it carefully, and sheathed it on his thigh. Then he carried a cup over to my bed.

"Drink," he said.

"What is it?" I could barely speak.

"Tonic," he said. "From a human doctor."

I drank. The first sip burned my throat again, but the second went down smoothly, and the third and fourth finished it.

"More?" he asked.

I nodded and he went to the counter and filled the cup. He came back with thin slices of vegetable and a cheese.

"This is all right?" he asked.

I didn't know. I drank more tonic and tried the vegetable. It went down and stayed.

The Lyrin smiled. He drew his knife and deftly sliced the cheese, then sheathed the blade again. Something in the action struck me funny. It was a potent tool to use in the kitchen. Most Lyrins wore one, but I'd never seen one drawn. I'd never seen a Lyrin smile before, either. I laughed weakly, a thin sound, given my throat and the state of my head.

The Lyrin looked startled, and then laughed himself.

"He's better," he said. "Laughter cures, yes?"

"Yes," I said. I lay back, cradling my cup on my chest. "Laughter cures." I smiled again to show I meant it, even though the room was slowly turning around me at the moment.

"Where is this?" I asked. I closed my eyes, and the room stopped moving. But then I started moving in it.

"This is home," he said.

Yes, I thought, home. Where is home? I tried to say it out loud—where is . . . But the swirling took me away.

I woke up several more times, drank more tonic, ate enough to stay alive. I found out that home was Sublevel Nine, Ring Twelve East, Donner Lane, 40. Low rent, subsidized, one room, one door. My old home had two rooms and a skylight. But my old home was on Sub Three. This was good enough, now.

On the day that I woke up hungry, I thought to ask his name. He was sitting at the table, mixing dyes in small jars, but he put that aside to bring me more tonic and offer food. I downed every slice as soon as he could cut it, until we both laughed at my appetite.

"Wait," he said, rising. He rummaged in the cupboard, found a real paring knife, and brought it back. He presented me with both knife and cheese, then helped me sit upright on the bench. He sat beside me as I stuffed the cheese into my mouth, holding the cup where I could reach it easily. When the worst of the craving had passed, I thought about his name.

He bowed, a formal gesture. It was a Lyrin gesture, but again the action struck me. He had fed me like a baby, wiped my face, mopped up my urine. Suddenly, when it came to names, he was formal, Lyrin.

"This one is Ayer," he said solemnly.

"Ayer," I repeated, trying to voice the y and roll the r as he had. He bowed again, then waited.

"Jensin Lord," I said. I realized this was a ceremony for him, this trading names. I kept my voice grave, and bowed.

"Jensin Lord," he repeated. He softened the j, but it sounded fine. "This one is Jensin Lord." Then he smiled again, became himself. "It is a long name," he said.

I smiled back.

"Jensin is enough," I said.

He nodded. "Jensin. Jensin."

"Ayer."

Suddenly, he touched my right hand, a soft touch with

just the stained tips of his fingers. But the welt was still there, still sore. I jerked back. He frowned.

"This Jensin is foolish," he said.

The way he said it made me blush.

"This Jensin is stupid," I said.

"Why?"

"Why stupid?" I asked.

He nodded. "Why make a fight?"

"Habit, I guess. I'm used to fighting for the little guy." He looked puzzled. "You," I said, pointing. "This one. Ayer. He cannot fight a Shivite."

"This Jensin can?" I couldn't read his expression, but I guessed he knew sarcasm. I shrugged.

"Six hours earlier, I could have," I said. "I forgot I had quit the force."

"This one, he is a peace officer." Ayer nodded, as if it answered some question.

"Was," I told him. "Was. I quit this morning. So they couldn't fire me."

"Fire?"

"Let go. Made to leave."

"Why should they?" They were direct, Lyrins. He hadn't shed that.

I thought about it. Why, indeed? Because I had tried reason when I should have used force. Because I had drawn my weapon when I should have tried reason. I had let people get hurt. I had shot first, thought later. Suddenly, after fifteen years, it all came down to kill or be killed. Or both.

"Impaired judgment," I said finally. "Loss of perspective. They'd call it something like that. I call it brain rot. Occupational insanity. Something small crawled in my ear and ate out my sense of balance." I took a deep breath. The room was spinning again. I settled back onto the pillow.

"What can I say?" I looked at the Lyrin, looked away. I couldn't read his thin black eyes. "I forgot how to do my job."

"So he fights with a Shivite." He laughed again, not unkindly. "That is, yes, loss of balance."

"You would have discussed things with it, I suppose."

"Talk with a Shivite? Who can think like a Shivite? No. It would have gone away, maybe."

"And if it didn't?"

"Ayer would go away."

That was Lyrin. "What were you doing there?" I asked.

"Painting." He didn't elaborate.

"I've never seen that done before," I said. "Is that something you do, your people?"

His eyes narrowed. "No. This is Ayer's, this painting."

"How come you're here? Why did you leave Lyra?"

He considered, then smiled. "Loss of balance," he said. "More food? Different food?"

I'm not sure I understood, any more than I understood the Shivite. He was right about that, at least—you can't talk to a Shivite. Or trust it to follow any human logic. Sometimes, you can face one down. Or maybe it just decides to do something else. Who can say? Lyrin at least are predictable. Even Ayer. They just bow and go away.

I was two weeks healing, and I counted myself lucky. Ayer never suggested I go to a hospital, and I never brought it up. I didn't question his kindness and didn't want to lose it. I had been living for a long time in a constant state of anger. His room was a haven, disorienting in its tranquility, but safe.

Once I could feed myself, he began to go out again, a few hours each day. He packed up his dyes and tube, a bottle of soapy water, a pan, all slung over his shoulder in a small box with scissored legs that opened into a stand. He came back spotted with color, with a jar full of loose change and small bills.

On the first day I could walk without swaying, I went out with him. Donner Lane took foot traffic only, a dark, narrow tunnel lined with doorways and never lit brighter than evenglow. I doubted many humans lived there. Certainly, no Lyrins. Ayer led me North and East and round the compass through a maze of dim narrow lanes and finally North again to a radial lane, where the light brightened to workday and there was a lift. We went up to Sub Six and caught an inbound local to Ring Three. It was a section of shops and offices similar to the neighborhood where I'd first found him, but halfway around the ring. I was weak and sweating by the time we got there.

Ayer found a place between two doorways and set up his stand. I sat back against the wall beside him and watched as a few curious shoppers paused to see what he was selling. When the first bubble lifted off his hand, the crowd grew. He held them for an hour, I guess, painting his brief creations, making them laugh or sigh at each shimmering globe. I laughed with them at the lively ones, sighed at the beauties, each an individual. And I watched them hover over Ayer's palm, watched his fingers paint without breaking the film, and wondered again.

Then a dark movement at the edge of the crowd caught my eye. The circle parted and a Shivite stepped forward. Its bright eyes caught mine a moment, then turned back to Ayer. It waited, tool arms crossed, whips coiled. Sweat chilled on my face.

Ayer lowered the tube from his lips, laughter gone now. He looked back at me, as if to see what I would do if he blew another bubble. I don't think either of us doubted what the Shivite would do. I shrugged. There was nothing I could do, except sit against the wall and sweat. I was still weak, and no longer so foolish. But I felt the old anger settle on me, the madness.

Ayer must have seen that. He put the tube aside and capped his jars. The crowd dispersed, as though glad there was nothing still to see. They gave the Shivite a wide berth. It stood there, three eyes watching, as Ayer closed up his stand and helped me rise. I felt them shimmer against my back as we turned and walked away.

The ride back seemed endless. My legs shook, from weakness and reaction. Blood whined in my ears. My vision narrowed to the small space before my feet. Then we were walking and the light dimmed and we entered the warren he called home. And finally we walked into Donner Lane, and I stopped wondering if Ayer would have to carry me. We were two steps from his door when someone spoke.

"Spare change?"

I lifted my head and forced myself to see.

The boy was thin and lank, with a scattering of beard. His eyes were dark and wet, his voice thick. He kept his hands in his pockets and peered up from hunched shoulders. He looked too pitiful to be dangerous, like me.

"Spare change?" he said again when we stopped. I leaned against the tunnel wall, wishing him gone. But Ayer set down his case and reached inside for the jar of coins. Then I heard footsteps behind us. I turned and saw thin boy had friends.

"I'll take that, Furry," one said. There were just two of them, but that made them one more than us. They were both human, both male. Their eyes shone like thin boy's, as if there was too much light. They were dark and hungry. The speaker eyed me once and decided I was easy. He stuck out his hand.

"The jar, Furry," he said. "I'll take it."

Ayer straightened slowly and bowed. He held out the jar, set it gently in the boy's hand. Thin boy came around to join his friends. The leader shook the jar and smiled.

"Thanks, Furry," he said. "That was real kind."

I watched them turn, raging at my shaking legs. Without thinking, I pushed off the wall and took one staggering step after them, reaching. But Ayer grabbed my shoulder and held me. I pulled against him, then realized my weakness and let him drag me back through his doorway.

I sank on the bench, fists clenched. He set his case on the table and opened it, took out the dyes and water.

"You could have stopped them," I said.

He added more color to the jars, replenished the soap solution.

"They were bluffing," I said, "play-acting. You could have stopped them cold."

"No," he said, but I didn't stop for an answer.

"They were half-starved sublife," I said, ranting now. "Empty handed. You could have drawn that damn knife and scared them off. Hell, you could have just touched the handle."

Ayer looked up at me. His eyes were narrowed, black lines.

"This one cannot use the knife," he said.

"Well then why the hell don't you leave it in the kitchen? What good is it if you can't use it?"

His right hand flashed to his thigh. The knife shimmered toward me, struck the wall beside my ear. Stuck there, ringing.

"This Jensin does not understand," Ayer said. "Can, but will not."

I pulled the knife from the wall. The edge was sharp, the balance perfect.

"Then why do you carry it?" I asked. I had stopped shouting.

He came to me, hand out, and I placed the handle in his palm. He sheathed the knife and went back to the table.

"To remember," he said. "It is there *not* to be drawn."

I closed my eyes and sank back on the bench. He made it sound easy. Too easy. I remembered the days I carried my own weapon and tried not to use it. And the days when I didn't give a damn.

"Jensin."

I opened my eyes. A bubble floated before them, cradled on Ayer's palm. He dabbed on colors, two, then three. His light touch made hollows in the film. The bubble bounced lightly, oval, then round, then oval. I couldn't help but smile. Then it popped, spattering my face.

"How do you do that?" I asked. "How do you make it stay there and not pop?"

"The wetness," he said. "Look, Jensin."

He blew a large bubble, as big as my head. Then he dipped his whole hand into the soap solution. He pressed it against the bubble, and it went through the film. He wore the bubble like a glove.

"No magic," he said. "Physics."

He pulled his hand out.

"But that," I said, pointing. "It floats above your hand. How do you do that?"

"Ah," he said, nodding. He lifted his hand gently, sent

the bubble floating across the room. The film wavered just before it popped. Then he blew another, smaller, and caught it deftly in the air over his palm. "This is different," he agreed. "This one might call magic."

For a moment, I believed him. Lyrins don't know humor. But this was Ayer.

"How do you do it?" I asked. "Is it levitation? What?"

"Levitation." He considered. "The bubble is made of water film," he said. "Around the bubble is thought film. The bubble is flown, the thought is formed. The thought rests on the hand. The bubble in a bubble. This is levitation?"

He drew his hand away and let the bubble sink to the floor. It shimmered a moment, a dome. Then popped.

"This is levitation," I said.

As simple as that. Blow a thought around a bubble. The armed forces of two dozen worlds would kill to have Ayer in their hands.

"Can you do this to other things?" I asked.

"People? Star ships?" He laughed. "This Jensin, he can lift a mountain?"

So. I felt relieved. "Ayer," I said. "If anyone else ever asks you, tell them it's a trick. Tell them it's all done with mirrors."

He smiled and bowed. "This one know, Friend."

His trust made me feel a dozen years healthier.

"Now," I said, "can you teach me?"

Yes and no, it turned out. He could show me. He could let me blow the bubbles and wield the dyes on tiny brushes made from his own fur. But he held the bubbles. First I held my hand below his, trying to sense . . . what? Something of the force that he shaped around the bubble. Then I held my hand above his, the bubbles riding a breath above my palm.

And after a while, I gave up. I stopped trying to grip each bubble in some kind of mental fist, stopped trying to float it on a cushion of thought. Because the real bubbles distracted me. The shining film caught my attention, held my eyes. I became aware of the patterns in the film, and how dyes could float on those patterns to make them whole. Or not. Many I made were flawed, but even they were beautiful. Ayer made suggestions, praised the ones that worked. I studied each as he drew his hand away and it floated free in the moments before it popped. And tried to make the next more perfect. Sometimes, I succeeded.

But once, I grabbed Ayer's hand when he started to move it away. "No," I told him. "One second more."

I reached for a different brush. But he moved his hand anyway, and the bubble soared. I chased it, vainly tried to touch on one more drop of color. It broke against the wall.

"Damn it!" I shouted. "It wasn't done."

He looked at me, pupils dilated to jet. Then he blew another bubble and held it patiently on his hand. I watched the film, saw a pattern, touched color here and there. Then again as the pattern changed. Then again as Ayer held his hand rock still beneath it. And stopped with my brush poised. Still Ayer held the bubble over his hand. But the colors grayed. The film blanched and went dull, like an eye open in death.

I drew back. And then Ayer moved his hand and let the bubble pop. The film poured in on itself and tumbled to the floor at my feet. I watched it fall, then looked up at Ayer.

"Each has a life," he said, "no shorter, no longer. That is most of the magic." I frowned, feeling stupid. "This Jensin, he knows the Shivite, yes?"

The memory made my hand ache. "Yes," I said.

"Remember the Shivite. Now, this one must eat."

Together we cleaned up the bottles and dyes, then made a meal. Ayer cooked a stew this time, deftly slicing ingredients with his knife. He talked about the dyes he used, the best places to set up the stand, which audiences left more money, which gave more laughter. I listened and helped, my eyes filled with iridescence.

We went out again the next day, to a spot near a park, where people could linger and enjoy his art. I watched avidly, seeing how he chose his points, which colors he used. But the Shivite came, and we packed up the dyes and left.

That night, I painted again while Ayer patiently held the bubbles. He insisted I blow them, and hold my hand above his, so the bubbles appeared to float over my palm.

"This will come," he said. "For now, pretend."

So I pretended until my eyes were tired and my breath ragged. And the next day we went back out, and Ayer let me paint before the crowd. Two times only, but they were good. I'd have done more, but the Shivite found us again.

I looked back as we walked away, and felt the old anger. My fists clenched, despite me. But Ayer walked calmly beside me and I matched his stride. I thought of bubbles floating in the air above my hand and kept walking away. It was not easy.

It was harder the next day, when the Shivite came and the crowd scattered, and the next, when we hadn't even set up the stand.

"What does he want with us?" I asked Ayer.

"Who can think like a Shivite?" he said. "Who can say this one is even the same?"

It was the same, I was sure of that. But he was right about the thinking. I tried to put it from my mind, to adopt Ayer's calm. I thought about bubbles. Bubbles within bubbles.

The next day, the Shivite was waiting for us at the lift station. It followed us into the lift and onto the shuttle, trailed us along the street and stood watching when we reached the spot Ayer had chosen. It stood back a tourist's distance and waited. Ayer started to walk away, but I stopped him.

He looked at me, curious. "This Jensin, he would stay?"

I looked at the Shivite, felt his third eye on me. I quelled my anger. I was strong again, but more than a fight, I wanted to paint.

"Yes," I said. "Yes, let's try it."

Ayer smiled and set up the stand.

He blew a bubble, and a crowd began to form. The Shivite stood in a pocket of space, silent, unmoving. I sat beside Ayer and watched him work. After a moment, I forgot the Shivite. I began to see the why of each move Ayer made, each color he chose. The bubbles floated up from his hand, performed for the crowd, and burst. I floated with them, once again more than a little mad.

Then Ayer handed me the tube. I stood and blew a bubble, held my hand under it, over his. I painted and let it go. Blew another, and painted. And another. I forgot the crowd and the Shivite. I forgot Ayer. I stood and painted and I forgot Ayer's hand. Until suddenly I saw he no longer stood beside me. I went still, the bubble floating above my palm, color whirling on its surface. Above my palm. His hand was gone, but the bubble floated there anyway, iridescent. A bubble in a bubble.

I almost lost it then, but I sent it up above the crowd to their applause.

My hand was shaking, but I blew another. And held it. And dipped my brush.

And then the Shivite struck.

The whip was there and gone, the bubble spattered on my face and dripping before I realized what had happened. I stared stupidly at my empty palm, then up at the Shivite. It loomed, quiet, blank. I saw myself reflected in its dark shell, and Ayer a white blur beside me.

"Jensin." He took me by the shoulder and tried to turn me. Eventually, I let him. I wiped my face and my palm and let Ayer hand me things to put away. I folded the stand and hung it over my shoulder. The crowd was gone already. Time to take our money and leave. I ignored the Shivite as best I could.

But it followed us, to the shuttle and the lift. And beyond, to the dark lanes where we lived. We pushed through the thinning crowd into the low and narrow alleys and it followed, face floating just below the ceiling, shining faintly in the evenglow.

I pulled Ayer into a crossing lane, away from our home.

"I don't want it waiting outside our door," I told him.

"It follows where it wants." His voice was calm as ever.

"We can lose it."

I began walking swiftly, pulling Ayer with me. He said nothing, only matched my stride, never fighting.

I turned down a side lane, then another, looped back onto yet a third. The dim corridors all looked the same—blank doors, low ceilings, features lost in the ever twilight. I was lost already, but I didn't care.

I heard the Shivite behind us, claws scratching the pavement, and went faster. Ayer lagged a step, then took my arm and turned me into an alley. He led, turning at every corner. We went right, left, left again, ducked through narrow alleys, dodged around bums half-seen against the walls. The stand banged against my hip, the strap cut my shoulder. The scratching followed, kept pace, unhurried behind us.

And finally I stopped at a tee, dim lanes leading off left and right, pulse beating in my ears. Ayer started left, but stopped when I didn't follow. He looked at me, waiting for direction. I had none to give.

I hit the wall with my fist, wishing it were someone's face. Then I turned, listening. The scratching came, turned the corner. The Shivite stood in the center of the lane, tool arms crossed, whips coiled above its gleaming eyes. Waiting.

I unslung the stand from my shoulder, held the folded legs in my hands. And stepped forward.

Ayer said something. I think it was "Friend." I didn't listen, didn't see. I took another step forward.

The Shivite struck then, right whip and then left. I took them on the stand, swinging it two-handed. It stepped closer. I held my ground.

And then Ayer grabbed me. He put both arms around me, chest high, and tried to pull me back. He spoke again, but I pulled against him, shouting. I twisted, spun around, trying to dislodge him. I showed my back to the Shivite, and Ayer clinging to me.

I felt the blow through him. Then the next and the next. I knew which whip. He stiffened and cried out. Then spasmed, nearly choking me as his muscles clenched. And falling away as they went limp. I spun, trying to catch him, but the stand was still in my hands and I hit him instead. He fell, mouth working.

I went to one knee beside him, and a whip cracked above my head.

I rolled to one side and came up facing the Shivite, took the next blow on the stand. It paused a second, third eye gleaming. Then it struck again.

I stepped in closer, beating the whips aside. It took a step back, but I was on it, swinging the stand with both hands. A blow above the eyes stunned it. I dodged to the side and hit it again at the base of the skull. The stand shattered. Dye splashed the black shell and ran down its shoulders. I hit it again with the legs and it sagged. And again and again until it fell slowly forward, twisting to lie askew on the pavement.

I stood there a moment, fists clenched on the broken legs of the stand. It didn't move. Then I went back to Ayer.

But he was already dead, eyes open and dull, white fur gone gray and spattered with dye. I took his stained hands and held them, shaking. Then I closed his eyes and took his knife and went back to the Shivite.

I stood over it, watching the dim light play in the dye that ran along its skull. It had several brains and more than one heart. I knew where they all were. The knife was long enough and sharp. But I took the left whip instead, and cut out the sting and the duct and the gland at its base that made the poison. Then I cleaned the knife and carried Ayer home.

The Shivite still follows me. It knows my doorway now and like as not will be there when I leave in the morning. If not, by midday at the latest, it finds me. It stands at the fringe of the crowd while I blow bubbles and send them soaring over its head. It trails me home at night. Usually, it lets me paint, my dark angel. If not, I leave.

I don't carry the knife. I'm not Ayer. I have a different view of things. It would be too easy. But I carry on his trade. And on the good days, I think I do him honor.

"THE ALIEN
IN THE LAKE"

Andrew Weiner

"The Alien in the Lake" was purchased by Gardner Dozois, and appeared in the September 1987 issue of IAsfm, *with an illustration by J.K. Potter. It was one of a long sequence of stories by Weiner that have appeared in the magazine under two different editors, and that have earned him a reputation as one of the most ingenious and slyly unorthodox new writers working in the field today. In "The Alien in the Lake" he offers us a wry, dark-humored examination of the sociological and interpersonal consequences of a series of Very Close Encounters.*

Andrew Weiner is one of science fiction's fastest rising young professionals, appearing frequently in IAsfm *and many other markets. In 1987, he published his first novel, the critically acclaimed* Station Gehenna. *Weiner lives in Toronto, Canada.*

1.

There was a police car parked down by the jetty, its
flashing lights reflecting off the rippling waters of the lake,
its radio murmuring softly of distant crimes. The night was
coming down, but the police officers in the boat could see
well enough to cast their net.

Other cars had pulled up on the lakeshore road. Their
drivers watched as the boat came in, dragging its strange
cargo.

2.

A man fishing in a small boat had seen the body floating
in the lake. At first he thought it was a bundle of old clothes.
But when he prodded it with an oar, it was altogether too
solid. And then an arm had floated up and there was no
longer any doubt.

The hand on the end of the arm was rather unusual, and
perhaps even frightening, having only three claw-like fingers. But the man in the boat did not notice that. It was
unusual and frightening enough for him to be finding a dead
body in the lake, let alone a dead alien.

3.

"God," said the police officer, as they tipped the body
out of the net and rolled it onto its back. "What happened
to his face?"

"Water can do funny . . ." his partner began, and then
suppressed the remark.

Water could do funny things to a corpse after a while,
but it could not give it an extra eye in the middle of its
forehead, or a six-inch-long trunk for a nose, or thick wavy
tendrils instead of hair sprouting from its head. Water could
not do those things.

4.

There were procedures to be followed in such cases, and they were followed in this one, despite the unusual circumstances.

The local coroner examined the body and quickly concluded that the alien had not drowned, but had in fact been murdered. The local coroner was only a country doctor, and there were considerable morphological differences between the body of the alien and the usual run of cadavers, but he had no great difficulty in establishing the cause of death. He had seen enough bullet wounds in his time, after all.

5.

The murdered alien had been wearing an overcoat, a thick bright green muffler, jeans, shirt, and underwear, all purchased from the local general store some months before, along with a pair of mittens which had not been recovered from the lake.

The store owner, Mr. Mills, recalled that the buyer of these items had been Lola Briggs. "Tall, good-looking blonde woman, early forties. I'd say," he told the police. "Comes into the store from time to time, although she lives up around the lake."

Lola Briggs was married to Gus Briggs, the caretaker for a complex of vacation cottages.

"Not that he takes much care of them," Mills said. "They're in very poor repair. And Briggs is always disappearing for weeks or months at a time, even at the height of the season, going off drinking and gambling and womanizing but mostly drinking, leaving her to take care of things. And when he's home he makes all kinds of trouble, there isn't a bar in town that will serve him anymore."

Briggs, apparently, was off on yet another of his little jaunts. Or at least, Mills had not seen him in months. Lola Briggs had come to the store alone to buy the clothes. He had wondered who they were for, because they were too small to fit Gus. Later he had found out.

He had been walking to church one Sunday with his wife, and they had seen them together, Lola and the man who had turned out not to be a man, strolling down the main street and looking in the windows. He had known immediately that it could not be Gus. Gus was all of six feet tall, where this man hardly came to Lola's shoulders.

The man was wearing the coat and he had the muffler wrapped tightly over his face. "I thought that was odd because it was quite warm, really unseasonably warm for the time of year," Mills said. "The fellow must have been sweltering under that muffler, and I said as much to my wife."

"Perhaps he doesn't want to be seen with her," Mrs. Mills had told him. "Not that it will do him any good when Gus comes back. He'll find out about all this and he'll find him, don't you worry. The temper on that man. But you can't blame the poor woman. You really can't."

She had not known then, of course, to what lengths Lola had been driven by her errant husband.

6.

Lola Briggs's nearest neighbor, old Mrs. Donnegan, was not surprised.

"I thought there was something funny about him," she told the police. "The way he always kept that scarf over his face, and the hat so low down on his head, always, no matter what the weather, he claimed he was bronchial. And the way he walked, scuttled more like. And he never did look you in the eye. And half the time he would never as much as say hello, and if he did it was in this funny high-pitched voice.

"Of course, Lola always did have funny tastes in men, that's for sure. Still, who would have thought she would take up with a Martian, or whatever?"

Mrs. Donnegan had not seen Gus Briggs, in, oh, six months. It was the longest time he had ever gone off on his wanderings, and this time, Lola had confided to her one day, he was gone for good. Or so she had believed. Good riddance, Mrs. Donnegan had thought.

The man in the muffler had just appeared on the scene one day. One day he wasn't there, the next he was. He didn't have a car, the nearest bus station was twenty miles away, and she hadn't seen a cab pull up, but one day there he was, coming out of the caretaker's cottage with Lola.

Lola had introduced him as her cousin, although Mrs. Donnegan hadn't believed her for a moment.

"He wasn't the first, you know," Mrs. Donnegan told the police. "A woman like that, she has certain needs, if you understand what I mean. And when the cat's away, and when you can't stand him even when he's home . . . Well, I've seen quite a few come and go over the years. He wasn't the first, but he sure was the strangest."

Sometimes she saw the two of them go out for a walk by the lake, or for a drive in Lola's car, but mostly they just seemed to stay home, behind drawn curtains. Lola had plenty of time on her hands, it being off-season and the cottages almost always empty.

She had wondered, of course, what they could be *doing* in there. And now, of course, she wondered even more.

And then one day, about a week ago, Gus had come home. Driven up his beat-up old pickup and gone into the house. And the next day Lola had had a terrible bruise on her face. And after that she had not seen the man in the muffler again.

She had not heard any gun shots. But her hearing was not the best these days.

7.

"Sure I did it," Gus said. The police had read him his rights when they entered the cottage, but he was very drunk at the time and may not have fully understood them. "Sure. You got some law against killing geeks?"

He had shot the alien down where he stood, on the living room carpet; there was still a funny green stain there under

the throw rug. The alien had offered no resistance. Later
he had dragged the body out and dumped it in the lake. He
had considered killing Lola too, but he had decided to forgive her, although he still couldn't bring himself to touch
her.

"What would you have done?" Gus demanded. "You
come home and find your wife shacked up with some alien
geek. What would you have done?"

Later, on advice from his lawyer, Gus would recant on
this confession and plead self-defense.

8.

The alien had left no belongings, no mechanical devices,
no documents. He had arrived with nothing, Lola told the
authorities, showing up at her door in the middle of the
night naked and green and dripping wet.

It was not even clear that the alien was intelligent, although Lola insisted that he was, and several townspeople
reported brief verbal exchanges with him.

"He talked mainly with his mind," Lola said. "Later I
taught him some words and he picked up some more from
the TV, but he wasn't much interested in them. Mostly he
would touch your mind, sort of, brush against it with pictures or feelings. That was how I knew not to be scared,
that first night when he showed up at my door."

Lola did not know how the alien had come to Earth.

"Some sort of spaceship, I suppose. How else would he
get here?"

A thorough search of the surrounding area failed to locate
any transportation device. If the alien had arrived via a
spaceship, it was no longer in evidence.

She did not know where, exactly, the alien had come
from.

"Some star or another," she said. "He pointed it out to
me one time, but I forget which one it was."

Neither was she able to recapture this information, even
under hypnosis.

There was no doubt, however, that the alien was indeed

an alien. Exhaustive study of his internal organs and genetic materials confirmed as much.

9.

The authorities, of course, were deeply concerned about the affair. They were concerned that the alien might have been a spy, the spearhead of an approaching alien invasion, although it was very hard to imagine what the alien could have been spying on, up there in the backwoods.

They were concerned, too, that even if the alien's intentions had been friendly, his alien comrades might now return to exact vengeance for his death.

Naturally, the authorities questioned Lola closely about the alien, and the nature of his mission on Earth. She was not, however, particularly helpful on this score.

"Sometimes I got the feeling that he was lost," she said. "Although maybe he only *felt* like he was lost, down here among all us strange folks, felt like a stranger even to himself. I've felt like that myself, sometimes."

As far as she could tell, the alien had not been making any systematic study of the planet and its civilizations.

"He didn't ask me questions or anything. Sometimes he liked to drive around and look at buildings and animals and things. He especially liked to watch the ducks down by the lake. But mostly he preferred to stay home, just the two of us.

"He watched quite a bit of TV, the game shows mainly, he couldn't get enough of them. And the soaps sometimes. He was never much on the news. And he liked listening to the country station. He especially liked Willie Nelson, he would hum the tunes to me sometimes when we were in bed."

The alien had liked her cooking, although it turned out that a lot of foods made him sick. Mostly what he ate was fish, he could hold that down well enough. And diet cola, he could go through that by the six-pack.

It made her cry just to think about it, him sitting there

on her couch guzzling diet cola and humming along in that
funny way of his to "Stardust."

That was his favorite song, "Stardust," although he was
also very partial to "Moonlight in Vermont."

10.

The scientists appointed by the authorities to investigate
the matter wanted to know what Lola had *done* with the
alien, other than take long walks and watch TV and listen
to country music. They wanted to know about the sexual
side of their relationship, if indeed there was such a side.

The scientists were by no means certain as to the alien's
sexual identity, if any. Autopsy results as to the alien's
means of reproduction had been ambiguous, to say the least,
with one camp concluding that it was essentially mammalian
while another found strong evidence of oviparous charac-
teristics and still another held out for parthenogenesis.

Later, in a similar spirit of inquiry although with less
purely scientific intent, a number of tabloid newspapers
would pose much the same questions. Lola was willing to
tell them all she could, talking freely in the case of the
government scientists, and in return for suitable recompense
in the case of the highest-bidding tabloid. But it was just
so hard for her to describe.

"Mostly he hummed to me, and burrowed deep into my
mind. Not literally you understand, he hardly laid a claw
on me, not that it would have bothered me, but with his
own mind, going real deep inside. And in a strange kind
of way, it was very sexy, you know. Sexier than any man
I'd ever known, and I've known a few.

"I don't know what it was like for him, but he seemed
to enjoy it. In my own way I loved the funny-looking thing.

"When Gus came home and found us together I told him,
honey it don't mean nothing. But it did, you know, it really
did.

"I warned him about Gus, of course, what Gus might
do to him if he ever came back. But he didn't seem worried
about it. And when Gus came in, he didn't try to run. He

just stood there and let him shoot. It was like, if he couldn't
have me, there was no place else he wanted to be."

11.

The trial of Gus Briggs went all the way to the Supreme
Court where the alien, in a landmark decision, was adjudged
to be under the protection of local criminal statutes. Briggs
was found guilty of murder in the second degree and sen-
tenced to seven years in jail, serving three before his parole.

Lola Briggs divorced her husband and moved to Florida,
where she bought a condo with the proceeds from the sale
of her memoirs. Subsequently she remarried, to a retired
milkman. Her new husband was quiet and gentle and made
her reasonably happy. But she still thought about the alien
from time to time, and how he had burrowed into her. And
she never could listen to "Stardust" again without coming
close to tears.

No alien invasion materialized, and no further aliens were
seen.

12.

The murder of the alien, and the trial of Gus Briggs,
naturally aroused great public interest. Leading national
commentators descended on the small resort town. They
talked a great deal about the futility of it all, of the alien
coming all that way, crossing that inconceivably vast distance, to die in some squalid domestic dispute in a backwoods resort town.

Why, they wondered, could the alien not have come to
New York, or some other major metropolis, to have intelligent and meaningful discourse with the country's finest
minds, to take in the ballet and the opera and dine in the
best restaurants?

Why had he chosen instead to shack up with an aging
blonde bimbo, to watch ducks and hum along with Willie
Nelson tunes and finally get himself gunned down by her
wretched excuse for a husband?

Why, why, why?

It was all, they agreed, so terribly futile.

And Lola Briggs, who had known him best, who alone had known him for what he was, could only say, "Maybe he knew what he was doing."

"A MIDWINTER'S TALE"

Michael Swanwick

"A Midwinter's Tale" was purchased by Gardner Dozois, and appeared in the December 1988 issue of IAsfm, *with an atmospheric cover and interior illustration by Terry Lee. Evocative, lyrical, and mysterious, the story was extremely popular with the magazine's readership—as proved by its easy victory as Best Short Story in that year's Davis Readers' Award poll.*

Michael Swanwick made his debut in 1980, and has gone on to become one of the most popular and respected of all the decade's new writers. He has several times been a finalist for the Nebula Award, as well as a finalist for the World Fantasy Award and the John W. Campbell Award. His fast-paced and evocative first novel, In the Drift, *was published in 1985 as part of the resurrected Ace Specials line. His most recent book is the critically acclaimed novel* Vacuum Flowers, *which was se-*

rialized in IAsfm, *and he has just finished work on a third novel,* Stations of the Tide. *Upcoming is a collection of his short fiction,* Gravity's Angels, *and a collection of his collaborative work with other writers,* Slow Dancing Through Time. *Swanwick lives in Philadelphia with his wife, Marianne Porter, and their young son, Sean.*

Maybe I shouldn't tell you about that childhood Christmas Eve in the Stone House, so long ago. My memory is no longer reliable, not since I contracted the brain fever. Soon I'll be strong enough to be reposted offplanet, to some obscure star light years beyond that plangent moon rising over your father's barn, but how much has been burned from my mind! Perhaps none of this actually happened.

Sit on my lap and I'll tell you all. Well then, my knee. No woman was ever ruined by a knee. You laugh, but it's true. Would that it were so easy!

The hell of war as it's now practiced is that its purpose is not so much to gain territory as to deplete the enemy, and thus it's always better to maim than to kill. A corpse can be bagged, burned, and forgotten, but the wounded need special care. Regrowth tanks, false skin, medical personnel, a long convalescent stay on your parents' farm. That's why they will vary their weapons, hit you with obsolete stone axes or toxins or radiation, to force your Command to stock the proper prophylaxes, specialized medicines, obscure skills. Mustard gas is excellent for that purpose, and so was the brain fever.

All those months I lay in the hospital, awash in pain, sometimes hallucinating. Dreaming of ice. When I awoke, weak and not really believing I was alive, parts of my life were gone, randomly burned from my memory. I recall standing at the very top of the iron bridge over the Izveltaya, laughing and throwing my books one by one into the river, while my best friend Fennwolf tried to coax me down. "I'll join the militia! I'll be a soldier!" I shouted hysterically. And so I did. I remember that clearly but just what led up to that preposterous instant is utterly beyond me. Nor can I remember the name of my second-eldest sister, though her face is as plain to me as yours is now. There are odd holes in my memory.

That Christmas Eve is an island of stability in my sea-changing memories, as solid in my mind as the Stone House itself, that neolithic cavern in which we led such basic lives that I was never quite sure in which era of history we dwelt. Sometimes the men came in from the hunt, a larl or two pacing ahead content and sleepy-eyed, to lean bloody spears against the walls, and it might be that we lived on Old Earth itself then. Other times, as when they brought in projectors to fill the common room with colored lights, scintillae nesting in the branches of the season's tree, and cool, harmless flames dancing atop the presents, we seemed to belong to a much later age, in some mythologized province of the future.

The house was abustle, the five families all together for this one time of the year, and outlying kin and even a few strangers staying over, so that we had to put bedding in places normally kept closed during the winter, moving furniture into attic lumberrooms, and even at that there were cots and thick bolsters set up in the blind ends of hallways. The women scurried through the passages, scattering uncles here and there, now settling one in an armchair and plumping him up like a cushion, now draping one over a table, cocking up a mustachio for effect. A pleasant time.

Coming back from a visit to the kitchen, where a huge woman I did not know, with flour powdering her big-freckled arms up to the elbows, had shooed me away, I surprised Suki and Georg kissing in the nook behind the great hearth. They had their arms about each other and I stood watching them. Suki was smiling, cheeks red and round. She brushed her hair back with one hand so Georg could nuzzle her ear, turning slightly as she did so, and saw me. She gasped and they broke apart, flushed and startled.

Suki gave me a cookie, dark with molasses and a single stingy, crystalized raisin on tóp, while Georg sulked. Then she pushed me away, and I heard her laugh as she took Georg's hand to lead him away to some darker forest recess of the house.

Father came in, boots all muddy, to sling a brace of game birds down on the hunt cabinet. He set his unstrung bow and quiver of arrows on their pegs, then hooked an elbow atop the cabinet to accept admiration and a hot drink from mother. The larl padded by, quiet and heavy and content. I followed it around a corner, ancient ambitions of riding the beast rising up within. I could see myself, triumphant before my cousins, high atop the black carnivore. "Flip!" my father called sternly. "Leave Samson alone! He is a bold and noble creature, and I will not have you pestering him."

He had eyes in the back of his head, had my father.

Before I could grow angry, my cousins hurried by, on their way to hoist the straw men into the trees out front, and swept me up along with them. Uncle Chittagong, who looked like a lizard and had to stay in a glass tank for reasons of health, winked at me as I skirted past. From the corner of my eye I saw my second-eldest sister beside him, limned in blue fire.

Forgive me. So little of my childhood remains; vast stretches were lost in the blue icefields I wandered in my illness. My past is like a sunken continent with only mountaintops remaining unsubmerged, a scattered archipelago of events from which to guess the shape of what was lost. Those remaining fragments I treasure all the more, and must pass my hands over them periodically to reassure myself that something remains.

So where was I? Ah, yes: I was in the north belltower, my hidey-place in those days, huddled behind Old Blind Pew, the bass of our triad of bells, crying because I had been deemed too young to light one of the yule torches. "Hallo!" cried a voice, and then, "Out here, stupid!" I ran to the window, tears forgotten in my astonishment at the sight of my brother Karl silhouetted against the yellowing sky, arms out, treading the roof gables like a tightrope walker.

"You're going to get in trouble for that!" I cried.

"Not if you don't tell!" Knowing full well how I worshipped him. "Come on down! I've emptied out one of the upper kitchen cupboards. We can crawl in from the pantry. There's a space under the door—we'll see everything!"

Karl turned and his legs tangled under him. He fell. Feet first, he slid down the roof.

I screamed. Karl caught the guttering and swung himself into an open window underneath. His sharp face rematerialized in the gloom, grinning. "Race you to the jade ibis!"

He disappeared, and then I was spinning wildly down the spiral stairs, mad to reach the goal first.

It was not my fault we were caught, for I would never have giggled if Karl hadn't been tickling me to see just how long I could keep silent. I was frightened, but not Karl. He threw his head back and laughed until he cried, even as he was being hauled off by three very angry grandmothers, pleased more by his own roguery than by anything he might have seen.

I myself was led away by an indulgent Katrina, who graphically described the caning I was to receive and then contrived to lose me in the crush of bodies in the common room. I hid behind the goat tapestry until I got bored—not long!—and then Chubkin, Kosmonaut, and Pew rang, and the room emptied.

I tagged along, ignored, among the moving legs, like a marsh bird scuttling through waving grasses. Voices clangoring in the east stairway, we climbed to the highest balcony, to watch the solstice dance. I hooked hands over the crumbling balustrade and pulled myself up on tiptoe so I could look down on the procession as it left the house. For a long time nothing happened, and I remember being annoyed at how casually the adults were taking all this, standing about with drinks, not one in ten glancing away from themselves. Pheidre and Valerian (the younger children had been put to bed, complaining, an hour ago) began a game of tag, running through the adults, until they were chastened and ordered with angry shakes of their arms to be still.

Then the door below opened. The women who were witches walked solemnly out, clad in hooded terrycloth robes as if they'd just stepped from the bath. But they were so silent I was struck with fear. It seemed as if something cold had reached into the pink, giggling women I had seen preparing themselves in the kitchen and taken away some warmth or laughter from them. "Katrina!" I cried in panic, and she lifted a moon-cold face toward me. Several of the men exploded in laughter, white steam puffing from bearded mouths, and one rubbed his knuckles in my hair. My second-eldest sister drew me away from the balustrade and hissed at me that I was not to cry out to the witches, that this was important, that when I was older I would understand, and in the meantime if I did not behave myself I would be beaten. To soften her words, she offered me a sugar crystal, but I turned away stern and unappeased.

Single-file the women walked out on the rocks to the east of the house, where all was barren slate swept free of snow by the wind from the sea, and at a great distance—you could not make out their faces—doffed their robes. For a moment they stood motionless in a circle, looking at one another. Then they began the dance, each wearing nothing but a red ribbon tied about one upper thigh, the long end blowing free in the breeze.

As they danced their circular dance, the families watched, largely in silence. Sometimes there was a muffled burst of laughter as one of the younger men muttered a racy comment, but mostly they watched with great respect, even a kind of fear. The gusty sky was dark, and flocked with small clouds like purple-headed rams. It was chilly on the roof and I could not imagine how the women withstood it. They danced faster and faster, and the families grew quieter, packing the edges more tightly, until I was forced away from the railing. Cold and bored, I went downstairs, nobody turning to watch me leave, back to the main room, where a fire still smouldered in the hearth.

The room was stuffy when I'd left, and cooler now. I lay down on my stomach before the fireplace. The flagstones smelled of ashes and were gritty to the touch, staining my fingertips as I trailed them in idle little circles. The stones were cold at the edges, slowly growing warmer, and then suddenly too hot and I had to snatch my hand away. The back of the fireplace was black with soot, and I watched the fire-worms crawl over the stone heart-and-hands carved there, as the carbon caught fire and burned out. The log was all embers and would burn for hours.

Something coughed.

I turned and saw something moving in the shadows, an animal. The larl was blacker than black, a hole in the darkness, and my eyes swam to look at him. Slowly, lazily, he strode out onto the stones, stretched his back, yawned a tongue-curling yawn, and then stared at me with those great green eyes.

He spoke.

I was astonished, of course, but not in the way my father would have been. So much is inexplicable to a child! "Merry Christmas, Flip," the creature said, in a quiet, breathy voice. I could not describe its accent; I have heard nothing quite like it before or since. There was a vast alien amusement in his glance.

"And to you," I said politely.

The larl sat down, curling his body heavily about me. If I had wanted to run, I could not have gotten past him, though that thought did not occur to me then. "There is an ancient legend, Flip, I wonder if you have heard of it, that on Christmas Eve the beasts can speak in human tongue. Have your elders told you that?"

I shook my head.

"They are neglecting you." Such strange humor dwelt in that voice. "There is truth to some of those old legends, if only you knew how to get at it. Though perhaps not all. Some are just stories. Perhaps this is not happening now; perhaps I am not speaking to you at all?"

I shook my head. I did not understand. I said so.

"That is the difference between your kind and mine. My kind understands everything about yours, and yours knows next to nothing about mine. I would like to tell you a story, little one. Would you like that?"

"Yes," I said, for I was young and I liked stories very much.

He began:

When the great ships landed—

Oh God. When—no, no, no, wait. Excuse me. I'm shaken. I just this instant had a vision. It seemed to me that it was night and I was standing at the gates of a cemetery. And suddenly the air was full of light, planes and cones of light that burst from the ground and nested twittering in the trees. Fracturing the sky. I wanted to dance for joy. But the ground crumbled underfoot and when I looked down the shadow of the gates touched my toes, a cold rectangle of profoundest black, deep as all eternity, and I was dizzy and about to fall and I, and I . . .

Enough! I have had this vision before, many times. It must have been something that impressed me strongly in my youth, the moist smell of newly opened earth, the chalky whitewash on the picket fence. It must be. I do not believe in hobgoblins, ghosts, or premonitions. No, it does not bear thinking about. Foolishness! Let me get on with my story.

—When the great ships landed, I was feasting on my grandfather's brains. All his descendants gathered respectfully about him, and I, as youngest, had first bite. His wisdom flowed through me, and the wisdom of his ancestors and the intimate knowledge of those animals he had eaten for food, and the spirit of valiant enemies who had been killed and then honored by being eaten, just as if they were family. I don't suppose you understand this, little one.

I shook my head.

People never die, you see. Only humans die. Sometimes a minor part of a Person is lost, the doings of a few decades, but the bulk of his life is preserved, if not in his body, then in another. Or sometimes a Person will dishonor himself, and his descendants will refuse to eat him. This is a great shame, and the Person will go off to die somewhere alone.

The ships descended bright as newborn suns. The People had never seen such a thing. We watched in inarticulate wonder, for we had no language then. You have seen the pictures, the baroque swirls of colored metal, the proud humans stepping down onto the land. But I was there, and I can tell you, your people were ill. They stumbled down the gangplanks with the stench of radiation sickness about them. We could have destroyed them all then and there.

Your people built a village at Landfall and planted crops over the bodies of their dead. We left them alone. They did not look like good game. They were too strange and too slow and we had not yet come to savor your smell. So we went away, in baffled ignorance.

That was in early spring.

Half the survivors were dead by midwinter, some of disease but most because they did not have enough food. It was of no concern to us. But then the woman in the wilderness came to change our universe forever.

When you're older you'll be taught the woman's tale, and what desperation drove her into the wilderness. It's part of your history. But to myself, out in the mountains and winter-lean, the sight of her striding through the snows in her furs was like a vision of winter's queen herself. A gift of meat for the hungering season, life's blood for the solstice.

I first saw the woman while I was eating her mate. He had emerged from his cabin that evening as he did every sunset, gun in hand, without looking up. I had observed him over the course of five days and his behavior never varied. On that sixth nightfall I was crouched on his roof when he came out. I let him go a few steps from the door, then leapt. I felt his neck break on impact, tore open his throat to be sure, and ripped through his parka to taste his innards. There was no sport in it, but in winter we will take game whose brains we would never eat.

My mouth was full and my muzzle pleasantly, warmly moist with blood when the woman appeared. I looked up, and she was topping the rise, riding one of your incomprehensible machines, what I know now to be a snowstrider. The setting sun broke through the clouds behind her and for an instant she was embedded in glory. Her shadow stretched narrow before her and touched me, a bridge of darkness between us. We looked in one another's eyes . . .

Magda topped the rise with a kind of grim, joyless satisfaction. I am now a hunter's woman, she thought to herself. We will always be welcome at Landfall for the meat we bring, but they will never speak civilly to me again. Good. I would choke on their sweet talk anyway. The baby stirred and without looking down she stroked him through the furs, murmuring, "Just a little longer, my brave little boo, and we'll be at our new home. Will you like that, eh?"

The sun broke through the clouds to her back, making the snow a red dazzle. Then her eyes adjusted, and she saw the black shape crouched over her lover's body. A very great distance away, her hands throttled down the snowstrider and brought it to a halt. The shallow bowl of land before her was barren, the snow about the corpse black with blood. A last curl of smoke lazily separated from the hut's chimney. The brute lifted its bloody muzzle and looked at her.

Time froze and knotted in black agony.

The larl screamed. It ran straight at her, faster than thought. Clumsily, hampered by the infant strapped to her stomach, Magda clawed the rifle from its boot behind the saddle. She shucked her mittens, fitted hands to metal that stung like hornets, flicked off the safety and brought the stock to her shoulder. The larl was halfway to her. She aimed and fired.

The larl went down. One shoulder shattered, slamming it to the side. It tumbled and rolled in the snow. "You sonofabitch!" Magda cried in triumph. But almost immediately the beast struggled to its feet, turned and fled.

The baby began to cry, outraged by the rifle's roar. Magda powered up the engine. "Hush, small warrior." A kind of madness filled her, a blind anesthetizing rage. "This won't take long." She flung her machine downhill, after the larl.

Even wounded, the creature was fast. She could barely keep up. As it entered the spare stand of trees to the far end of the meadow, Magda paused to fire again, burning a bullet by its head. The larl leaped away. From then on it varied its flight with sudden changes of direction and unexpected jogs to the side. It was a fast learner. But it could not escape Magda. She had always been a hothead, and now her blood was up. She was not about to return to her lover's gutted body with his killer still alive.

The sun set and in the darkening light she lost sight of the larl. But she was able to follow its trail by two-shadowed moonlight, the deep, purple footprints, the darker spatter of blood it left, drop by drop, in the snow.

It was the solstice, and the moons were full—a holy time. I felt it even as I fled the woman through the wilderness. The moons were bright on the snow. I felt the dread of being hunted descend on me, and in my inarticulate way I felt blessed.

But I also felt a great fear for my kind. We had dismissed the humans as incomprehensible, not very interesting creatures, slow-moving, bad-smelling, and dull-witted. Now, pursued by this madwoman on her fast machine, brandishing a weapon that killed from afar, I felt all natural order betrayed. She was a goddess of the hunt, and I was her prey.

The People had to be told.

I gained distance from her, but I knew the woman would catch up. She was a hunter, and a hunter never abandons wounded prey. One way or another, she would have me.

In the winter, all who are injured or too old must offer themselves to the community. The sacrifice rock was not far, by a hill riddled from time beyond memory with our burrows. My knowledge must be shared: The humans were dangerous. They would make good prey.

I reached my goal when the moons were highest. The flat rock was bare of snow when I ran limping in. Awakened by the scent of my blood, several People emerged from their

dens. I laid myself down on the sacrifice rock. A grand-
mother of the People came forward, licked my wound,
tasting, considering. Then she nudged me away with her
forehead. The wound would heal, she thought, and winter
was young; my flesh was not yet needed.

But I stayed. Again she nudged me away. I refused to
go. She whined in puzzlement. I licked the rock.

That was understood. Two of the People came forward
and placed their weight on me. A third lifted a paw. He
shattered my skull, and they ate.

Magda watched through power binoculars from atop a
nearby ridge. She saw everything. The rock swarmed with
lean black horrors. It would be dangerous to go down among
them, so she waited and watched the puzzling tableau below.
The larl had wanted to die, she'd swear it, and now the
beasts came forward daintily, almost ritualistically, to taste
the brains, the young first and then the old. She raised her
rifle, thinking to exterminate a few of the brutes from afar.

A curious thing happened then. All the larls that had eaten
of her prey's brain leaped away, scattering. Those that had
not eaten waited, easy targets, not understanding. Then
another dipped to lap up a fragment of brain, and looked
up with sudden comprehension. Fear touched her.

The hunter had spoken often of the larls, had said that
they were so elusive he sometimes thought them intelligent.
"Come spring, when I can afford to waste ammunition on
carnivores, I look forward to harvesting a few of these
beauties," he'd said. He was the colony's xenobiologist,
and he loved the animals he killed, treasured them even as
he smoked their flesh, tanned their hides, and drew detailed
pictures of their internal organs. Magda had always scoffed
at his theory that larls gained insight into the habits of their
prey by eating their brains, even though he'd spent much
time observing the animals minutely from afar, gathering
evidence. Now she wondered if he were right.

Her baby whimpered, and she slid a hand inside her furs
to give him a breast. Suddenly the night seemed cold and
dangerous, and she thought: What am I doing here? Sanity

returned to her all at once, her anger collapsing to nothing, like an ice tower shattering in the wind. Below, sleek black shapes sped toward her, across the snow. They changed direction every few leaps, running evasive patterns to avoid her fire.

"Hang on, kid," she muttered, and turned her strider around. She opened up the throttle.

Magda kept to the open as much as she could, the creatures following her from a distance. Twice she stopped abruptly and turned her rifle on her pursuers. Instantly they disappeared in puffs of snow, crouching belly-down but not stopping, burrowing toward her under the surface. In the eerie night silence, she could hear the whispering sound of the brutes tunneling. She fled.

Some frantic timeless period later—the sky had still not lightened in the east—Magda was leaping a frozen stream when the strider's left ski struck a rock. The machine was knocked glancingly upward, cybernetics screaming as they fought to regain balance. With a sickening crunch, the strider slammed to earth, one ski twisted and bent. It would take extensive work before the strider could move again.

Magda dismounted. She opened her robe and looked down on her child. He smiled up at her and made a gurgling noise.

Something went dead in her.

A fool. I've been a criminal fool, she thought. Magda was a proud woman who had always refused to regret, even privately, anything she had done. Now she regretted everything: Her anger, the hunter, her entire life, all that had brought her to this point, the cumulative madness that threatened to kill her child.

A larl topped the ridge.

Magda raised her rifle, and it ducked down. She began walking downslope, parallel to the stream. The snow was knee deep and she had to walk carefully not to slip and fall. Small pellets of snow rolled down ahead of her, were overtaken by other pellets. She strode ahead, pushing up a wake.

The hunter's cabin was not many miles distant; if she

could reach it, they would live. But a mile was a long way in winter. She could hear the larls calling to each other, soft coughlike noises, to either side of the ravine. They were following the sound of her passage through the snow. Well, let them. She still had the rifle, and if it had few bullets left, *they* didn't know that. They were only animals.

This high in the mountains, the trees were sparse. Magda descended a good quarter-mile before the ravine choked with scrub and she had to climb up and out or risk being ambushed. Which way? she wondered. She heard three coughs to her right, and climbed the left slope, alert and wary.

We herded her. Through the long night we gave her fleeting glimpses of our bodies whenever she started to turn to the side she must not go, and let her pass unmolested the other way. We let her see us dig into the distant snow and wait motionless, undetectable. We filled the woods with our shadows. Slowly, slowly, we turned her around. She struggled to return to the cabin, but she could not. In what haze of fear and despair she walked! We could smell it. Sometimes her baby cried, and she hushed the milky-scented creature in a voice gone flat with futility. The night deepened as the moons sank in the sky. We forced the woman back up into the mountains. Toward the end, her legs failed her several times; she lacked our strength and stamina. But her patience and guile were every bit our match. Once we approached her still form, and she killed two of us before the rest could retreat. How we loved her! We paced her, confident that sooner or later she'd drop.

It was at night's darkest hour that the woman was forced back to the burrowed hillside, the sacred place of the People where stood the sacrifice rock. She topped the same rise for the second time that night, and saw it. For a moment she stood helpless, and then she burst into tears.

We waited, for this was the holiest moment of the hunt, the point when the prey recognizes and accepts her destiny. After a time, the woman's sobs ceased. She raised her head and straightened her back.

Slowly, steadily she walked downhill.

• • •

She knew what to do.

Larls retreated into their burrows at the sight of her, gleaming eyes dissolving into darkness. Magda ignored them. Numb and aching, weary to death, she walked to the sacrifice rock. It had to be this way.

Magda opened her coat, unstrapped her baby. She wrapped him deep in the furs and laid the bundle down to one side of the rock. Dizzily, she opened the bundle to kiss the top of his sweet head, and he made an angry sound. "Good for you, kid," she said hoarsely. "Keep that attitude." She was so tired.

She took off her sweaters, her vest, her blouse. The raw cold nipped at her flesh with teeth of ice. She stretched slightly, body aching with motion. God it felt good. She laid down the rifle. She knelt.

The rock was black with dried blood. She lay down flat, as she had earlier seen her larl do. The stone was cold, so cold it almost blanked out the pain. Her pursuers waited nearby, curious to see what she was doing; she could hear the soft panting noise of their breathing. One padded noiselessly to her side. She could smell the brute. It whined questioningly.

She licked the rock.

Once it was understood what the woman wanted, her sacrifice went quickly. I raised a paw, smashed her skull. Again I was youngest. Innocent, I bent to taste.

The neighbors were gathering, hammering at the door, climbing over one another to peer through the windows, making the walls bulge and breathe with their eagerness. I grunted and bellowed, and the clash of silver and clink of plates next door grew louder. Like peasant animals, my husband's people tried to drown out the sound of my pain with toasts and drunken jokes.

Through the window I saw Tevin-the-Fool's bonewhite skin gaunt on his skull, and behind him a slice of face—sharp nose, white cheeks—like a mask. The doors and walls pulsed with the weight of those outside. In the next room,

children fought and wrestled, and elders pulled at their long
white beards, staring anxiously at the closed door.

The midwife shook her head, red lines running from the
corners of her mouth down either side of her stern chin.
Her eye sockets were shadowy pools of dust. "Now push!"
she cried. "Don't be a lazy sow!"

I groaned and arched my back. I shoved my head back
and it grew smaller, eaten up by the pillows. The bedframe
skewed as one leg slowly buckled under it. My husband
glanced over his shoulder at me, an angry look, his fingers
knotted behind his back.

All of Landfall shouted and hovered on the walls.

"Here it comes!" shrieked the midwife. She reached
down to my bloody crotch, and eased out a tiny head, purple
and angry, like a goblin.

And then all the walls glowed red and green and sprouted
large flowers. The door turned orange and burst open, and
the neighbors and crew flooded in. The ceiling billowed up,
and aerialists tumbled through the rafters. A boy who had
been hiding beneath the bed flew up laughing to where the
ancient sky and stars shone through the roof.

They held up the child, bloody on a platter.

Here the larl touched me for the first time, that heavy
black paw like velvet on my knee, talons sheathed. "Are
you following this?" he asked. "Can you separate truth
from fantasy, tell what is fact and what the mad imagery
of emotions we did not share? No more could I. All that,
the first birth of human young on this planet, I experienced
in an instant. Blind with awe, I understood the personal
tragedy and the communal triumph of that event, and the
meaning of the lives and culture behind it. A second before,
I lived as an animal, with an animal's simple thoughts and
hopes. Then I ate of your ancestor and was lifted all in an
instant halfway to godhood.

"As the woman had intended. She had died thinking of
the child's birth, in order that we might share in it. She
gave us that. She gave us more. She gave us *language*. We
were wise animals before we ate her brain, and we were

People afterward. We owed her so much. And we knew what she wanted from us.'' The larl stroked my cheek with his great, smooth paw, the ivory claws hooded but quivering slightly, as if about to awake.

I hardly dared breathe.

"That morning I entered Landfall, carrying the baby's sling in my mouth. It slept through most of the journey. At dawn, I passed through the empty street as silently as I knew how. I came to the First Captain's house. I heard the murmur of voices within, the entire village assembled for worship. I tapped the door with one paw. There was sudden, astonished silence. Then slowly, fearfully, the door opened.''

The larl was silent for a moment. "That was the beginning of the association of People with humans. We were welcomed into your homes, and we helped with the hunting. It was a fair trade. Our food saved many lives that first winter. No one needed know how the woman had perished, or how well we understood your kind.

"That child, Flip, was your ancestor. Every few generations we take one of your family out hunting, and taste his brains, to maintain our closeness with your line. If you are a good boy and grow up to be as bold and honest, as intelligent and noble a man as your father, then perhaps it will be you we eat.''

The larl presented his blunt muzzle to me in what might have been meant as a friendly smile. Perhaps not; the expression hangs unreadable, ambiguous in my mind even now. Then he stood and padded away into the friendly dark shadows of the Stone House.

I was sitting staring into the coals a few minutes later when my second-eldest sister—her face a featureless blaze of light, like an angel's—came into the room and saw me. She held out a hand, saying, "Come on, Flip, you're missing everything.'' And I went with her.

Did any of this actually happen? Sometimes I wonder. But it's growing late, and your parents are away. My room is small but snug, my bed warm but empty. We can burrow deep in the blankets and scare away the cave-bears by playing the oldest winter games there are.

You're blushing! Don't tug away your hand. I'll be gone soon to some distant world to fight in a war for people who are as unknown to you as they are to me. Soldiers grow old slowly, you know. We're shipped frozen between the stars. When you are old and plump and happily surrounded by grandchildren, I'll still be young, and thinking of you. You'll remember me then, and our thoughts will touch in the void. Will you have nothing to regret? Is that really what you want?

I thought once that I could outrun the darkness. I thought—I must have thought—that by joining the militia I could escape my fate. But for all that I gave up my home and family, in the end the beast came anyway to eat my brain. Now I am alone. A month from now, in all this world, only you will remember my name. Let me live in your memory.

Come, don't be shy. Let's put the past aside and get on with our lives. That's better. Blow the candle out, love, and there's an end to my tale.

All this happened long ago, on a planet whose name has been burned from my memory.

"DINOSAURS"

Walter Jon Williams

"Dinosaurs" was purchased by Gardner Dozois, and appeared in the June 1987 issue of IAsfm, *with a double-page illustration by Gary Freeman. Williams is regarded as one of the hottest new talents in science fiction, and certainly he has proved to be one of the most popular with the readership of the magazine, where the bulk of his short fiction has been appearing since 1986. "Dinosaurs"—along with the Hugo and Nebula finalist "Surfacing"—was a popular story even for Williams; in it, he takes us six million years into a very bizarre future, to meet some of our own distant descendants.*

Walter Jon Williams was born in Minnesota and now lives in Albuquerque, New Mexico. His novels include Ambassador of Progress, Knight Moves, Hardwired, The Crown Jewels, Voice of the Whirlwind, House of Shards, *and* The Last Deathship Off Antares. *His most recent book is a collection of his short work—most of it from* IAsfm—Facets.

The Shars seethed in the dim light of their ruddy sun. Pointed faces raised to the sky, they sniffed the faint wind for sign of the stranger and scented only hydrocarbons, far-off vegetation, damp fur, the sweat of excitement and fear. Weak eyes peered upward, glistened with hope, anxiety, apprehension, and saw only the faint pattern of stars. Short, excited barking sounds broke out here and there, but mostly the Shars crooned, a low ululation that told of sudden onslaught, destruction, war in distant reaches, and now the hope of peace.

The crowds surged left, then right. Individuals bounced high on their third legs, seeking a view, seeing only the wide sea of heads, the ears and muzzles pointed to the stars.

Suddenly, a screaming. High-pitched howls, a bright chorus of barks. The crowds surged again.

Something was crossing the field of stars.

The human ship was huge, vaster than anything they'd seen, a moonlet descending. Shars closed their eyes and shuddered in terror. The screaming turned to moans. Individuals leaped high, baring their teeth, barking in defiance of their fear. The air smelled of terror, incipient panic, anger.

War! cried some. *Peace!* cried others.

The crooning went on. *We mourn, we mourn,* it said, *we mourn our dead billions.*

We fear, said others.

Soundlessly, the human ship neared them, casting its vast shadow. Shars spilled outward from the spot beneath, bounding high on their third legs.

The human ship came to a silent rest. Dully, it reflected the dim red sun.

The Shars crooned their fear, their sorrow. And waited for the humans to emerge.

These? Yes. These. Drill, the human ambassador, gazed through his video walls at the sea of Shars, the moaning, leaping thousands that surrounded him. Through the mass a group was moving with purpose, heading for the airlock as per his instructions. His new Memory crawled restlessly in the armored hollow atop his skull. *Stand by*, he broadcast.

His knees made painful crackling noises as he walked toward the airlock, the silver ball of his translator rolling along the ceiling ahead of him. The walls mutated as he passed, showing him violet sky, far-off polygonal buildings, cold distant green . . . and here, nearby, a vast, dim plain covered with a golden tissue of Shars.

He reached the airlock and it began to open. Drill snuffed wetly at the alien smells—heat, dust, the musky scent of the Shars themselves.

Drill's heart thumped in his chest. His dreams were coming true. He had waited all his life for this.

Mash, whimpered Lowbrain. Drill told it to be silent. Lowbrain protested vaguely, then obeyed.

Drill told Lowbrain to move. Cool, alien air brushed his skin. The Shars cried out sharply, moaned, fell back. They seemed a wild, sibilant ocean of pointed ears and dark, questing eyes. The group heading for the airlock vanished in the general retrograde movement, a stone washed by a pale tide. Beneath Drill's feet was soft vegetation. His translator floated in the air before him. His mind flamed with wonder, but Lowbrain kept him moving.

The Shars fell back, moaning.

Drill stood eighteen feet tall on his two pillarlike legs, each with a splayed foot that displayed a horny underside and vestigial nails. His skin was ebony and was draped in folds over his vast naked body. His pendulous maleness swung loosely as he walked. As he stepped across the open space he was conscious of the fact that he was the ultimate product of nine million years of human evolution, all leading to the expansion, diversification, and perfection that was now humanity's manifest existence.

He looked down at the little Shars, their white skin and golden fur, their strange, stiff tripod legs, the muzzles raised to him as if in awe. *If your species survives*, he thought benignly, *you can look like me in another few million years*.

• • •

The group of Shars that had been forging through the crowd were suddenly exposed when the crowd fell back from around them. On the perimeter were several Shars holding staffs—weapons, perhaps—in their clever little hands. In the center of these were a group of Shars wearing decorative ribbon to which metal plates had been attached. *Badges of rank,* Memory said. *Ignore.* The shadow of the translator bobbed toward them as Drill approached. Metallic geometries rose from the group and hovered over them.

Recorders, Memory said. *Artificial similarities to myself. Or possibly security devices. Disregard.*

Drill was getting closer to the party, speeding up his instructions to Lowbrain, eventually entering Zen Synch. It would make Lowbrain hungrier but lessen the chance of any accidents.

The Shars carrying the staffs fell back. A wailing went up from the crowd as one of the Shars stepped toward Drill. The ribbons draped over her sloping shoulders failed to disguise four mammalian breasts. Clear plastic bubbles covered her weak eyes. In Zen Synch with Memory and Lowbrain, Drill ambled up to her and raised his hands in friendly greeting. The Shar flinched at the expanse of the gesture.

"I am Ambassador Drill," he said. "I am a human."

The Shar gazed up at him. Her nose wrinkled as she listened to the booming voice of the translator. Her answer was a succession of sharp sounds, made high in the throat, somewhat unpleasant. Drill listened to the voice of his translator.

"I am President Gram of the InterSharian Sociability of Nations and Planets." That's how it came through in translation, anyway. Memory began feeding Drill referents for the word "nation."

"I welcome you to our planet, Ambassador Drill."

"Thank you, President Gram," Drill said. "Shall we negotiate peace now?"

President Gram's ears pricked forward, then back. There was a pause, and then from the vast circle of Shars came a mad torrent of hooting noises. The awesome sound lapped over Drill like the waves of a lunatic sea.

They approve your sentiment, said Memory.

I thought that's what it meant, Drill said. *Do you think we'll get along?*

Memory didn't answer, but instead shifted to a more comfortable position in the saddle of Drill's skull. Its job was to provide facts, not draw conclusions.

"If you could come into my Ship," Drill said, "we could get started."

"Will we then meet the other members of your delegation?"

Drill gazed down at the Shar. The fur on her shoulders was rising in odd tufts. She seemed to be making a concerted effort to calm it.

"There are no other members," Drill said. "Just myself."

His knees were paining him. He watched as the other members of the Shar party cast quick glances at each other.

"No secretaries? No assistants?" the President was saying.

"No," Drill said. "Not at all. I'm the only conscious mind on Ship. Shall we get started?"

Eat! Eat! said Lowbrain. Drill ordered it to be silent. His stomach grumbled.

"Perhaps," said President Gram, gazing at the vastness of the human ship, "it would be best should we begin in a few hours. I should probably speak to the crowd. Would you care to listen?"

No need. Memory said. *I will monitor.*

"Thank you, no," Drill said. "I shall return to Ship for food and sex. Please signal me when you are ready. Please bring any furniture you may need for your comfort. I do not believe my furniture would fit you, although we might be able to clone some later."

The Shars' ears all pricked forward. Drill entered Zen Synch, turned his huge body, and began accelerating toward the airlock. The sound of the crowd behind him was like the murmuring of wind through a stand of trees.

Peace, he thought later, as he stood by the mash bins

and fed his complaining stomach. *It's a simple thing. How long can it take to arrange?*

Long, said Memory. *Very long.*

The thought disturbed him. He thought the first meeting had gone well.

After his meal, when he had sex, it wasn't very good.

Memory had been monitoring the events outside Ship, and after Drill had completed sex, Memory showed him the outside events. *They have been broadcast to the entire population,* Memory said.

President Gram had moved to a local elevation and had spoken for some time. Drill found her speech interesting— it was rhythmic and incantorial, rising and falling in tone and volume, depending heavily on repetition and melody. The crowd participated, issuing forth with excited barks or low moans in response to her statements or questions, sometimes babbling in confusion when she posed them a conundrum. Memory only gave the highlights of the speech. "Unknown . . . attackers . . . billions dead . . . preparations advanced . . . ready to defend ourselves . . . offer of peace . . . hope in the darkness . . . unknown . . . willing to take the chance . . . peace . . . peace . . . hopeful smell . . . peace." At the end the other Shars were all singing "Peace! Peace!" in chorus while President Gram bounced up and down on her sturdy rear leg.

It sounds pretty, Drill thought. *But why does she go on like that?*

Memory's reply was swift.

Remember that the Shars are a generalized and social species, it said. *President Gram's power, and her ability to negotiate, derives from the degree of her popular support. In measures of this significance she must explain herself and her actions to the population in order to maintain their enthusiasm for her policies.*

Primitive, Drill thought.

That is correct.

Why don't they let her get on with her work? Drill asked.

There was no reply.

• • •

After an exchange of signals the Shar party assembled at the airlock. Several Shars had been mobilized to carry tables and stools. Drill sent a Frog to escort the Shars from the airlock to where he waited. The Frog met them inside the airlock, turned, and hopped on ahead through Ship's airy, winding corridors. It had been trained to repeat "Follow me, follow me" in the Shars' own language.

Drill waited in a semi-reclined position on a Slab. The Slab was an organic sub-species used as furniture, with an idiot brain capable of responding to human commands. The Shars entered cautiously, their weak eyes twitching in the bright light. "Welcome, Honorable President," Drill said. "Up, Slab." Slab began to adjust itself to place Drill on his feet. The Shars were moving tables and stools into the vast room.

Frog was hopping in circles, making a wet noise at each landing. "Follow me, follow me," it said.

The members of the Shar delegation who bore badges of rank stood in a body while the furniture-carriers bustled around them. Drill noticed, as Slab put him on his feet, that they were wrinkling their noses. He wondered what it meant.

His knees crackled as he came fully upright. "Please make yourselves comfortable," he said. "Frog will show your laborers to the airlock."

"Does your Excellency object to a mechanical recording of the proceedings?" President Gram asked. She was shading her eyes with her hand.

"Not at all." As a number of devices rose into the air above the party, Drill wondered if it were possible to give the Shars detachable Memories. Perhaps human bioengineers could adapt the Memories to the Shar physiology. He asked Memory to make a note of the question so that he could bring it up later.

"Follow me, follow me," Frog said. The workers who had carried the furniture began to follow the hopping Frog out of the room.

"Your Excellency," President Gram said, "may I have

the honor of presenting to you the other members of my delegation?''

There were six in all, with titles like Secretary for Syncopated Speech and Special Executive for External Coherence. There was also a Minister for the Dissemination of Convincing Lies, whose title Drill suspected was somehow mistranslated, and an Opposite Secretary-General for the Genocidal Eradication of Alien Aggressors, at whom Drill looked with more than a little interest. The Opposite Secretary-General was named Vang, and was small even for a Shar. He seemed to wrinkle his nose more than the others. The Special Executive for External Coherence, whose name was Cup, seemed a bit piebald, patches of white skin showing through the golden fur covering his shoulders, arms, and head.

He is elderly, said Memory.

That's what I thought.

''Down, Slab,'' Drill said. He leaned back against the creature and began to move to a more relaxed position.

He looked at the Shars and smiled. Fur ruffled on shoulders and necks. ''Shall we make peace now?'' he asked.

''We would like to clarify something you said earlier,'' President Gram said. ''You said that you were the only, ah, conscious entity on the ship. That you were the only member of the human delegation. Was that translated correctly?''

''Why, yes,'' Drill said. ''Why would more than one diplomat be necessary?''

The Shars looked at each other. The Special Executive for External Coherence spoke cautiously.

''You will not be needing to consult with your superiors? You have full authority from your government?''

Drill beamed at them. ''We humans do not have a government, of course,'' he said. ''But I am a diplomat with the appropriate Memory and training. There is no problem that I can foresee.''

''Please let me understand, your Excellency,'' Cup said. He was leaning forward, his small eyes watering. ''I am elderly and may be slow in comprehending the situation.

But if you have no government, who accredited you with this mission?"

"I am a diplomat. It is my specialty. No accreditation is necessary. The human race will accept my judgment of any matter of negotiation, as they would accept the judgment of any specialist in his area of expertise."

"But why *you*. As an individual?"

Drill shrugged massively. "I was part of the nearest diplomatic enclave, and the individual without any other tasks at the moment." He looked at each of the delegation in turn. "I am incredibly happy to have this chance, honorable delegates," he said. "The vast majority of human diplomats never have the chance to speak to another species. Usually we mediate only in conflicts of interest between the various groups of human specialties."

"But the human species will abide by your decisions?"

"Of course." Drill was surprised at the Shar's persistence. "Why wouldn't they?"

Cup settled back in his chair. His ears were down. There was a short silence.

"We have an opening statement prepared," President Gram said. "I would like to enter it into our record, if I may. Or would your Excellency prefer to go first?"

"I have no opening statement," Drill said. "Please go ahead."

Cup and the President exchanged glances. President Gram took a deep breath and began.

Long. Memory said. *Very long*.

The opening statement seemed very much like the address President Gram had been delivering to the crowd, the same hypnotic rhythms, more or less the same content. The rest of the delegation made muted responses. Drill drowsed through it, enjoying it as music.

"Thank you, Honorable President," he said afterwards. "That was very nice."

"We would like to propose an agenda for the conference," Gram said. "First, to resolve the matter of the cease-fire and its provisions for an ending to hostilities. Second, the establishment of a secure border between our two species, guaranteeing both species room for expansion. Third, the establishment of trade and visitation agreements. Fourth, the matter of reparations, payments, and return of lost territory.''

Drill nodded. "I believe," he said, "that resolution of the second through fourth points will come about as a result of an understanding reached on the first. That is, once the cease-fire is settled, that resolution will imply a settlement of the rest of the situation.''

"You accept the agenda?''

"If you like. It doesn't matter.''

Ears pricked forward, then back. "So you accept that our initial discussions will consist of formalizing the disengagement of our forces?''

"Certainly. Of course I have no way of knowing what forces you have committed. We humans have committed none.''

The Shars were still for a long time. "Your species attacked our planets, Ambassador. Without warning, without making yourselves known to us.'' Gram's tone was unusually flat. Perhaps, Drill thought, she was attempting to conceal great emotion.

"Yes," Drill said. "But those were not our military formations. Your species were contacted only by our terraforming Ships. They did not attack your people, as such—they were only peripherally aware of your existence. Their function was merely to seed the planets with lifeforms favorable to human existence. Unfortunately for your people, part of the function of these lifeforms is to destroy the native life of the planet.''

The Shars conferred with one another. The Opposite Secretary-General seemed particularly vehement. Then President Gram turned to Drill.

"We cannot accept your statement, your Excellency," she said. "Our people were attacked. They defended themselves, but were overcome.''

"Our terraforming Ships are very good at what they do,'' Drill said. "They are specialists. Our Shrikes, our Shrews, our Sharks—each is a master of its element. But they lack intelligence. They are not conscious entities, such as ourselves. They weren't aware of your civilization at all. They only saw you as food.''

"You're claiming that you *didn't notice us?*" demanded Secretary-General Vang. "*They didn't notice us as they were killing us?*" He was shouting. President Gram's ears went back.

"Not as such, no," Drill said.

President Gram stood up. "I am afraid, your Excellency, your explanations are insufficient," she said. "This conference must be postponed until we can reach a united conclusion concerning your remarkable attitude."

Drill was bewildered. "What did I say?" he asked.

The other Shars stood. President Gram turned and walked briskly on her three legs toward the exit. The others followed.

"Wait," Drill said. "Don't go. Let me send for Frog. Up, Slab, up!"

The Shars were gone by the time Slab had got Drill to his feet. The Ship told him they had found their own way to the airlock. Drill could think of nothing to do but order the airlock to let them out.

"Why would I lie?" he asked. "Why would I lie to them?" Things were so very simple, really.

He shifted his vast weight from one foot to the other and back again. Drill could not decide whether he had done anything wrong. He asked Memory what to do next, but Memory held no information to comfort him, only dry recitations of past negotiations. Annoyed at the lifeless monologue, Drill told Memory to be silent and began to walk restlessly through the corridors of his Ship. He could not decide where things had gone bad.

Sensing his agitation, Lowbrain began to echo his distress. *Mash*, Lowbrain thought weakly. *Food. Sex.*

Be silent, Drill commanded.

Sex, sex, Lowbrain thought.

Drill realized that Lowbrain was beginning to give him an erection. Acceding to the inevitable, he began moving toward Surrogate's quarters.

Surrogate lived in a dim, quiet room filled with the murmuring sound of its own heartbeat. It was a human subspecies, about the intelligence of Lowbrain, designed to comfort voyagers on long journeys through space, when carnal access to their own subspecies might necessarily be limited. Surrogate had a variety of sexual equipment designed for the accommodation of the various human subspecies and their sexes. It also had large mammaries that gave nutritious milk, and a rudimentary head capable of voicing simple thoughts.

Tiny Mice, that kept Surrogate and the ship clean, scattered as Drill entered the room. Surrogate's little head turned to him.

"It's good to see you again," Surrogate said.

"I am Drill."

"It's good to see you again, Drill," said Surrogate. "It's good to see you again."

Drill began to nuzzle its breasts. One of Surrogate's male parts began to erect. "I'm confused, Surrogate," he said. "I don't know what to do."

"Why are you confused, Drill?" asked Surrogate. It raised one of its arms and began to stroke Drill's head. It wasn't really having a conversation: Surrogate had only been programmed to make simple statements, or to analyze its partners' speech and ask questions.

"Things are going wrong," Drill said. He began to suckle. The warm milk flowed down his throat. Surrogate's male part had an orgasm. Mice jumped from hiding to clean up the mess.

"Why are things going wrong?" asked Surrogate. "I'm sure everything will be all right."

Lowbrain had an orgasm, perceived by Drill as scattered, faraway bits of pleasure. Drill continued to suckle, feeling a heavy comfort beginning to radiate from Surrogate, from the gentle sound of its heartbeat, its huge, wholesome, brainless body.

Everything will be all right, Drill decided.

"Nice to see you again, Drill," Surrogate said. "Drill, it's *nice* to see you again."

· · ·

The vast crowds of Shars did not leave when night fell. Instead they stood beneath floating globes dispersing a cold reddish light that reflected eerily from pointed ears and muzzles. Some of them donned capes or skirts to help them keep warm. Drill, watching them on the video walls of the command center, was reminded of crowds standing in awe before some vast cataclysm.

The Shars were not quiet. They stood in murmuring groups, but sometimes they began the crooning chants they had raised earlier, or suddenly broke out in a series of shrill yipping cries.

President Gram spoke to them after she had left Ship. "The human has admitted his species' attacks," she said, "but has disclaimed responsibility. We shall urge him to adopt a more realistic position."

"Adopt a position," Drill repeated, not understanding. "It is not a position. It is the truth. Why don't they understand?"

Opposite Minister-General Vang was more vehement. "We now have a far more complete idea of the humans' attitude," he said. "It is opposed to ours in every way. We shall not allow the murderous atrocities which the humans have committed upon five of our planets to be forgotten, or understood to be the result of some inexplicable lack of attention on the part of our species' enemies."

"That one is obviously deranged," thought Drill.

He went to his sleeping quarters and ordered the Slab there to play him some relaxing music. Even with Slab's murmurs and comforting hums, it took Drill some time before his agitation subsided.

Diplomacy, he thought as slumber overtook him, was certainly a strange business.

In the morning the Shars were still there, chanting and crying, moving in their strange crowded patterns. Drill watched them on his video walls as he ate breakfast at the mash bins. "There is a communication from President

Gram,'' Memory announced. ''She wishes to speak with you by radio.''

''Certainly.''

''Ambassador Drill.'' She was using the flat tones again. A pity she was subject to such stress.

''Good morning, President Gram,'' Drill said. ''I hope you spent a pleasant night.''

''I must give you the results of our decision. We regret that we can see no way to continue the negotiations unless you, as a representative of your species, agree to admit responsibility for your peoples' attacks on our planets.''

''Admit responsibility?'' Drill said. ''Of course. Why wouldn't I?''

Drill heard some odd, indistinct barking sounds that his translator declined to interpret for him. It sounded as if someone other than President Gram were on the other end of the radio link.

''You admit responsibility?'' President Gram's amazement was clear even in translation.

''Certainly. Does it make a difference?''

President Gram declined to answer that question. Instead she proposed another meeting for that afternoon.

''I will be ready at any time.''

Memory recorded President Gram's speech to her people, and Drill studied it before meeting the Shar party at the airlock. She made a great deal out of the fact that Drill had admitted humanity's responsibility for the war. Her people leaped, yipped, chanted their responses as if possessed. Drill wondered why they were so excited.

Drill met the party at the airlock this time, linked with Memory and Lowbrain in Zen Synch so as not to accidentally step on the President or one of her party. He smiled and greeted each by name and led them toward the conference room.

''I believe,'' said Cup, ''we may avoid future misunderstandings, if your Excellency would consent to inform us about your species. We have suffered some confusion in regard to your distinction between 'conscious' and 'unconscious' entities. Could you please explain the difference, as you understand it?''

"A pleasure, your Excellency," Drill said. "Our species, unlike yours, is highly specialized. Once, eight million years ago, we were like you—a small, nonspecialized species type is very useful at a certain stage of evolution. But once a species reaches a certain complexity in its social and technological evolution, the need for specialists becomes too acute. Through both deliberate genetic manipulation and natural evolution, humanity turned away from a generalist species, toward highly specialized forms adapted to particular functions and environments. We understand this to be a natural function of species evolution.

"In the course of our explorations into manipulating our species, we discovered that the most efficient way of coding large amounts of information was in our own cell structure— our DNA. For tasks requiring both large and small amounts of data, we arranged that, as much as possible, these would be performed by organic entities, human subspecies. Since many of these tasks were boring and repetitive, we reasoned that advanced consciousness, such as that which we both share, was not necessary. You have met several unconscious entities. Frog, for example, and the Slab on which I lie. Many parts of my Ship are also alive, though not conscious."

"That would explain the smell," one of the delegation murmured.

"The terraforming Ships," Drill went on, "which attacked your planets   these were also designed so as not to require a conscious operator."

The Shars squinted up at Drill with their little eyes. "But why?" Cup asked.

"Terraforming is a dull process. It takes many years. No conscious mind could possibly enjoy it."

"But your species would find itself at war without knowing it. If your explanation for the cause of this war is correct, you already have."

Drill shrugged massively. "This happens from time to time. Sometimes other species which have reached our stage of development have attacked us in the same way. When it does, we arrange a peace.''

"You consider these attacks normal?" Opposite Minister-General Vang was the one who spoke.

"These occasional encounters seem to be a natural result of species evolution," Drill said.

Vang turned to one of the Shars near him and spoke in several sharp barks. Drill heard a few words: "Billions lost . . . five planets . . . atrocities . . . *natural result!*"

"I believe," said President Gram, "that we are straying from the agenda."

Vang looked at her. "Yes, honorable President. Please forgive me."

"The matter of withdrawal," said President Gram, "to recognized truce lines."

Species at this stage of their development tend to be territorial, Memory reminded Drill. *Their political mentality is based around the concept of borders. The idea of a borderless community of species may be perceived as a threat.*

I'll try and go easy on them, Drill said.

"The Memories on our terraforming Ships will be adjusted to account for your species," Drill said. "After the adjustment, your people will no longer be in danger."

"In our case, it will take the disengage order several months to reach all our forces," President Gram said. "How long will the order take to reach your own Ships?"

"A century or so." The Shars stared. "Memories at our exploration bases in this area will be adjusted first, of course, and these will adjust the Memories of terraforming Ships as they come in for maintenance and supplies."

"We'll be subject to attack for *another hundred years?*" Vang's tone mixed incredulity and scorn.

"Our terraforming Ships move more or less at random, and only come into base when they run out of supplies. We don't know where they've been till they report back. Though they're bound to encounter a few more of your planets, your species will still survive, enough to continue your species evolution. And during that time you'll be searching for and occupying new planets on your own. You'll probably come out of this with a net gain."

"Have you no respect for life?" Vang demanded. Drill considered his answer.

"All individuals die, Opposite Minister-General," he said. "That is a fact of nature which no species has been able to alter. Only species can survive. Individuals are easily replaceable. Though you will lose some planets and a large number of individuals, your species as a whole will survive and may even prosper. What more could a species or its delegated representatives desire?"

Opposite Minister-General Vang was glaring at Drill, his ears pricked forward, lips drawn back from his teeth. He said nothing.

"We desire a cease-fire that is a true cease-fire," President Gram said. Her hands were clasping and unclasping rhythmically on the edge of her chair. "Not a slow, authorized extermination of our species. Your position has an unwholesome smell. I am afraid we must end these discussions until you alter it."

"Position? This is not a position, honorable President. It is truth."

"We have nothing further to say."

Unhappily, Drill followed the Shar delegation to the airlock. "I do not lie, honorable President," he said, but Gram only turned away and silently left the human Ship. The Shars in their pale thousands received her.

The Shar broadcasts were not heartening. Opposite Minister-General Vang was particularly vehement. Drill collected the highlights of the speeches as he speeded through Memory's detailed remembrance. "Callous disregard . . . no common ground for communication . . . casual attitude toward atrocity . . . displays of obvious savagery . . . no respect for the individual . . . defend ourselves . . . this stinks in the nose."

The Shars leaped and barked in response. There were strange bubbling high-pitched laughing sounds that Drill found unsettling.

"We hope to find a formula for peace," President Gram said. "We will confer with all the ministers in session." That was all.

That night, the Shars surrounding Ship moaned, moving slowly in a giant circle, their arms linked. The laughing sounds that followed Vang's speech did not cease entirely. He did not understand why they did not all go home and sleep.

Long, long, Memory said. No comfort there.

Early in the morning, before dawn, there was a communication from President Gram. "I would like to meet with you privately. Away from the recorders, the coalition partners."

"I would like nothing better," Drill said. He felt a small current of optimism begin to trickle into him.

"Can I use an airlock other than the one we've been using up till now?"

Drill gave President Gram instructions and met her in the other airlock. She was wearing a night cape with a hood. The Shars, circling and moaning, had paid her no attention.

"Thank you for seeing me under these conditions," she said, peering up at him from beneath the hood. Drill smiled. She shuddered.

"I am pleased to be able to cooperate," he said.

Mash! Lowbrain demanded. It had been silent until Drill entered Zen Synch. Drill told it to be silent with a snarling vehemence that silenced it for the present.

"This way, honorable President," Drill said. He took her to his sleeping chamber—a small room, only fifty feet square. "Shall I send a Frog for one of your chairs?" he asked.

"I will stand. Three legs seem to be more comfortable than two for standing."

"Yes."

"Is it possible, Ambassador Drill, that you could lower the intensity of the light here? I find it oppressive."

Drill felt foolish, knowing he should have thought of this himself. "I'm sorry," he said. "I will give the orders at once. I wish you had told me earlier." He smiled nervously as he dimmed the lights and arranged himself on his Slab.

"Honorable ambassador." President Gram's words seemed hesitant. "I wonder if it is possible . . . can you tell me the meaning of that facial gesture of yours, showing me your teeth?"

"It is called a smile. It is intended as a gesture of benevolent reassurance."

"Showing of the teeth is considered a threat here, honorable Ambassador. Some of us have considered this a sign that you wish to eat us."

Drill was astonished. "My goodness!" he said. "I don't even eat meat! Just a kind of vegetable mash."

"I pointed out that your teeth seemed unsuitable for eating meat, but still it makes us uneasy. I was wondering . . ."

"I will try to suppress the smile, yes. Eating meat! What an idea. Some of our military specialists, yes, and of course the Sharks and Shrikes and so on . . ." He told his Memory to enforce a strict ban against smiling in the presence of a Shar.

Gram leaned back on her sturdy rear leg. Her cape parted, revealing her ribbons and badges of office, her four furry dugs. "I wanted to inform you of certain difficulties here, Ambassador Drill," she said. "I am having difficulty holding together my coalition. Minister-General Vang's faction is gaining strength. He is attempting to create a perception in the minds of Shars that you are untrustworthy and violent. Whether he believes this, or whether he is using this notion as a means of destabilizing the coalition, is hardly relevant—considering your species' unprovoked attacks, it is not a difficult perception to reinforce. He is also trying to tell our people that the military is capable of dealing with your species."

Drill's brain swam with Memory's information on concepts such as "faction" and "coalition." The meaning of the last sentence, however, was clear.

"That is a foolish perception, honorable President," he said.

"His assurances on that score lack conviction." Gram's

eyes were shiny. Her tone grew earnest. "You must give me something, ambassador. Something I can use to soothe the public mind. A way out of this dilemma. I tell you that it is impossible to expect us to sit idly by and accept the loss of an undefined number of planets over the next hundred years. I plead with you, ambassador. Give me something. Some way we can avoid attack. Otherwise . . ." She left the sentence incomplete.

Mash, Lowbrain wailed. Drill ignored it. He moved into Zen Synch with Memory, racing through possible solutions. Sweat gathered on his forehead, pouring down his vast shoulders.

"Yes," he said. "Yes, there is a possibility. If you could provide us with the location of all your occupied planets, we could dispatch a Ship to each with the appropriate Memories as cargo. If any of our terraforming Ships arrived, the Memories could be transferred at once, and your planets would be safe."

President Gram considered this. "Memories," she said. "You've been using the term, but I'm not sure I understand."

"Stored information is vast, and even though human bodies are large we cannot always have all the information we need to function efficiently even in our specialized tasks," Drill said. "Our human brains have been separated as to function. I have a Lowbrain, which is on my spinal cord above my pelvis. Lowbrain handles motor control of my lower body, routine monitoring of my body's condition, eating, excretion, and sex. My perceptual centers, short-term memory, personality, and reasoning functions are handled by the brain in my skull—the classical brain, if you like. Long-term and specialized memory is the function of the large knob you see moving on my head, my Memory. My Memory records all that happens in great detail, and can recapitulate it at any point. It has also been supplied with information concerning the human species' contacts with other nonhuman groups. It attaches itself easily to my nervous system and draws nourishment from my body. Specific memories can be communicated from one living Mem-

ory to another, or if it proves necessary I can simply give
my Memory to another human, a complete transfer. I have
another Memory aboard that I'm not using at the moment,
a pilot Memory that can navigate and handle Ship, and I
wore this Memory while in transit. I also have spare Memories in case my primary Memories fall ill. So you see, our
specialization does not rule out adaptability—any piece of
information needed by any of us can easily be transferred,
and in far greater detail than by any mechanical medium."

"So you could return to your base and send out pilot
Memories to our planets," Gram said. "Memories that
could halt your terraforming ships."

"That is correct." Just in time, Memory managed to stop
the twitch in Drill's cheeks from becoming a smile. Happiness bubbled up in him. He was going to arrange this
peace after all!

"I am afraid that would not be acceptable, your Excellency," President Gram said. Drill's hopes fell.

"Whyever not?"

"I'm afraid the Minister-General would consider it a na-
ïve attempt of yours to find out the location of our populated
planets. So that your species could attack them, ambassador."

"I'm trying very hard, President Gram," Drill said.

"I'm sure you are."

Drill frowned and went into Zen Synch again, ignoring
Lowbrain's plaintive cries for mash and sex, sex and mash.
Concepts crackled through his mind. He began to develop
an erection, but Memory was drawing off most of the available blood and the erection failed. The smell of Drill's sweat
filled the room. President Gram wrinkled her nose and
leaned back far onto her rear leg.

"Ah," Drill said. "A solution. Yes. I can have my Pilot
memory provide the locations to an equivalent number of
our own planets. We will have one another's planets as
hostage."

"Bravo, ambassador," President Gram said quietly. "I
think we may have a solution. But—forgive me—it may

be said that we cannot trust your information. We will have to send ships to verify the location of your planets.''

''If your ships go to my planet first,'' Drill said, ''I can provide your people with one of my spare Memories that will inform my species what your people are doing, and instruct the humans to cooperate. We will have to construct some kind of link between your radio and my Memory . . . maybe I can have my Ship grow one.''

President Gram came forward off her third leg and began to pace forward, moving in her strange, fast, hobbling way. ''I can present it to the council this way, yes,'' she said. ''There is hope here.'' She stopped her movement, peering up at Drill with her ears pricked forward. ''Is it possible that you could allow me to present this to the council as my own idea?'' she asked. ''It may meet with less suspicion that way.''

''Whatever way is best,'' said Drill. President Gram gazed into the darkened recesses of the room.

''This smells good,'' she said. Drill succeeded in suppressing his smile.

''It's nice to see you again.''
''I am Drill.''
''It's nice to see you again, Drill.''
''I think we can make the peace work.''
''Everything will be all right, Drill. Drill, I'm sure everything will be all right.''
''I'm so glad I had this chance. This is the chance of a lifetime.''
''Drill, it's *nice* to see you again.''

The next day President Gram called and asked to present a new plan. Drill said he would be pleased to hear it. He met the party at the airlock, having already dimmed the lights. He was very rigid in his attempts not to smile.

They sat in the dimmed room while President Gram presented the plan. Drill pretended to think it over, then acceded. Details were worked out. First the location of one human planet would be given and verified—this planet, the

Shar capital, would count as the first revealed Shar planet. After verification, each side would reveal the location of two planets, verify those, then reveal four, and so on. Even counting the months it would take to verify the location of planets, the treaty should be completed within less than five years.

That night the Shars went mad. At President Gram's urging, they built fires, danced, screamed, sang. Drill watched on his Ship's video walls. Their rhythms beat at his head.

He smiled. For hours.

The Ship obligingly grew a communicator and coupled it to one of Drill's spare Memories. The two were put aboard a Shar ship and sent in the direction of Drill's home. Drill remained in his ship, watching entertainment videos Ship received from the Shars' channels. He didn't understand the dramas very well, but the comedies were delightful. The Shars could do the most intricate, clever things with their flexible bodies and odd tripod legs—it was delightful to watch them.

Maybe I could take some home with me, he thought. *They can be very entertaining.*

The thousands of Shars waiting outside Ship began to drift away. Within a month only a few hundred were left. Their singing was quiet, triumphant, assured. Sometimes Drill had it piped into his sleeping chamber. It helped him relax.

President Gram visited informally every ten days or so. Drill showed her around Ship, showing her the pilot Memory, the Frog quarters, the giant stardrive engines with their human subspecies' implanted connections, Surrogate in its shadowed, pleasant room. The sight of Surrogate seemed to agitate the President.

"You do not use sex for procreation?" she asked. "As an expression of affection?"

"Indeed we do. I have scads of offspring. There are never enough diplomats, so we have a great many couplings among our subspecies. As for affection . . . I think I can say that I have enjoyed the company of each of my partners.''

She looked up at him with solemn eyes. ''You travel to the stars, Drill,'' she said. ''Your species expands randomly in all directions, encountering other species, sometimes annihilating them. Do you have a reason for any of this?''

''A reason?'' Drill mused. ''It is natural to us. Natural to all intelligent species, so far as we know.''

''I meant a conscious reason. Is it anything other than what you do in an automatic way?''

''I can't think of why we would need any such reasons.''

''So you have no philosophy of constant expansion? No ideology?''

''I do not know what those words mean,'' Drill said.

Gram closed her eyes and lowered her head. ''I am sorry,'' she said.

''No need. We have no conflicts in our ideas about ourselves, about our lives. We are happy with what we are.''

''Yes. You couldn't be unhappy if you tried, could you?''

''No,'' Drill said cheerfully. ''I see that you understand.''

''Yes,'' Gram said. ''I scent that I do.''

''In a few million years,'' Drill said, ''these things will become clear to you.''

The first Shar ship returned from Drill's home, reporting a transfer of the Memory. The field around Ship filled again with thousands of Shars, crying their happiness to the skies. Other Memories were now taking instructions to all terraforming bases. The locations of two new planets were released. Ships carrying spare Memories leaped into the skies.

It's working, Drill told Memory.

Long, Memory said. *Very long.*

But Memory could not lower Drill's joy. This was what he had lived his life for, and he knew he was good at it. Memories of the future would take this solution as a model for negotiations with other species. Things were working out.

• • •

One night the Shars outside Ship altered their behavior. Their singing became once again a moaning, mixed with cries. Drill was disturbed.

A communication came from the President. "Cup is dead," she said.

"I understand," Drill said. "Who is his replacement?"

Drill could not read Gram's expression. "That is not yet known. Cup was a strong person, and did not like other strong people around him. Already the successors are fighting for the leadership, but they may not be able to hold his faction together." Her ears flickered. "I may be weakened by this."

"I regret things tend that way."

"Yes," she said. "So do I."

The second set of ships returned. More Memories embarked on their journeys. The treaty was holding.

There was a meeting aboard Ship to formalize the agreement. Cup's successor was Brook, a tall, elderly Shar whose golden fur was darkened by age. A compromise candidate, President Gram said, his election determined after weeks of fighting for the successorship. He was not respected. Already pieces of Cup's old faction were breaking away.

"I wonder, your Excellency," Brook said, after the formal business was over, "if you could arrange for our people to learn your language. You must have powerful translation modules aboard your ship in order to learn our language so quickly. You were broadcasting your message of peace within a few hours of entering real space."

"I have no such equipment aboard Ship," Drill said. "Our knowledge of your language was acquired from Shar prisoners."

"Prisoners?" Shar ears pricked forward. "We were not aware of this," Brook said.

"After our base Memories recognized discrepancies," Drill said, "we sent some Ships out searching for you. We seized one of your ships and took it to my home world. The prisoners were asked about their language and the location of your capital planet. Otherwise it would have taken me months to find your world here, and learn to communicate with you.''

"May we ask to arrange for the return of the prisoners?''

"Oh.'' Drill said. "That won't be possible. After we learned what we needed to know, we terminated their lives. They were being kept in an area reserved for a garden. The landscapers wanted to get to work.'' Drill bobbed his head reassuringly. "I am pleased to inform you that they proved excellent fertilizer for the gardens. The result was quite lovely.''

"I think,'' said President Gram carefully, "that it would be best that this information not go beyond those of us in this room. I think it would disturb the process.''

Minister-General Vang's ears went back. So did others'. But they acceded.

"I think we should take our leave,'' said President Gram.

"Have a pleasant afternoon,'' said Drill.

"It's important.'' It was not yet dawn. Ship had awakened Drill for a call from the President. "One of your ships has attacked another of our planets.''

Alarm drove the sleep from Drill's brain. "Please come to the airlock,'' he said.

"The information will reach the population within the hour.''

"Come quickly,'' said Drill.

The President arrived with a pair of assistants, who stayed inside the airlock. They carried staves. "My people will be upset,'' Gram said. "Things may not be entirely safe.''

"Which planet was it?'' Drill asked.

Gram rubbed her ears. "It was one of those whose location went out on the last peace shuttle.''

"The new Memory must not have arrived in time.''

"That is what we will tell the people. That it couldn't have been prevented. I will try to speed up the process by which the planets receive new Memories. Double the quota.''

"That is a good idea.''

"I will have to dismiss Brook. Opposite Minister-General

Vang will have to take his job. If I can give Vang more power, he may remain in the coalition and not cause a split."

"As you think best."

President Gram looked up at Drill, her head rising reluctantly, as if held back by a great weight. "My son," she said. "He was on the planet when it happened."

"You have other offspring," Drill said.

Gram looked at him, the pain burning deep in her eyes. "Yes," she said. "I do."

The fields around Ship filled once again. Cries and howls rent the air, and dirges pulsed against Ship's uncaring walls. The Shar broadcasts in the next weeks seemed confused to Drill. Coalitions split and fragmented. Vang spoke frequently of readiness. President Gram succeeded in doubling the quota of planets. The decision was a near one.

Then, days later, another message. "One of our commanders," said President Gram, "was based on the vicinity of the attacked planet. He is one of Vang's creatures. On his own initiative he ordered our military forces to engage. Your terraforming Ship was attacked."

"Was it destroyed?" Drill asked. His tone was urgent. There is still hope, he reminded himself.

"Don't be anxious for your fellow humans," Gram said. "The Ship was damaged, but escaped."

"The loss of a few hundred billion unconscious organisms is no cause for anxiety," Drill said. "An escaped terraforming Ship is. The Ship will alert our military forces. It will be a real war."

President Gram licked her lips. "What does that mean?"

"You know of our Shrikes and so on. Our military people are worse. They are fully conscious and highly specialized in different modes of warfare. They are destructive, carnivorous, capable of taking enormous damage without impairing function. Their minds concentrate only on tactics, on destruction. Normally they are kept on planetoids away from the rest of humanity. Even other humans find their proximity too . . . disturbing." Drill put all the urgency in his speech that he could. "Honorable President, you must give me the locations of the remaining planets. If I can get Memories to each of them with news of the peace, we may yet save them.''

"I will try. But the coalition . . ." She turned away from the transmitter. "Vang will claim a victory."

"It is the worst possible catastrophe," Drill said.

Gram's tone was grave. "I believe you," she said.

Drill listened to the broadcasts with growing anxiety. The Shars who spoke on the broadcasts were making angry comments about the execution of prisoners, about flower gardens and values Drill didn't understand. Someone had let the secret loose. President Gram went from group to group outside Ship, talking of the necessity of her plan. The Shars' responses were muted. Drill sensed they were waiting. It was announced that Vang had left the coalition. A chorus of triumphant yips rose from scattered members of the crowd. Others only moaned.

Vang, now simply General Vang, arrived at the field. His followers danced intoxicated circles around him as he spoke, howling their responses to his words. "Triumph! United will!" they cried. "The humans can be beaten! Treachery avenged! Dictate the peace from a position of strength! We smell the location of their planets!"

The Shars' weird cackling laughter followed him from point to point. The laughing and crying went on well into the night. In the morning the announcement came that the coalition had fallen. Vang was now President-General.

In his sleeping chamber, surrounded by his video walls, Drill began to weep.

"I have been asked to bear Vang's message to you," Gram said. She seemed smaller than before, standing unsteadily even on her tripod legs. "It is his . . . humor."

"What is the message?" Drill said. His whole body seemed in pain. Even Lowbrain was silent, wrapped in misery.

"I had hoped," Gram said, "that he was using this simply as an issue on which to gain power. That once he had the

Presidency, he would continue the diplomatic effort. It appears he really means what he's been saying. Perhaps he's no longer in control of his own people.''

"It is war," Drill said.

"Yes."

You have failed, said Memory. Drill winced in pain.

"You will lose," he said.

"Vang says we are cleverer than you are."

"That may be the case. But cleverness cannot compete with experience. Humans have fought hundreds of these little wars, and never failed to wipe out the enemy. Our Memories of these conflicts are intact. Your people can't fight millions of years of specialized evolution.''

"Vang's message doesn't end there. You have till nightfall to remove your Ship from the planet. Six days to get out of real space.''

"I am to be allowed to live?" Drill was surprised.

"Yes. It is our . . . our custom."

Drill scratched himself. "I regret our efforts did not succeed.''

"No more than I." She was silent for a while. "Is there any way we can stop this?"

"If Vang attacks any human planets after the Memories of the peace arrangement have arrived," Drill said, "the military will be unleashed to wipe you out. There is no stopping them after that point.''

"How long," she asked, "do you think we have?"

"A few years. Ten at the most."

"Our species will be dead."

"Yes. Our military are very good at their jobs."

"You will have killed us," Gram said, "destroyed the culture that we have built for thousands of years, and you won't even give it any thought. Your species doesn't think about what it does any more. It just acts, like a single-celled animal, engulfing everything it can reach. You say that you are a conscious species, but that isn't true. Your every action is . . . instinct. Or reflex.''

"I don't understand," said Drill.

Gram's body trembled. "That is the tragedy of it," she said.

An hour later Ship rose from the field. Shars laughed their defiance from below, dancing in crazed abandon.

I have failed, Drill told Memory.

You knew the odds were long, Memory said. *You knew that in negotiations with species this backward there have only been a handful of successes, and hundreds of failures.*

Yes, Drill acknowledged. *It's a shame, though. To have spent all these months away from home.*

Eat! Eat! said Lowbrain.

Far away, in their forty-mile-long Ships, the human soldiers were already on their way.

"TRUE COLORS"

Kathe Koja

"True Colors" was purchased by Gardner Dozois, and appeared in the January 1990 issue of IAsfm, with an illustration by Will Brown. A new writer, Koja has proved unusually adroit at exploring interpersonal relationships, including alien-human relationships; "True Colors" is her most subtle and accomplished handling of this difficult theme to date.

Kathe Koja made her first sale to IAsfm in 1988 with a story called "Distances," which was immediately picked up by two of the three science fiction "Best of the Year" anthologies that year. She has subsequently made four more sales to IAsfm, and is receiving wide attention as one of the most exciting new writers around. Coming up is her first novel, The Cipher. She lives in Willowbrook, Illinois.

Lake wind on Susin's lips, pale brown hair rustling like
weeds, long brown legs ankle-crossed on the porch rail.
This was her favorite place, this porch that hung like a
sagging barnacle from the beach cottage, and this was her
favorite time, the day over and Poole beside her. Poole was
not his name, of course, or even close to it, only a syllable
he had liked and kept. She had invented her name, too, or
at least its spelling.

Faint pale ripple of his skin, long pupils' pulse to division,
merging again as she watched. Sometimes she imagined she
could see in his eyes not herself, but his real self, not the
mannish shape he wore but him. She never got tired of
watching him, of being with him.

He was the most important thing in her life, had been
since the winter's morning she found him, dried skin sluggish and grainy to the touch, slick cadaver eyes peering up
at her through a scum of lake debris. It took him almost a
day to finally speak, throat working like a bellows, his voice
so thick with sussuration she could barely understand him
or how he came to be there. He had obviously been elsewhere, and not so far away either; in his oblique way, he
made it plain how travel distressed him, after his long,
original trip. She sat, skin shivering, listening to all he said,
then made a careful nest of sleeping bag and blankets in the
empty pantry room off the kitchen, and by doing so told
him that he had come to stay. She never questioned for a
moment what she did or why. She knew why.

His coming changed for her even the things he did not
directly touch: the town, its people, its bland routine and
blander tourists, as changeless as the lake. Susin had lived
there all her life; it had never been her home. She moved
among them even more as an outsider now, wearing the
pride of her difference like a chip on her shoulder, thinking,
if you knew, if you only knew.

Now, without looking, she felt Poole changing, the faint
damp copper scent of his skin turning colors. She turned to
face him like facing the sun, his skin not warm reds or golds
but frigid gray, indigo, a slippery sinister purple, and then
crawling patterns, austere, risky, like the skin of a snake.

She sat with her body thrust forward, hands out not to touch but to mime touching.

"Beautiful," she said, "it's so beautiful." Poole nodded, once and solemnly, a learned motion, like shaking his head, like shrugging or smiling. He had learned them all and well, and used them easily.

He made more colors for her, until it was very dark, the water's sound rising with the wind. He sat changing, his skin chilling so the colors muddied, and Susin said, "Let's go in, okay?" and he followed her, screen door and paint-scratched front door, closing out the rest of the world.

Susin parked at the IGA, quick impatient slew of the rusty Dodge into a slim space between a Corvette and a Jeep. Across the street, she saw another in a summerlong parade of sidewalk Rembrandts, sketching like mad outside the plastic driftwood arch of She Sells Sea Shells (sweatshirts for the whole family, Gulls and Buoys). No big crowd, but if his work was pedestrian enough, ha ha, there surely would be. Let me guess, she thought. Seascapes, or Your Picture Five Dollars?

People buying hot dog buns, beer, big dusty bags of charcoal imprinted with a grinning bear in a chef's hat; Susin greeted no one, pushed her spavined cart like an icebreaker, spinach greens, ginger ale. Still no one watching the artist as she loaded the car, three greasy-feeling plastic sacks, and on impulse she walked over, sandals slapping, sweat on the back of her neck.

The work stopped her three feet from the easel: rich eerie colors, blues thick and juicy as blood, spidery lavender lines like the whorl of a desiccated shell. Shirtless, his back muscles working strongly as back and forth went the chalk, heavy swipes of red like the end of the world.

He saw or felt her, turned to regard her with a smileless gravity that swallowed her first sardonic comment ("Welcome to Philistine Valley"). His eyes unseen, covered by sunglasses someone else would have worn as a Halloween joke, nose richly sunburned, long hair pulled back in a

messy plait, half-curly, half-straight, the color of expensive
wine.

"I like your pictures," Susin said. It seemed inane after
she had said it, but it was simply true: the colors reminded
her of Poole.

"I like them too. Sometimes."

"You can't sell them here." That surprised them both,
and, annoyed at herself, she said, "I mean, no one will *buy*
them here." You think that's *better?* "I *mean*," forehead
red, "the people here generally run to Norman Rockwell-
type stuff, the dregs of the dregs. You know?"

He considered his pictures as with a customer's eye.
"Well," and she heard more plainly the sinuous accent,
the sea, not the lake, and summer suns hotter than the one
burning overhead, "it's still fun to do them."

He plucked a piece of sweetest yellow chalk, worked it
in a slippery vertical line, and Susin stepped farther back,
watching as much the movements he made, the slight
compression of his lips—full red underlip, like a child's—
as the motion of the chalk. Two women came out from She
Sells and edged Susin back, one step, three, and stood
watching with heads cocked like busy birds. Susin made a
hard little smile.

"If it's not on a T-shirt," she told Poole that night, slicing
day-old rye bread for them both, "they can't understand it.
The tourists are the worst, but the *locals*—" All her life,
she had called them the locals. "He'll be gone in a week,"
she said.

A yellow flicker ran Poole's length. His tiny tongues
extruded as he placed between them a slice of bread. "It's
good for you," Poole said, "to see what the other ones
miss." Susin smiled. It took an alien mind to know hers.

The artist was not gone, though. There were many drawings taped to the easel back, fresh new fluttering papers,
and it seemed all the originals were still there too. He was
sweating, squinting without his sunglasses, and his drawing
was as hot as the pavement. Without stopping, he said to
Susin, "You were right."

"I told you." It sounded smug, and she shook her head

in private dismay. "I'm sorry—I think your work is beautiful." Two boys, skinny legs, boombox, expensive running shoes, their sneer expert as they passed, but Susin did not deign to sneer back at them. "I'd like to buy one of your pictures. That one—" pointing on impulse to a wash of ivory and gray, speared with long plinths of iridescent lime.

"That's an old one. You can have it."

"No," firmly. "I want to buy it."

"No good unless it costs you, huh?" She shook her head, then saw his smile, pliant choirboy curve. He shrugged when she handed him a twenty. "I can't make change for that."

"Then I'll buy you a coffee."

It was too hot for coffee, so they sat in the stuffy shade of her car, drinking Cokes. His name was Robin, and he smiled again when she told him her name, spelling it. He talked, in his faint rounded drawl, not of adventures but situations, a gas station, a swimming pool, an empty field. And all the time one hand, blunt, long-fingered, picked and flattened the fraying upholstery, unconscious creation.

"Where are you staying now?" she asked him.

"The King's Shore," he said. "Pretty fancy name for a place with plastic bedspreads." He drank the last of his Coke, wiped his mouth on his sleeve like a child. "Thanks again," and slid across the seat, out the door, bending to smile once more into the open passenger window.

As soon as she got home, she showed the picture to Poole. He did not speak or praise, but from the depths of his throat came the faint atonal keening that marked emotion, and his hands on the paper pulsed its colors, held it so long that Susin, namelessly disturbed, reached to take it back. At once, he leaned away from her, the lines of his body taut, uneasy.

"You can have it, if you want," Susin said. She had stepped back unconsciously, stepped away from him, and when she saw this, stepped consciously forward. "Put it in your room, if you want to."

He did, and that night slept beneath it, face turned as if to catch its light. He spent much of his time crouched under it, his color almost null, only a faint freckling of green beneath his blinkless eyes. She was almost sorry she had given the picture to him—sorrier when, seeing her watching him, he deliberately closed his door.

He said little for the next few weeks, not seeming to mind that she was away, now, more than formerly. She watched Robin's colors now, as she had once watched Poole's: intently, eyes half-closed and rich with the sting of them. She tried once or twice to explain her absences to Poole, apologize if he was feeling neglected, but he shook his head. No, he did not mind, he said, it was very peaceful there in the cottage alone.

"What do you do?" Susin asked, and Poole gave her a look. Read, he told her, pointing to the neat rectangle of newspapers beside his sleeping place. Read and listen to the water. And think, he added, with an involuntary look upward, at Robin's picture.

It was unusually hot the next day, the sky a charcoal color, almost liquid in its humidity. Susin drove past She Sells, but Robin was gone. Frowning, she turned for the motel, asked at the desk for his room number.

"He moved out," the clerk told her, attention on the newspaper beneath his hands. "Couldn't make the rent, you wanna know."

"Moved out where?" Susin said sharply.

"How should I know?" He leaned forward over the counter. "You're the one lives out on the beach, right? He your boyfriend or something?" and he grinned, started to laugh a little. "Is that right?"

She pushed hard at the door, careless of its heavy glass slam, felt rain on her face. The sky was starting to crack, a slick sullen trench heavy with rain. She stared down the line of identical doors, number after number and none to show which had been his. Her heart was beating hard. She looked at the doors again.

And saw him, shiny something in his hand, peering around a door marked 16. Her heart beat harder still, she smiled, walked fast and faster to his door. "They said you were gone," she said, and the rain started in full, deep drape of water in unbroken lines from top to bottom, sky to ground. It fell so hard it leaped up again with impact, and he put one hand on her arm and tugged her inside.

His room—he had made it a lair: covered as if by shed skins, drawings everywhere. Some pictures on the wall, not his, cheaply-framed prints of bland seaside oils, but even these transformed by the hand of his art: a sheet of colored plastic taped over one, changing it to cool sepia, a string of glittering broken rosary beads, gull feathers, and two blood-red plastic roses adorned the other. On the table lamp, an incongruous false sheaf of hair, curled like a question mark and tied with a bow. A scatter of cassettes beside a K-mart tape player, beside them a pile of creased paperbacks, and in the center of the stained bedspread two plastic IGA sacks jumbled with clothing, the torn sleeve of a windbreaker hanging out as if exhausted. He pushed the bags aside, sat, gathered into his lap his old leather portfolio, his hands stroking it as if it were a mistreated dog. "I'm supposed to be out by now," he said, glancing at the rain past the half-pulled curtains, "but I don't want to go in this."

She sat beside him, smelling the faint musk of his skin, echoed by the scent of the sheets. "Where are you going?" Her voice came out higher than normal, fiercely casual. His feet were bare, and she saw a long fresh cut on his instep.

Shrugging, not answering, his hands paint-scarred and gentle on the portfolio, and Susin said, her voice higher still, tight in her throat, "Come stay with me. Until you find another place."

His hands stilled. Very slowly he looked at her, eyes blue and calm and full on hers, and he smiled. "I'd like that," he said.

"Well, then let's get going," and nervously she started packing, piling up the paperbacks and tapes, taking the embellishments from the dreary pictures She did not want to think of what Poole might say. Or do. What else could I *do*, she argued with his image, I can't just let him go, out in the rain.

On the drive there, streets already starting to eddy and worse as they drew closer to the beach, he spoke a little, saying that he was thankful, saying other things that she could not hear. The closer she got to the cottage, to Poole, the faster her heart beat, a long sustained gallop that was almost painful. A sharp wet smell rose from under her arms. She pulled up close beside the cottage, spoke without looking at Robin.

"I'll be out in a minute. Just wait here, all right? Wait in the car," and she pushed open the door, ran to the cottage through the cold blow of rain. Her hair hung half in her face, and her hands shook on the wet key.

"Poole!" she called. "Poole, I have to talk to you. Poole?" tracking through the cottage, empty kitchen, empty sleeping bag. Her sneakers made small wet sounds on the bare floors. "Poole—"

"Someone *else* is here."

He came up from nowhere, stood before her in the hallway like an apparition, absolutely still. There was no expression in his eyes, no clue in his color, dun. He had never, not even from the first, seemed as alien as this.

"Poole—"

Nothing: no flicker, no shine, no pulse of dividing pupils. Thunder outside.

"Poole, I would never have brought him if I didn't think it was safe, safe for you." Lie. She had *not* thought, not of Poole, before asking, only that Robin would be gone, only how to stop that from happening. "He won't tell anyone, I swear it."

Poole's voice, low vibration, strange clicking sounds, anger? distress? between the words. "I was once before found this way and it was hard—" A sound she had never heard before, it swept gooseflesh down her skin, more as his long mouth opened and his two tongues fluttered to be still, to make the sounds that she could understand. He could barely speak, now, for agitation; the only word she could make out was "hurt."

Firmly, as strongly as she could with her shaking voice, her trembling hands: "I will never let him hurt you, Poole, never."

He passed her, slipping into the kitchen, going, she knew, to his pantry-retreat, hiding there, and a tenderness rose in her, almost maternal in its ferocity, and a great ache of fear for what she had done. What *had* she done? Slowly, as if through unfamiliar territory, she went back out, slowly through the rain as if she could not feel it slapping her skin, matting her hair. She took her seat behind the wheel and turned to face Robin with that same abstracted slowness.

"Before we go in," she said, "I have to tell you something."

She did it just that baldly, the fact of Poole's presence, what he was, how he had come. She told it in less than ten sentences, short sharp words in a dry voice, and sat back to see what he would do. Her heart pounded so terribly the blood was like pain in her ears.

Robin said nothing. Head bent, he considered his feet, picked at a loose seam on his cutoffs. "I don't care if you believe me or not," Susin said, her voice unraveling, "I don't *care* what—"

"Susin," very softly, almost shy. "Do you think . . . do you think he would let me talk to him?"

"I can ask." Was he humoring her? There was no way to tell. They left the bags where they were and went inside, the door slamming loud in the utter quiet of the cottage. "Poole," Susin called, "Robin wants to talk to you, please. *Please,* Poole."

Picking his way, steppingstone walk, Robin headed for the kitchen, obeying Susin's directing nod. She stood in the living room, hands pressed together against her stomach, feeling a rising pocket of sickness there. Should she go with him? He was in the kitchen now, she could hear him saying Poole's name, not in a tone stretched and trembling like hers, but in a quiet respectful way, his drawl softer somehow, pliable as wax.

Poole's answering sound made her start, guttural, half a groan, and then Robin's voice again, startled and pleased: "*I* painted that!" More sounds from Poole. Robin's answer, indistinct, and then something she had not heard before: Robin's laugh, deeper than his voice, deep with delight. "Oh!" she heard him cry, "oh yeah!" and another laugh, and cautiously she went to the kitchen, went to stand by the pantry door.

To see Robin, face alight, eyes filled with the color of Poole, who was showing in a fanlike spread the colors of Robin's picture, more beautiful than it, more beautiful than human skill could reproduce. "*Oh,*" Robin said again, and tears came from his eyes to shine like rain on his cheeks.

She leaned back against the pantry door, relief so strong it made her feel sick, her muscles stringy and weak. Neither looked at her. Poole's colors pulsed and rose, and Robin watched, wept, smiled. Some time later, she stepped back from the door, shivering, then, with reaction, tears in her own eyes, but neither glanced her way, or watched her as she left the cottage to collect the bags.

Robin's studio, they called it: the half of the kitchen abutting the pantry, easel and papers and the smell of chalk dust and paint, richer than the odor of food. The table and two mismatched chairs were pushed into a corner to make room, the meager counters crowded, but Susin was so happy she would have torn down the house if they had suggested it. Them both, and together, and she between them, it was so much more than she had ever hoped for. Some nights she lay awake, simply smiling into the dark, hearing the faint sounds of Robin, breathing in dreams on the couch, and the voiceless murmurs of Poole in his sleeping bag nest. Rich, she was rich, she was immensely full.

All Robin's work, now, was of Poole: not his shape, or the physical; but his *colors,* living palette, constantly changing, whisper or glory or muted gleam, stopping only for Poole to rest. Robin was very strict: Poole must not be overtaxed, Poole must have everything just the way he liked it.

"God, you're something, you know?" he would say, hands busy, eyes full of color, and Poole would answer not in words but in a hum, a sweet foreign sound that Susin had not heard before.

"What's that, Poole?" she asked, and Robin said, "It's

like his, his purr. Didn't you know that?'' and Susin had smiled and shook her head. Poole's purr.

Robin was almost as unobtrusive a roommate as Poole, clean as a cat and tidy, rolling up his bedclothes every morning, using one coffee cup all day long. Susin cooked for everyone, an easy job since no one but she ever seemed to be hungry: too busy, Robin would say, patting her back, her shoulder. Later, 'kay? Later would come, and she, yawning, would climb into bed to the counterpoint of their quiet conversation and the paint's perfume. They had quickly developed a work language, a kind of artist's patois, augmented by gestures. One morning Susin saw Robin bend and dip his head gracefully, like a bird, twice, and Poole repeated the gesture twice, and, intrigued, she asked what they were doing.

''It's a way of,'' Robin at a loss, circling motion of his hand as if to say I know but I can't explain, ''a way of saying, like, I understand, or I know what you mean.'' Poole made a tiny crow and Robin laughed, and Susin laughed too, bewildered. She stayed watching for a few more minutes, but neither turned to her, spoke in any sort of gesture, and finally she wandered away.

One night she woke to hear tiny sounds, soft and distressful, and, frightened, she slipped out of bed, hurried on cold feet to the kitchen. In Poole's pantry, he lay curled in a painful circle, and Robin sat beside him, stroking the sorrowful bluish body, crooning half-song, half-words, his voice very deep.

''What's wrong?'' Susin said sharply, and Robin hushed her just as sharply.

''Don't talk so loud!'' and then, even more quietly, ''He's upset. He's homesick.''

''Homesick?''

''Well,'' and beneath the drawl a slight disbelief at her wonder, ''wouldn't *you* be? He's awful far from home,'' and again the croon, like a lullaby, over and over, until the blue skin washed to lavender and the eyes emptied and closed. In the living room, as Robin crawled wearily onto the couch, pulling up his blankets, Susin paused, arms crossed over her breasts, looking down at him.

"How did you know he was homesick?"

"How could I not know?" Robin sighed, rubbed his eyes. "Listen, we talk a lot, when we're working—"

"Yes," more pointedly than she had intended, "I've noticed."

"Well then." Rubbing his eyes, and a big pink yawn. "You see how it is."

I see how it is, she thought, walking the dark hall back to bed. It might be nice if you'd see a few things, too.

The mornings chilled, the nights were filled with long winds and the whisper of the moving sand. Susin took her ceremonial last swim of the summer, pulling strongly through the gray-blue water that echoed the long empty sweep of the sky. She came out shivering, running back to the cottage and warmth, pushed open the door to a quality of silence she had not heard before. Soft and careful, into the kitchen, and, unimaginable, a color she could not believe, an intensity she could not fathom, and Robin, rapt, working hard and rapidly, trying to blend an approximate, and she stood as rapt and watched, stood dripping and cold for almost an hour. Finally her trembling recalled her to herself, she left for a towel, rubbed herself dry.

"—like it?" Robin was saying; she edged her door open and stood beside it, listening. "It's your real color, isn't it? The color you really are."

Poole made a murmur, then, "My color," with a wistfulness so acute that Susin's breath caught, snagged on a pain in her throat. "Where I was, there are so many, many colors. I wish I could show them to you."

"I wish," with equal longing, "that I could see them."

Slowly, she closed the door. She sat on her bed for a long time, past dinner, into dark. The sounds from the kitchen ceased, she heard Robin, yawning, call his good-night, move into the living room. All her motions deliberate, she undressed, walked silently into the living room, stood in the dark above him. "Robin," she said, very quietly.

"Mmm?" half-asleep already; they must have worked

very hard tonight. He pushed himself half-upright, then sat very straight and still when he saw her. "Susin?" like a question, his face half turned from the paleness of her, the warmth of her body displayed. "What—"

"It's cold out here," she said softly. Her hands were very cold, loose at her sides, palms turned in. "Why don't you come in my room."

Silence. It almost seemed he would reach for her, rise to take what she offered; in the lines of his body he spoke without speaking, but then did speak, saying gently, "Susin—no, honey. I don't think—"

Now the cold crept up her arms, into her chest, making it hard to talk. "You don't think what?"

"I just don't think it's a good idea." He ran his hands over his face, pulling at the skin, pushing back his hair. "Don't be mad, Susin, please. Okay? Will you please not—"

"No," she said, and turned as the cold seeped through to her stomach, lay like lead in her thighs, "no," as she walked, very slowly, back to her room, as slowly shut the door until it clicked, a small and final sound.

The next day, she rose late, stayed late in her room to emerge in the midafternoon, bright, brisk as if nothing had happened, but with an edge to her smile. Poole sat silently, his gaze following Susin as she moved around the room. After a few long minutes, he went into his pantry and shut the door, something he had not done since Robin moved in.

"What's the matter?" Susin asked Robin, thumb pointed at Poole's door. Robin shook his head, and Susin laughed, a short little laugh. "Don't you know?"

"No," steadily, "I don't. But what I think is, he's upset because *you're* upset."

"Well, that *is* thoughtful. But I'm not upset." She left the kitchen, the cottage, and began to walk, feet digging deep into the wettish sand, grinding it with her passage, arms swinging like a soldier, aiming for the pointed yellow roof of the restaurant far down at the public beach. Smaller than a caret at this distance, but two hours' hard walking would get her there.

Her jeans were wet to the calf when she got there, her sneakers clumsy with sand. It was early dinner hour, there

were no seats in the dining area. Would she care to take a seat
at the bar? She would. She did not know what to order. The
man next to her asked for a screwdriver, and she did too.

She was thirsty from her long walk. The drink tasted all
right, faintly sour, but the juice was kind to her empty stomach. She studied the tiny clinging pulp on the sides of the
glass. The bar end of the restaurant directly fronted the lake,
and from where she sat she could watch the gathering of long
clouds, a bleak smear of darkening bluish-gray. Maybe Robin
was out painting it, right now. Maybe a storm would come and
blow him into the lake, and Poole too, the fucking ingrate.

The man next to her left. She ordered another drink. She
was unaccustomed to drinking, and was briefly surprised that
she did not feel more from the first screwdriver. The waitress
told her there was a table available in the dining room; no
thanks, Susin said. Not right now.

The bar was filling up. Two men, young men, loud, came
in, scanned the row of stools. They sat, deliberately casual, on
either side of Susin. She recognized one, vaguely, the other
not at all. They both smelled like beer.

"Gettin' cold out there," the one on her right said. "Tem-
perature's droppin' like a stone." He touched her glass with
one short finger. "What're you drinking there? Isn't your
name Susan?"

"Yes, it is," she said, with vast warm dignity. She remembered him now. "You work at the gas station," she told him.
"In the booth."

"That's right," he agreed, grinning as if she had just told a
particularly clever joke. "Takin' money, day in and day
out."

"But not today," the one on her left said, and they both
laughed.

A bright bayonet of lightning, and coughing thunder; Susin
jumped at the flash, and the two flanking her laughed again.
"Don't be scared, Susan," said the one on her right.

She noticed her glass was almost empty. "Why don't I buy
you a drink?" the one on the right said. Susin felt a snicker
bubbling up inside; it felt hot, and barbed.

"Go ahead," she said.

It rained, through sundown and into dark. Susin never made it into the dining room. Instead, she sat with Mike and Danny, her two new friends, chuckling in small mean bursts, laughing not at their jokes but at what they thought was humor. The drinks had begun to blossom, and the cold inside, while not melting, was at least starting to fray.

Mike, on her right, was winding up a story about his landlord: " 'n so I told him, why don't you send me a fuckin' *bill?*" and he crowed a laugh, and Danny laughed too. Susin did not laugh. "Hey," Mike said. "For what he's charging me, he can afford to eat a little shit."

"I don't have that problem." More thunder, heavy rumble like a drumful of boulders. It seemed painfully loud.

"Yeah, you live in that beach house, don't you?" They both leaned toward her, as if excessively interested. "All by yourself?"

Susin laughed then, a bray that startled all three of them. "I have," she said, when the laugh was past, "a friend staying with me now." They teased her: Friend, huh? What kind of friend? The real good kind?

"No," she said. "Just somebody I know."

"He from around here, maybe?" nudging each other, grinning. Three more drinks fresh and slippery on the bar before them.

"No, he's not." Her voice was loud, peculiar in her ears. "He's from very very *very* far away. Farther than you've ever been."

"Is that right?" Elaborate courtesy, both of them suppressing smiles. "Maybe he's E.T.," said Danny, and he and Mike laughed, loud beery whoops.

Susin did not laugh, but smiled, an ugly little motion. "Maybe he is," she said.

When her drink was done she pushed off the stool, distantly startled by the looseness of her muscles. Her bones felt like wire. "I'm going home now," she said. "Thanks for the drinks."

Mike pointed to the rain, increasing now, its force beginning to churn the water. "Why don't you wait for the rain to stop?'' With great cunning, he slipped an arm around Susin's shoulders. ''Too bad to drive right now.''

Susin's cheeks turned red, a dull color. ''I didn't drive,'' she said sullenly. ''I walked.''

''Walked!'' She couldn't walk back in *this*, they said, fumbling for keys, slurping up the dregs of foam, no kind of weather for walking! They would drive her home. She slipped out of Mike's hold; he smiled behind her back at Danny, thought she did not see, but she did. She saw everything. ''All right,'' she said, slowly. ''Let's go.''

Crammed into the front seat, thighs mashed between them, she felt her heart, brightly pounding, thump thump, but so cold. One of the windshield wipers was broken. She watched its crooked arc, back and forth, thump thump. Something, like nausea but not, curled in her belly, and it too was very cold.

The makeshift drive beside the house was thickly puddled, and empty. *Empty*, Susin thought, and said, in a dull cold voice, ''My car's gone.''

''Maybe your boyfriend took it,'' Danny said.

''Drove it back to Mars,'' Mike added, and they both laughed, a tandem sound like two trained dogs.

''My car's gone,'' Susin said again, louder this time, and louder still, ''My fucking *car's* gone! I'll call the police!'' The last word seemed somehow too big for the car, and suddenly Mike and Danny seemed very uneasy. She did not hear, did not listen to what they said, only sat in a cold circle of rage until Mike said, ''Listen Susan, we'll see you later, okay? Okay?'' as Danny opened the passenger door, hopped out to let her exit, impatient in the downpour. As he slipped past her to get back in, she heard Mike's voice, indistinct: ''—one DUI already.'' The car sprayed her, lightly, with water and gravel as it backed up, but she did not turn, kept walking, up the porch, jammed the key and had to try again.

As soon as the door was open, she cried, ''Poole!'' and, without waiting, aimed for the kitchen, her walk ragged, her heart pounding now a different way. She fumbled at the pantry door, pulled it open too hard, almost lost her balance. *"Poole!"*

His nest was empty.

"Poole Poole Poole," screaming it through the house, "Poole *Poole!*" kicking newspapers, ripping at bedclothes, slamming doors open and then shut. She looked everywhere, places absurd in their size, places he could not possibly be, ended back at the pantry. "Poole!" she clawed the thin chain, jerked on the light.

Robin's picture was gone.

Clumsy pivot, staring around the kitchen: the easel was gone, the supplies, but not all, a hurried job of packing. Robin's windbreaker, still limp on a chairback. Some sketches still magnetted to the refrigerator. She leaned against the pantry door, the cold melting now, running in the heat of her sickness, the hard gurgling feel of nausea as she ran to the sink, tears in her eyes. How did they know, how did they *know,* better than she, and faster, what she was capable of doing? She vomited, a loud ugly blurt of sound in the silent house, then stood, crying silently, hands on either side of the sink. *Had* they known, or only feared, choosing the danger of flight as the lesser fear? She would never know, now.

She was sick for a long time. She thought dimly she might never stop being sick.

She never called the police. They called her.

"The computer lists the VIN number on your registration," the officer said, her voice very brisk. "The car was found in—" pause "—Buckman."

Buckman, ninety miles north. From there, where? Anywhere.

When Susin did not speak, the officer spoke again. "The car's not damaged. According to the report, there's even a little gas in the tank." Pause. Uncomfortable with Susin's silence: "The police in Buckman found the car empty. Do you have any idea who might have taken it?"

Susin closed her eyes. "No," she said. "No, I don't."

The wind had risen, and the screen door was banging, a

rhythmic gentle sound. Susin locked it, leaning for a moment into the cold wind. After a moment, she shut the door, and went into the pantry to gather up the sleeping bag and blankets.

She would need them now.

"TRADING POST"

Neal Barrett, Jr.

"Trading Post" was purchased by Gardner Do-
zois, and appeared in the October 1986 issue of
IAsfm, with an illustration by J.K Potter. This was
Barrett's first sale to IAsfm, and the first of a long
series of stories—including the gonzo cult classic
"Perpetuity Blues"—that would make him one of
the magazine's most popular writers in the last half
of the 1980's, and gain him wide critical acclaim.
Here he examines what an alien-dominated Earth
would feel like to the people who would have to
live in it, with a hard-edged, hard-eyed, unsenti-
mental intelligence rare to the genre.

Born in San Antonio, Texas, Neal Barrett, Jr.
grew up in Oklahoma City, Oklahoma, spent sev-
eral years in Austin, hobnobbing with the likes of
Lewis Shiner and Howard Waldrop, and now
makes his home with his family in Fort Worth,
Texas. He made his first sale in 1959, and has been
a full-time freelancer for the past twelve years. His
books include Stress Pattern, Karma Corps, *and*
the four-volume Aldair *series. His most recent*

books are the critically acclaimed novel Through
Darkest America *and its sequel,* Dawn's Uncertain
Light.

With the glasses, lying on the flat gravel roof across the
street, he could follow ant dramatics on the worn brick
facing of the center. The place looked thoroughly abandoned. Dry summer grass followed cracks along the broad
parking lot, sprouting in small explosions. Wild azalea had
taken hold in rusted cars. He slipped the binoculars into his
pack and out of the heat. The South Texas sun bleached the
sky of any color and there was no shade at all on the roof.
He thought about beer in sweaty bottles. He'd tried making
beer but it was flat, both in chemistry and emotion. Fruit
jars lacked the ambiance of TV taverns.

What the Snakes had done was set up their operation in
an old shopping mall on the far edge of Beaumont, close
to the Port Arthur road. There was a K-mart and a Safeway
and a discount appliance store, and a dozen smaller shops
all connected by an inside mall. Josh was sure they weren't
using the whole place. The real operation would be hidden
in some inaccessible corner, past a wall that had crumbled
on its own or gotten help. You could walk through rubble
all day and satisfy yourself there was nothing to see. Proper
measures would be taken.

A noise from the street brought him about and he bellied
across the roof and parted a tangle of dead vines. A one-
wheeler took the corner fast, raising white dust and heading
south. The motor was strangely flat in humid air. The Snake
sat high on his perch, awkward as Orville Wright. The sun
glanced off copper scales. His whip-tail snapped in the
breeze. A moment later, the convoy followed. Nine boxy
shapes painted the familiar vomit yellow. They made no
sound and rode meters above the road.

There was nothing else to see. He backed off and dropped

through a hole in the roof. The store was dark and cool. He laid on his pack and slept amid the ghosts of plumbing supplies. He dreamed that a dog came in and saw him. When it was dark he slipped out and walked back to the Neches River. The black gelding was hobbled in a thick grove of willows near the water. The mount jerked away when he approached; he held its nose and spoke to it quietly. A few miles north he turned west and followed Black Creek into the Thicket. A big magnolia grew near the creek, as broad as three men. He stepped down and allowed himself a smoke.

That was how they worked it, then; the convoy turning right past the mall had shown him the answer. The Snakes had a small repair base out past the Eastex Freeway. He had no idea what they repaired. The fact that it was there had gotten him thinking about how his buddy Howard Johnson ran his scam. Traffic came off the base and past the mall. All Howard had to do was bring his goods out the mall's back door, circle around and edge in a convoy going south. The Snakes had a setup over east of Sabine Pass, a fair-sized town and a landing pad for the big space freighters that took everything in and out of the Gulf Coast. Howard would grease some palms and his stuff would go out clean with everything else. Someone would pick up the goods at the other end. Fucking larceny among the lizards. So much for advanced civilizations.

He mounted up again and took a long pull from the bottle he kept in his pack. The moon was nearly full. He could see flat water, a dense stand of thick-boled cypress. The mosquitoes found him out and he kicked the gelding into a trot.

He was up and out back splashing his face with cold water out of the bucket before the sun came over the trees, regretting the fact that he'd ridden in late and finished off the whiskey on the way. One of the men was chopping wood and the sound rang sharply over the clearing. The smell of breakfast led him into the cabin.

"Dry off before you sit," Ellie told him. She didn't turn

from the stove. He wiped his dark beard on a cloth and filled his plate with fried fish and biscuits and sorghum. The hands had already eaten. He'd seen their plates stacked on a stump.

"You had to go and see," Ellie said. "That's what this is all about."

"Don't start on me now."

Ellie faced him, a big wooden spoon in her hand. She was a long-limbed girl with a country-strong jaw and yellow hair. "What good did it do. Will you just tell me that?"

"I know old Howard's a crook."

"Big surprise."

"Ellie. I wanted to see how he does it."

Ellie turned back to the stove.

"He's got a slick operation which is how he better do it. They ever catch him at it, they'll make him into eighty dollar shoes and a belt."

"And what'll they do to you?"

"Commerce is a risk."

"The way you do it it is."

He got up and pushed back his chair and walked up behind her and touched her waist. She stiffened slightly under his hands.

"You didn't bathe this morning. You smell like whiskey and horses."

"You smell pretty good. Like flour and a woman in heat."

"That last part's wishing." She squirmed out of his grasp. Josh saw her flush and knew evening would find her content. He drank down his coffee and walked out into the yard. The land below the cabin sloped down to a narrow inlet, the water there still and dark as slate. The wind had picked up right at dawn and the fog had burned off early. Moss bearded tall oak trees at the edge of the water. The world came to an end twenty yards into the swamp, choked off in dense vegetation. When the sun broke through, the feeble light was pale as butter.

Sol and Jim and the two new hands were waiting in the shade of the live oak that spread its branches over the cabin and the barn, the smokehouse and the hands' quarters back past the corral. The red flag was down; Ellie had taken breakfast out to the men and disarmed the traps. Still, they waited past the last white line. They seldom came closer unless they were asked.

Josh didn't much care for the new hands but Sol said they were all right. They came from up past Votaw and Sol was vaguely related to them both. Which said nothing at all, as everyone in the Thicket was somebody's cousin. The two would bear watching. They both had the tallow-colored skin and spare frames of back country men who were never more than a day this side of hungry. They knew who Josh was and what he had, and they wouldn't stop thinking about that.

Sol and Jim stood as Josh appeared. The new men followed their lead, one deliberately slower than the other.

"We got a lot to do," Josh said without greeting. "I want those horses fit and clean. Jim, you see the trading stock gets some extra feed." He turned to the new hands. "You all get started on those stumps past the barn. I want that patch flat as a table."

One of the men looked down at his feet. The other faced Josh for an instant and scratched at his chin. He didn't want to chop out stumps. It was backbreaking work in the heat of summer.

Sol stayed on when the others left. "Anything special you want me to do today, Josh?"

It was part of their morning rite. Josh would give him paper and a pinch of tobacco in acknowledgment of his status as top hand. Sol would roll a smoke and carefully put it away. Josh had never seen him light up. Sol took his pleasure in private, or did a little trading of his own.

"That storm last week took some cedar shakes off the barn," Josh said. "You can see it from right here. In the unlikely event it ever rains again we'll have a ton of sour feed to fork out."

Sol looked down at his hands. It was something he should have noticed and he knew it. "I'll get right to that, Josh. I sure will."

"I found a bee tree yesterday evening coming back. Two miles down past that stand of palmetto. You might take a look at that."

"Right after I get to that roof," said Sol. "You have any luck out in the bush? See anything at all?" He pretended the question had suddenly struck him, but it wasn't a thing he did well at all.

"A little sign, maybe," Josh told him. "There's wild porkers out there. One day I'll get 'em."

"You take me out I'll find them. I got a good nose for game."

"I might do that," said Josh. Sol knew it was a lie. He hadn't gone out three days looking for pigs that didn't exist.

Josh stood and Sol sprang up like his shadow. He showed Josh an open cheerful grin. A dog eager to fetch. "All right, get to it," Josh told him. Sol trotted off and Josh rolled a smoke. You couldn't help but like Sol and it was better to have a snoop on the property who was easy than one who wasn't. It had to be Sol that told everything he knew to Martin Bregger. Jim was too dumb. Nobody could act that ignorant unless he was.

Josh sighed and walked back to the house. The sun was up strong, the air already too thick to breathe. On one side he had Martin Bregger, who ran everything clear up to the Red River and over east to Louisiana. Martin was too smart to try and kill the golden goose, but he wouldn't mind at all if the goose was his own man instead of Josh. And on the other end he had the Snakes, Howard Johnson and whoever else was in it. He wasn't sure which he trusted the least. If either one got foolish he was standing in the middle. He tossed down the smoke and stubbed it out. Maybe he was getting too old for this business. Except the only other business was going hungry, and he was sure as hell too old for that.

It seemed like a night for a treat; no good reason except Beaumont had left him feeling edgy. That, and Ellie's disapproval. When he finished up his rounds and locked up he ran the patch of red cloth above the roof. The flag told the hands and whoever might decide to wander in that he'd armed the traps again and it wouldn't be smart to poke around. No one had since the boys from Liberty County had decided to come in and try for the horses. Martin Bregger said it wouldn't happen again and had come down himself to look at the bodies. Josh knew Bregger had likely sent them himself to see what the traps could do.

He went to the cellar and got the Herradura Añejo tequila, ninety-two proof and still in the bottle, that and two good joints, and then climbed to the bedroom upstairs. Ellie was moving about fluffing pillows. She slept in the raw year round, as he did himself, there being little need for bedclothes in the Thicket. The lamp was out but there was a candle. He liked the way the light kissed her skin. She turned and saw the bottle and the joints and gave him a curious smile.

"What's the occasion, something special?"

"Make one up if you want."

She got a single glass from beside the bed and watched him pour, then waited while he lit up the joints, closing her eyes and drawing smoke into her lungs.

"God, it isn't going to take much of that."

"It's all right, is it?"

"Better than all right."

Josh tasted the tequila on his tongue. Quick picture of a fountain, red-tiled roof and bright color.

"I'm sorry my leaving upset you."

"I don't ever like you going. Specially if it's got to do with a town. That wasn't something you really had to do."

"Maybe not."

"I don't like staying here, Josh. Making a little circle around the house."

"Isn't any other way I know to do it."

"I still don't have to like it." She flipped ash on the floor, using her whole arm in the motion. He gave her the glass again and she held it in both hands, bringing it to her mouth like a child. Her eyes came up and she caught him checking her out.

"You didn't need to get out the goodies. I can be had."

"Isn't what it was for."

"Well, then. Let's pretend it was." She touched his chest and smiled. "I'll fight you off a little."

"Not if you finish that toke."

"Then I guess I finish the toke. I can get you whenever I want."

"That's true."

"While you were gone Sol acted real funny."

"Funny how?"

"Walking around the yard all the time, stopping to get a rock out of his shoe. That kind of thing."

Josh grinned. "He's trying to map out the traps. I've caught him at it before."

"You think it's funny?"

"Ellie, you know how to find the traps? Step on 'em. That's not a practical solution." There were two trap perimeters around the cabin. When he was gone, Ellie armed the outside perimeter day and night, and shut off the inside perimeter during the day. It left her a little room to walk around, and was better than being shut up in the house.

"You're not going again soon, are you?" she asked.

"No, you know I'm not."

"Good. Just don't." She pinched out the candle and came in close against his shoulder. The loving was good and they surprised each other with their needs. When Ellie was asleep he looked up at the ceiling and thought about Sol. He was getting a little cocky. He never did anything he wasn't told to do so Martin was egging him on. Pushing him into something or maybe nothing at all. The whole idea was to keep Josh from getting any sleep and sometimes it worked better than others.

He spent his days mostly in the cellar, getting his goods in order for Howard Johnson's next visit, the squares on his homemade calendar diminishing much faster than he liked. The cellar was as large as the cabin space above, lined with concrete blocks Josh had hauled in from Batson by team and wagon three summers before. It was caulked, painted and generally proof against the wet ground pressing on every side, and had the virtue of being twenty degrees cooler in the summer. Ellie was from northern Minnesota and had no tolerance for hot and humid weather. More than once he'd been tempted to bring her down, when her skin flushed red and she could hardly get a breath. He hated to see her suffer but it was a rule he couldn't break. He'd made it clear to Martin that no one but himself had ever been in the cellar or knew how to get in or what was there. It was the only way he had of protecting Ellie. After the boys from Liberty County had taken the short course in fragmentation mines and other surprises, Josh had broken his rule about no one in the cabin. He had brought Martin in and shown him the heavy steel door to the cellar, which was really the front half of a safe, and let him read the sign he'd painted just above the combination:

WARNING!
NO ONE CAN OPEN THIS BUT ME. EVEN IF YOU
HAD THE COMBINATION THE DOOR IS RIGGED
TO BLOW THE WHOLE FUCKING CABIN UN-
LESS THE DOOR IS FIRST DISARMED IN SEV-
ERAL PLACES.
SINCERELY YOURS,
JOSHUA T. RAINES

Martin had seemed impressed. He had stopped looking crazed for several moments. Of course the flaw in all this was if Martin somehow got past the traps outside and got to Ellie he could make Josh open up the door. If things ever went that far it was over anyway and wouldn't matter. The best guarantee against trouble was that Martin was a businessman first and a looney-tune second. That, and the fact that he was scared to death of the Snakes. Josh knew this for certain. It was easier just to let him keep dealing with Howard Johnson than try to cut him out and learn what he traded to the Snakes. Sol's little capers simply reflected Martin's feeling that Josh ought to worry a little more. It was a sound corporate tactic. One that told him Martin was probably only marginally unhinged.

• • •

The flyer dipped low over the swamp, scaring up bright-colored birds from the trees. The craft was a dull mustard yellow, shaped like half a melon, its power source vaguely asthmatic, a man sucking air through his teeth. It settled on runners in the clearing where Josh had whitewashed a circle. A blister set asymmetrically forward was tinted against the sun. It slid back to reveal the four Snakes. Pilot. Two armed guards. Howard Johnson stepped out and came quickly toward Josh, walking in the springy deliberate manner that make Snakes appear to move in slow-motion—even when they ran as fast as deer, which Josh had watched them do from a distance.

Josh differed from Martin in that he feared them for what they were, and not for the way they looked. Reasonably they were no more alien than upright chameleons. Seven-foot lizards that talked. Rust-sienna skin, salmon under-belly. Whip tail and apparently no use for any clothing. Howard Johnson wore a weapon, slung from a decorative webbing about his throat. To Josh, it looked like a lubri-cating tool, but would likely prove effective.

The Snake came to a stop. Forty-weight eyes found Josh. "Have a nice day," said Howard.

"Right, Coke is it," said Josh. "Hang on, I'll get the stuff." He left the Snake standing in the yard and went in and got his goods, packed on a dolly and covered with a tarp. Ellie didn't come out of the kitchen. Howard Johnson made her nervous. Josh wheeled the dolly across the yard and into the barn, waited until Howard was inside and shut the door. Sol and Jim and the new hands were off in the woods. They had left before sunup with no urging. In the hot, heavy air of the barn, Howard smelled musty and slightly sweet. Dead leaves and pollen. Josh pulled back the tarp and set his wares on a weathered plank table. Light from the slanted window was slightly muted.

"Some real good items this time," he told Howard. "You're lucky. First-rate stuff isn't all that easy to find. Rats get to the canvas. They take to that pigment like candy." As he talked he fooled with the paintings, turning one a little to the light, brushing at the frame of another.

"I like the people dancing," said Howard.

"Well sure," said Josh, "that's a Degas."

"Degas is good, I think."

"Degas is good." He knew Howard really didn't care about names. While he talked about dancers his eyes were flicking over the other paintings. It irritated the hell out of Josh that the Snake had a fine critical eye. Bluebonnets and moon-eyed children wouldn't cut it. Howard knew better. Josh had only tried it on him once.

"Just five, Josh?" Howard shook his head sadly in human imitation. "This is all?"

Not unexpected, but a direction Josh had hoped they might avoid. "We're talking masterpieces, Howard. These are first-rate goods."

"I know that, Josh."

"Then what are we saying here?"

"Last time there were nine."

"It can't be the same every time," Josh said patiently. "You know that. It depends on what I find."

"Five is not enough, Josh." His voice was slightly nasal, the words faintly musical and extended, as if he might have learned English from a Chinese waiter.

Josh studied the paintings while he thought about what to do next. He couldn't tell Howard he had only found two the last trip, that the others were from his hold-back stash. Besides the Degas he had the Miro and the Klee and the Andrew Wyeth, and a Lennart Anderson that looked as good as Gauguin. Back in the cellar he had the Freilicher landscape and the Cézanne and what he thought was maybe a Titian. And that was it. He wanted to tell Howard Johnson that it hadn't been his idea to flatten Houston. That devastation hindered the earnest collector. He was fast running out of museums, concentrating now on well-to-do residential rubble. This last avenue hit or miss, wealth not always reflecting taste.

He showed Howard the other stuff he had, the Kazak carpet and the three good Téotihuacán heads and a Minoan beaker jug, a salesman winding up his pitch and saving a little kicker for the last. Howard had a weakness for good glass, and he brought out the Baccarat crystal and held it up to the light, flipping the rim so Howard could hear it ring. A tulip-shaped glass, clear as air and whisper-thin.

"Oh yes very nice," said Howard. He took the piece carefully from Josh. Their hands didn't touch. He held the crystal by its base, fingers long and spatulate at the tips. Needles of light flecked his skin, for a moment a disco lizard.

"I would like more of these. In other shapes as well."

"So would I," Josh said carefully. Howard had an ear for human inflection. "I found this item in a shop that handled fine crystal and china. Spode and Waterford, Steuben, everything the best. Two floors of it. I never saw so much broken glass in my life. This was the only piece intact."

"You should find other shops such as that."

"That's a real good idea. As a matter of fact I'm working on another site now. There might be something, I can't promise."

The other site was pure fiction and maybe Howard knew it. If there was a Mason jar left in Houston Josh couldn't find it. In the cellar he had a single, exquisite Lalique, a crystal piece with a frosted satin finish that would knock the Snake on his tail. Howard would expect something big next time and he'd have to bring it out.

The Snakes came in from the flyer and loaded everything up, packing the items carefully under Howard's watchful eye. Josh handed Howard the envelope with his samples for next time, then loaded up the goods Howard had brought him and wheeled the dolly into the house.

Howard was waiting in the yard.

"Bring Ellie outside," he told Josh.

"Ellie? What for?"

It shook Josh badly and Howard caught his concern. "I'm not going to hurt her, Josh. I am going to take her up in the flyer. I will bring her back safely. She can look at the countryside and see the Gulf from great heights."

"Howard, I don't think Ellie'd like to do that."

"Bring her out, Josh."

He was overcome by a terrible fear, a helpless rage. There was nothing he could do and there was no use asking the Snake what he wanted. He turned and went inside. Ellie looked up from the kitchen table and read his face. She stood quickly and Josh held her shoulders and sat her down and told her.

"Oh Jesus . . ." She looked like a bird caught in a trap.

"You'll be all right," he said. "If he was going to do something he'd just do it. That's his way. I can't stop him, Ellie."

She pulled away and stood and walked out of the cabin, past Howard without looking. Howard nodded to Josh and followed Ellie. Josh watched the flyer lift from the clearing and bank out of sight above the trees. He went inside and found the Remington 12-gauge which he wasn't supposed to have and leaned it by the door. Howard was trying to tell him something. He didn't much care what it was. If he didn't bring Ellie back safe he'd try to kill him. Pointless. But the only gesture he could imagine.

It was a full two hours before he heard the flyer again. It settled in afternoon shadow and Howard got out and then Ellie. Josh ran out to meet her. Her face looked pale and unfinished. She'd thrown up and stained the front of her dress.

"Ellie . . ."

"Just leave me the fuck alone, all right?" She pushed him off and walked shakily to the cabin.

"She became ill," said Howard.

"Yeah, I can see that. You want to tell me what this is all about?"

"Let's walk," said Howard. He left the front of the house and started past the barn to the corral. The horses shied and trotted away at his approach, bunching up at the far side of the pen, afraid of the unfamiliar smell. There were six pack animals and nine riding horses. Howard drew his weapon and began firing methodically into the pens. Josh stared in dismay, certain this was something he only imagined. A

big sorrel mare went down heavily and thrashed in the dust.
The other animals went crazy with fear. They shrieked and
kicked out at each other and ran blindly into the fence.
Howard killed five of the riding horses. He left the pack
animals alone, a point not wasted on Josh. Finally, he put
the weapon away. Josh couldn't take his eyes from the
corral.

"It was not a good idea to approach my place of business," said Howard. "I am greatly concerned about this,
Josh."

Josh made no attempt to deny it, or ask Howard how
he'd found him out. That's what it was all about, then. Ellie
and the horses. Things could be taken from him. Returned
or not returned.

"All right, you made your point," said Josh. "Here's
one you maybe didn't consider. People see you and me
having trouble, that isn't good for business. It gives them
ideas."

"You'd better take care of that."

"You got any suggestions?"

Howard nodded toward the corral. "Fresh meat is scarce.
Give some to Martin Bregger." He had never mentioned
Bregger before. He was letting Josh know something else.

"I will be back in one month," Howard announced.
"One instead of four. Have more goods ready."

"Now Christ, that doesn't make sense!" Josh was tired
of holding back his anger. "I can't make a run that fast and
you know it. What are you trying to do?"

"If the canvases are difficult to find you may substitute
crystal for some of the paintings. One good piece will equal
three paintings."

"It doesn't work like that. The glass is just as scarce."

"Try harder, Josh."

"All right, I don't know. I'll do what I can."

"I know you will. Goodbye, Josh."

He waited until the flyer disappeared and then turned and
stomped back into the cabin and armed the traps, not even
bothering to raise the flag. Maybe Sol would come back

and blow off his ass. Ellie was upstairs. She had changed clothes and washed herself off. The bedroom smelled sour.

"You all right?" He knew it was a useless thing to say.

"I got sick and threw up and passed out. I've never been so scared in my life. I'm fine, Josh."

"I'm sorry, Ellie."

"He shoot all the horses?"

"Just the ones I don't need for business."

"Beaumont. Your goddamn adventure."

"How do you know that?"

"He told me."

"If you want I can get you something to eat. Some soup or I'll fry up those potatoes."

"No thanks. You want you can bring me the rest of the Herradura."

"I wish this hadn't of happened."

"So do I." She looked at him for the first time and he saw less anger there than despair. "I'll be okay. Just leave me alone for awhile."

Sol and Jim and the new hands came in before dark. The new man took one look at the corral and ran off into the woods. Josh got Sol and Jim butchering before the flies could do more damage. Sol knew better than to ask any questions. Martin would know something had happened here before morning.

Josh took his goods off the dolly and into the cellar, lit a lamp and locked himself in. The way the operation worked, Josh would give Howard a few grams of what he wanted and Howard would work it up. The goods came back in square plastic containers. Some standard Snake measure that came out to roughly four and a half gallons. The Snakes were clearly hotshot chemists; anything Josh had in mind they could make it. Howard never seemed concerned with the sample packets. All he told Josh was the process was risky and expensive; Josh had to take his word for that.

The Snakes leveled the cities with sonic disaster, some weapon that shattered buildings and fine crystal. The best casualty figures Josh had heard were eighty percent. Maybe more, and the same for other countries. The Snakes went away and let pestilence take its course. Disease and famine took another hefty percent. Survivors looted shopping centers and homes and grocery stores. Cattle and pigs quickly vanished. Cats and dogs. Nine years later, the Snakes came again, quashing feeble resistance and settling in to stay. They left people alone and went about doing whatever they did. Howard Johnson caught Josh looting a 7–11 ruin and made him a deal. Supply determined trade. Most items were spoiled or lost forever. Canned goods, Hershey bars and Sprite. Josh concentrated his efforts on items that had lasted. Salt. Sugar. Tea. Coffee. Tobacco. Isolated pockets of whiskey and wine. Seeds that would still come up. Occasional caches of gasoline. Marijuana, and selected recreational and medicinal drugs. Some of the food items had gone stale but nobody cared. Josh gave samples to Howard Johnson and Howard brought the goods back in bulk. There was never very much. Maybe seven hundred pounds each trip.

So Josh traded art to Howard Johnson, which Howard smuggled out to distant worlds. Howard made formerly staple items which Josh traded off to Martin Bregger. Martin stayed in power through control of rare goods. He gave Josh vegetables and fruit, flour and clothing and nails, axe handles and protection from Martin Bregger. Howard Johnson got paid in some measure; Josh had never even thought about that. All he needed to know was that Howard would never let him out of the business. If he couldn't get out, he had to make certain he stayed in. An indispensable link in the chain of commerce and trade. Why was Howard suddenly making that difficult to do? It could be the Beaumont thing or something else. Maybe lizards thought like Martin Bregger. Keep Josh from getting any sleep. It had a perverse sense of logic, the ring of truth.

Martin appeared in the yard with the morning fog. Four men, a wagon and a team were in the clearing. One man held Martin's reins while he stood under the trees and waited for Josh. Josh had the goods ready and waiting, stacked on wooden pallets a few yards past his inside perimeter of traps. The goods had been transferred from the Snakes' plastic containers to canvas sacks, Josh having skimmed off portions for personal use.

Josh appeared in the door and Martin nodded. "Morning, friend. It's going to be a scorcher."

"Martin . . ."

Bregger was tall and stringy, a man with possum eyes. His height seemed wrong, as if something might have stretched him out of shape. One leg was shorter than the other, causing him to stand like a tree grown up in the wind. This didn't bother Martin; other men found themselves leaning off balance to catch his eye.

"Josh, my boys blow up if they get those goods?"

"Not now they won't, Martin."

Martin smiled in appreciation. He nodded and his crew brought over the wagon and loaded up. As soon as the pallets were empty, they filled them with the goods they'd brought along. Sweet corn and tomatoes, sacks of onions, strips of metal strapping and bolts of cloth. The men worked quickly. They didn't like walking in Josh's yard. Once they were clear, Josh ducked inside and armed the perimeter again, making a big show of raising the flag. Martin was still standing in his spot.

"Understand you had some trouble," he said to Josh.

"Nothing I can't handle."

"That's good to know."

"I got you some fresh meat. Be a good idea to start it smoking or eat it fast."

"Sure kind of you. Hate to see you shoot prime horses just for me." Josh waited for Bregger to get to it. "Your trouble with the Snakes goin' to interfere with business?"

"I can handle the Snakes just fine."

A wide possum grin. "I know you can, Josh."

He decided there was no use putting it off. "I'll need a couple of escorts, Martin. Sunup four days from now. I'm going back to Houston."

Martin smiled. "Did put the screws to you, didn't he?"

"The business that doesn't grow stands still."

"Uh-huh." Martin picked at a tooth. "I'll have the boys here. Pleasant trip to you." He turned back to the wagon, listing to the right. A man handed over the reins and he mounted up. Sol and Jim brought meat out of the barn and slung it off their shoulders into the wagon. Blood had soaked the sacking and left stains along their arms. Sol pretended he didn't know Martin or the others.

Ellie seemed better. There was still a distance between them. Maybe that would change with time. She walked through her days like a woman coming back from a sickness, brushing against life out of habit. Josh would find her standing in the kitchen in a pool of morning light, clutching a spoon or teacup to her breast. He sensed she was drawing some strength from the familiar.

She was reconciled to the trip; that, or too much within herself to show concern. "I'll be all right," she told him. "Don't worry about me."

"I do worry, Ellie."

"Worry about yourself. And come back safe." She rested her hands on his shoulders. The action seemed an effort. When she kissed him, her lips were dry as paper.

Sol and Jim had the packhorses ready. Josh had decided on three. He'd likely find goods to warrant one, but no use advertising that. Martin Bregger's two men were waiting under the big stand of cypress by the road. The older of the two reached up and flicked at moss with his knife. Josh had worked with the pair before. Sol brought over the black gelding and told Josh he'd hold down the fort. Sol's open, boyish grin irritated Josh more than usual.

By early mid-morning they had passed the marshy lake with its forest of skeletal trees. Yellow iris dotted the shore. The way south snaked through willows and sharp-leaved holly. Farther, the willows gave way to a steep hammock of pine and welcome shade. A sound like applause startled Josh and he turned to see hundreds of white herons overhead. Birds reassured him. Wildlife was apparently holding its own, the hunger less intense across the land. Creatures mating and reproducing, faster than people could eat them. He kept a running tally of survivors. Grey squirrels. Swamp rabbits. No more deer or wild turkey, but now and then a possum or a coon. Coons were as sly as people. He told himself the Thicket was no place to take a poll. Wildlife had always gathered here and what he saw didn't reflect true conditions.

He didn't talk to Martin's riders. There was nothing he had to say. They were there to protect him, make sure he and the horses got to Houston and back safe. Raiders were always about; protecting Josh was essential to Martin's business. The men carried pistols but never showed them. It wasn't smart to let another see you owned something of such great value.

Josh picked up the pace and led them through a tricky piece of swamp. Gnats followed the men and the horses. The trip was settling down in his head. Going back this soon wouldn't hurt. He was running out of goods; Howard had simply nudged him into action, a little sooner than he liked. The Beaumont business or something else entirely— it didn't matter. Motives here were futile. A lizard mind was razorblade jelly.

Just after noon he called a halt and stepped out of the saddle. He ate biscuits and honey and sat down under a tree and listened to the lazy sound of cicadas. The riders ate and kept to themselves. Branches crowded in overhead; the air itself was lemony yellow. Cinnamon fern grew thickly under the trees. Josh saw a canebrake rattler slip through the grass. There were still plenty of snakes—the other kind. Snapping turtles and frogs, and 'gators back in the worst parts of the swamp. He wondered how Snakes viewed the reptile population. Probably the same way people thought of apes.

A hundred years before, black bear had roamed the Thicket. Bears couldn't run as fast as hogs. They tracked the razorbacks and caught them when they bedded down for the night. Bit the back of the neck and started eating. Wild hogs feared nothing in the world except bears. Josh remembered the taste of bacon. Pleasures now extinct seemed all the sweeter.

He was coming to his feet when the unmistakable sound reached his ears. He looked at Martin's riders. They led the animals quickly back in the trees, held the reins and squatted on their heels. Josh crawled up through the brush. He'd come due south through the Thicket, intending to skirt 90 and cross over past the Liberty County line. The Snakes kept 90 open for their convenience. Now there was traffic on the road. Four landcars and three flyers overhead. The striped cursive symbol was one everyone knew. Lizard law and order. They'd have to hole up or go back. Travel was out of the question.

The direction of the traffic worried Josh. East, into Beaumont or past it, and past it wasn't likely. He could tell himself it had nothing to do with Howard Johnson but making himself believe it was something else. Avoidance seemed a temperate solution. Reptile fuzz was the worst kind of trouble you could find.

He walked back and squatted by the riders. "I'll catch up with you later," he told them. "Don't expect me till noon maybe tomorrow. Take the horses back up Jackson Creek and wait for me there."

The older of the two looked at Josh. "We're supposed to stay with you."

"You're supposed to stay with me if I go to Houston. We can't go to Houston right now."

The man wore a straw hat frayed at the edges. "Where is it you're going?"

"That's not your business. You don't want to go."

The man thought about that, putting together the Snakes' appearance and Josh's sudden change of plans. Coming up with indeterminate answers. Each possibility worse than the last.

"We'll be at the creek," he said finally.

"Don't get attached to those horses," Josh told him. "They don't belong to you."

The shopping center was no longer deserted. A flyer sat untended near the rows of rusted cars. The three squat sedans reminded Josh of boll weevils. Three at the Safeway, one farther down at the K-Mart entrance. Winking yellow lights illumined Snakes on official errands. There was no more room for question. Howard Johnson was busted. Which meant, essentially, that Josh was busted too. They'd want to know connections and Howard would tell them. There was no way to guess whether they had him—Josh had to assume they didn't, that he still had time to get Ellie out of the cabin and into the Thicket. He backed away from the broken fence. The gelding was in an alley, two blocks away and to his right. He stood and started back across the street. Light stabbed out of the dark, nearly catching him in the open. He leaped for the cover of tall weeds. The one-wheelers drew tight circles on the road, came to a stop in a line. Josh guessed four, maybe five. They made Snake-talk and purred their engines. They weren't looking for him but they clearly didn't intend to go away. Someone had told them to keep everyone clear of the center.

Josh considered. There was no way to get across the street. Ahead, a warehouse wall blocked the way. He would have to follow the ditch to the back of the mall. Go all the way around and hope for no Snakes on the other side. It would take a good hour. He needed to be heading for the Thicket.

A building had collapsed leaving a mountain of broken brick. Debris lapped the rear of the center. Box-like carriers nosed the concrete dock where K-Mart shoppers had loaded their goods. The carriers floated just above the ground. Bright cones of light illumined the dock, the reef-like strands of rubble. Josh viewed the scene without pleasure. He could easily break his neck if he climbed the rubble. The area near the docks was bright as day. Josh watched the procedure. Workers wheeled dollies out of the mall, loaded them into carriers, turned and went back for more. More what? Josh wondered. The Snake cops were hauling off a hell of a lot of goods. What else was Howard into besides art?

One way out. If he kept to the shadow below the dock, worked his way under the carriers past the rubble to the other end of the center. He watched the routine once more. There were maybe four minutes when all the Snakes were gone. Loading up inside or going back with empty dollies. Check it out again. He saw he was losing his nerve, waiting for intercession. He took a deep breath and bolted from cover.

The Snakes loaded a dolly directly above. The carrier dipped slightly under the weight. When they left, he made for the next carrier in line. A barrier of rubble intervened. For a moment he was level with the floor of the dock itself. He hesitated, checked quickly for Snakes. Poked his head inside the carrier for a look. The space was packed with long rectangular containers. Pressure-sealed in plastic, accordion ridges along the sides. They reminded Josh of crackers. Individual packs for locked-in flavor. The packs were different sizes. Two feet square on up. It was a bad idea but he knew he was going to do it. Pulling himself up, he slipped inside and moved to the far back wall. With his knife, he cut through the translucent plastic. Stretching the ridges apart, he got a glimpse of a very nice Utrillo. He'd traded it to Howard in March. Behind the Utrillo was another. Not really another, the same one. And after that another, the same painting. Josh tried another, slightly larger container. Grant Wood. All identical down to a wavy scratch on the frame.

He didn't picture for a moment a roomful of busy Snake forgers. The little bastards had a duplicating device. Something that could stamp out paintings like cookies. Josh ran a gallery operation; Howard had dime-store distribution. The egg-shaped containers to his left would be Pre-Columbian jars. Aztec culture by the gross. So much for hard-working chemists, miserly portions of pot. Howard could turn it out by the ton.

He heard them coming and knew he couldn't make it to the front. Crouching behind Utrillo, he waited until they wheeled the new load inside. They had to jockey things around to make room. For a moment, the containers hid him from view. He moved up as the load moved back. The dolly was flush against the carrier, stacked high with containers. No way to drop back to the ground. He went to his knees and crawled through the stacks, waited, then darted into the mall.

The mall was a mess. Storefronts gutted and crowded with rubble. Dark except for lights set up farther down. He ducked inside a store. Hickory Farms, the shelves stripped for more than twenty years. He guessed the big lights were where Howard had stored his goods. The lizard cops were looking it over. Part of the roof had collapsed. A cavern hung with rusted steel vines. It allowed Josh to move through stores without going back to the mall. Discount shoes, Doubleday. A shop for skiers and divers. Loaded dollies passed in the mall. The stench hit him at Penney's. Something was recently dead; it would be deader tomorrow in the heat.

He could hear Snake voices and see the lights in the mall. He was right next door or close to it, much too bright and he moved to the back of the store. Clothing, he decided, from the jungle of empty racks. Light cast a narrow dusty beam on the floor. It came from a fist-sized puncture in the wall. The hole sprouted old electric wiring. The smell here was bad. He held his breath and went to his knees, turning his head to see in the hole. He backed off fast, throwing up in one violent constriction after another. His body was helpless to stop. Cries of alarm reached his ears and he knew the Snakes had heard him. He tried to crawl away. The Snake poked him with something hard. Josh turned and saw a muzzle that resembled a garden hose. Two more Snakes arrived quickly. Josh wiped his face with his shirt. The Snakes gave way to another; he wore ornamental webbing around his throat. He turned a flash on Josh, then bent to study him closer. Standing, he gave quick instructions to the others and walked away.

The Snakes pulled him roughly to his feet, took his knife and his belongings and hustled him out of the store into the mall. Outside, they opened the rear door of a landcar, tossed him in and shut him up in the dark.

Josh tried not to think, a process that only served to sharpen mental pictures. The store was full of Ellies.

Hundreds of dead Ellies under a white hot light. The Snakes were dragging them by the legs and tossing them in mustard-colored dumpsters. The Ellies wore blue cotton dresses and jogging shoes . . .

"*Jesus!*" The image was too sharp, too bright. His stomach lurched again. There was nothing left to give. He took off his shirt and tossed it away. His hands were shaking and wouldn't stop. The landcar started up smoothly. He felt it turn left, leave the lot and go north. The Ellies wouldn't go away. Dead Ellies in the store. One back at the cabin, but *which one?* He saw her in light. Sunlight finding her in the kitchen. A candle by the bed. If he looked at her *now*, touched her again, would she be the same? *Ellie, Ellie* . . . His throat tightened just short of closing. He shut his eyes and tried to push the image aside. He wasn't sure he wanted the answer. Maybe that wasn't a problem. The way things were going it probably wasn't a question he'd ever get to ask.

The ride seemed to last half an hour. When the landcar stopped, the Snakes came back and let him out. Dark pines shadowed the rutted dirt road. Josh smelled stagnant water. A flash shined in his eyes and the Snakes motioned him forward. One brought up the rear. He watched the other spring along in an awkward, peculiarly graceful manner. Finally, he stopped and motioned Josh to a halt. A square boxy light sat on the ground. It illuminated two more Snakes. They were digging a shallow grave.

Josh felt a quick little motion under his heart. Breaking glass. He'd guessed where they were going, but a guess is a speculation. A hole is to the point.

When the grave was complete, the guards and the digger left. Josh heard steps, turned and saw the official-looking Snake from the mall.

"You are the one named Josh," he said abruptly. "You worked with Howard Johnson. You gathered artifacts and traded them for goods. Howard Johnson produced the goods."

"Yes. I did." Josh saw no reason to deny it.

"The female. She came from your place? She left at some time with Howard Johnson?"

"Yes."

"And Howard Johnson brought her back."

"Yes."

"You'd like to know if she is real, or if Howard left a copy."

"The thought occurred."

" 'Real' is a personal observation."

"Is that supposed to be an answer?"

"An answer is not a solution. That was a very foolish decision on Howard's part. Smuggling is one thing. Duplicating a being is something else. This is why I put him out of business."

"A humanitarian gesture."

"A contradiction in terms."

"Look. What was Howard going to *do* with them?"

"Do with what?"

"With the Ellies."

"Trust me. You don't want to know." The Snake drew his weapon. "This is your burial spot. No one will see you again."

Josh felt himself unravel. The Snake pointed the weapon in the hole and fired twice.

Josh looked at him.

"Take a shovel and fill it up."

Josh did. The Snake held the light. Josh was wet all over when he finished. The Snake tossed him his knife and his belongings.

"Baskin Robbins. Is that a name?"

"I guess it is."

"Then you will call me Baskin Robbins. Don't go back and get your horse. Walk home. Tomorrow afternoon, I will officially discover your cabin and destroy it from a flyer. Don't take anything with you. Sol will guide you and the female to a place where someone will meet you and pick you up."

"*Sol* will?"

"Sol worked for the Bregger person. But mostly he

worked for Howard Johnson. Now he works for me. Basically, we start all over from scratch. I have to burn those goods we took from the mall. I still have Howard's originals. I think. Doesn't matter. You can't work in Houston anymore. I want you out of the district. We'll set you up somewhere else. Maybe San Francisco. Denver.''

''You're going to keep the operation like it is?''

''Yes, of course. Why not?''

Josh sat down on his grave and made a smoke. ''All right,'' he said, ''let's talk business. There are some things you got to know about art . . .''

"PEOPLE LIKE US"

Nancy Kress

"People Like Us" was purchased by Gardner Dozois, and appeared in the September 1989 issue of IAsfm, *with an illustration by N. Taylor Blanchard. It was the latest in a long sequence of elegant and incisive stories by Kress that have appeared in* IAsfm *under four different editors over the last decade, since her first* IAsfm *sale to George Scithers in 1979—stories that have made her one of the most popular of all the magazine's writers. Here, with her usual cool expertise, she offers us a wry study of the true meaning of compatibility.*

Born in Buffalo, New York, Nancy Kress now lives with her family in Brockport, New York. Her books include the novels The Prince of Morning Bells, The Golden Grove, The White Pipes, *and* An Alien Light, *and the collection* Trinity and Other Stories. *Her most recent book is the novel* Brain Rose. *She has frequently been a finalist for science fiction's major awards, and won a Nebula Award for her story "Out of All Them Bright Stars."*

Parker brought the car around at seven; George was going
to meet the dinner guests at the station. Sarah said incred-
ulously, "They're coming up by *train?*"

"Buddy Calucci broke his wrist last week and can't
drive," George said, "and his wife has some kind of phobia
about it. And the alien of course can't drive either."

Of course. Of course *not*. Couldn't drive, couldn't wear
pants, probably couldn't eat anything Sarah had had Cook
prepare for dinner either. All the alien could do was put her
poor old George's firm out of business with its strange
advanced fuel products, whatever they were. Sarah stood
before the fireplace and regarded her husband as he picked
up his coat from a leather chair.

"If it's supposed to be such a discreet meeting that you
can't have it in the city, why are they taking the *train?* Why
didn't your Mr. Calucci order a car and driver?"

"I don't think it would occur to him."

"This is going to be horrible, George. It really is. I'd
just as soon have Parker and Cook and Cook's criminal
brother-in-law. The one in Attica."

George shrugged into his coat, crossed the room, and put
his hands on Sarah's shoulders. "I know, darling; it's too
bad. But necessary. And if they come by train, they can't
stay late. The last train back is the 10:42. That's something,
at least."

"At least," Sarah said. But she made herself smile at
George; it wasn't his fault, after all, and whining like this
was really terribly unattractive. These . . . people were coming, and that was that. Just the same, with George's florid
face inches from her own, she suddenly remembered something Louise Henderson had said to her just that week at
the gallery. *You know, darling, George is getting awfully
fat. He should go back to tennis instead of golf. If he's not
careful, he'll start to look like that man that runs the hardware store.* Sarah had laughed; Louise had a wicked eye.
But Sarah had been stung, too: George *did* look a little like
the man in the hardware store. The same shape to the brow,
the same chin. Friends had joked about it before.

After George had left for the station, Denise brought in

a tray of canapes and fresh ice. Sarah made herself a Scotch and water, drank half of it, poked at the fire, finally settled on a chair. The living room looked well by firelight, she thought. She loved this house, even if it had seemed a little empty since Emily had gone off to Rosemary Hall four years ago. Brass and mahogany gleamed in the firelight; wainscotting and molding took on subtle curves; the colors of the old Orientals glowed. In the bookcases leather bindings and Chinese vases jumbled comfortably against each other, both slightly dusty. Emily's violin leaned against one corner. Had Emily, home for the weekend, practiced today? Probably not; too busy with the horses. Sarah smiled, finished her Scotch, and considered moving a pile of old *Smithsonians* and *Forbes* off the wing chair beside the violin. She decided against it.

She heard the car, and they were here. Sarah rose to meet her guests. "Hello."

"My wife, Sarah," George said. "Darling, Mr. Calucci, Mrs. Calucci, Mr. C'Lanth."

"Call me Buddy," Calucci boomed at the same moment that his wife said, "Pleased to meet you, I'm sure. I'm Mabel." Buddy Calucci seized Sarah's hand and pumped it. He wore a coat with hugely padded shoulders and a bright yellow tie, carefully knotted, printed with daisies. Mabel Calucci wore heart-shaped glasses and a red satin dress cut so low that Sarah blinked. She avoided altogether looking at the alien. Not just yet.

"Nice place you got here," Calucci boomed. "Looks real homey." His eyes, Sarah saw, missed nothing, scrutinizing the portraits as if appraising them.

"My, yes," Mabel Calucci said. Her mouth pursed slightly at the magazines tossed on the wing chair.

Sarah said, "Would you like a drink?" and started towards the sideboard. Calucci's words stopped her.

"No, no, Mabel and I never touch the stuff. Christian Temperance. But you folks go right ahead—feel free."

"You don't drink?"

"Lips that touch liquor shall never touch mine," Mabel said roguishly. "This must be your dog—let him right into the living room, do you?'' Her eyes moved to the spot by the fireplace where Brandy usually lay; Labrador hair clung to the Oriental.

"We got a dog, too," Calucci said. "Doberman. Meanest guard dog you ever saw. Not that we need it now with the new security system on the country home. Del EverGuard. Seven thousand for the fencing alone."

"How interesting," Sarah murmured. George threw her a warning glance. She poured herself another Scotch and water, then one for George.

The alien said, "I'd like one, too, please."

Sarah turned in surprise. She had assumed that an alien wouldn't drink alcohol. Not that she actually knew much about the aliens, really—she hadn't kept up. The television set, a small black and white, had broken a few months ago, and with Emily only home occasional weekends Sarah hadn't yet gotten around to getting it repaired. She didn't watch TV.

"Scotch and water is fine," the alien said. He had a deep, slightly hoarse voice. Sarah made herself look at him. Standing with his back to the fire, balancing with what looked like careless ease on both legs and the curving, muscular tail, he wasn't quite as bad as Sarah had expected. The aliens she had seen on the now-dead TV had worn odd-looking, shiny clothes on the top halves of their bodies, nothing below. But this one wore a soft white shirt, no tie, and a tweed jacket cut long enough to cover all but his hairy legs. His head hair, too, didn't look as strange as on the TV aliens; she supposed that a barber must have cut it. It fell thickly from a side part to just over the tops of his ears. Sarah handed him the drink.

"Didn't know you folks imbibed," Calucci said to the alien. He sat on the sofa, pulling up his pant legs at the knees: preserving the crease. "Didn't see *that* on TV."

"We just got a new set," Mabel Calucci said. "Sony. Hundred-inch screen, remotes, stereo, everything."

"Have to have you all to our big Super Bowl party in January," Calucci said. "C'Lanth, your folks like football?"

"No," C'Lanth said. Calucci waited, but the alien said no more, sipping his drink and smiling faintly. Sarah smothered a grin.

"Probably not your native pastime," Calucci said. "Stands to reason. What sports do you guys like? Earth sports, I mean. When in Rome, I always say."

"I like tennis."

"Tennis?" George said, looking surprised.

C'Lanth smiled. "Yes. I'm afraid I've become something of a fanatic. But I'm also afraid I have an unfair advantage— something about the joints of our thumbs. Do you play?"

"Not as much as I used to." George said ruefully.

"Mrs. Atkinson?"

"Yes," Sarah said, wondering where C'Lanth had learned such good English. But didn't she remember something in the papers about the aliens being natural mimics as well as shrewd businessmen? And about their avidly studying just everything? "I play, but not very seriously, I'm afraid. I prefer sailing."

"Buddy and I bowled in a league," Mabel Calucci said. Her plump rouged face clouded over. "In St. Pete I mean. Before we moved to New York. Now—I don't know." She suddenly looked wistful.

"Are there bowling alleys in this cute little country town of yours, George?" Calucci asked.

"I'm afraid I wouldn't know."

There was a slight pause. Then Calucci and the alien spoke simultaneously: "Well, now, let's get down to business!" and "I met a friend of yours, Mrs. Atkinson, at an art gallery board meeting Tuesday. Louise Henderson."

George said to Calucci, "Oh, I rather think later might be better, Buddy."

Sarah said to C'Lanth, "You were at the gallery board meeting?"

"Not as a member, of course. Kyle Van Dorr was just showing me around. A tourist." He smiled; Sarah would have sworn it was a self-deprecating smile.

"When *do* we get down to business then?" Calucci said. His big body shifted restlessly. When he lowered his head like that, Sarah thought, it was the exact shape of a garden trowel. "We have to act fast on this one, George, if we're going to have any kind of alliance here. Before *your* pals—" he nodded at C'Lanth "—have their little rule-making meeting on mergers."

"We believe in competition," C'Lanth said mildly. He finished his drink and held out the glass, mouthing "Please?" George made him another Scotch and water. In front of the fireplace Brandy stretched, turned in a circle, and farted. Mabel Calucci looked delicately away, mouth pursed; C'Lanth smiled. Sarah found herself smiling back. What kind of nitwit acted so affected as to be offended by a dog? Denise came to the door and announced dinner.

Sarah ate little. She watched. C'Lanth also ate sparingly, but he tried everything. Mabel Calucci, in the presence of food, turned garrulous; each course seemed to swell her verbally, words coming out at the same rate that calories went in. She talked about her little grandson—"Cute as a button, and smart as a whip! He can already tell a Caddy from a Buick"; about the redecoration of her kitchen in apple-blossom pink; about a woman on a game show who had won $100,000, had a heart attack, and had to sell the prizes to pay her medical bills; about the street they used to live on in St. Pete when Buddy and her were first married, where people were so friendly they didn't even knock on each others' doors before visiting. Not like here, where you couldn't even see the houses from the street. Not that that was true in New York, of course, where they had their new penthouse, with the cutest terrace you ever saw twelve stories up and just filled with fresh flowers. Buddy Calucci let his wife talk, his eyes appraising the room's furniture, pictures, wallpaper, silver. George, good host that he always was, listened to Mabel Calucci, nodding and smiling.

The five of them had just returned to the living room when Emily came in with her boyfriend, the Walker boy, both of them in jeans and sweaters, laughing. Emily's dark hair had escaped its barrette and fallen around her face, thick and shining. She showed no reaction to finding an alien in her parents' living room beyond a friendly smile.

Sarah felt her heart swell. Her daughter was beautiful, and smart, and mannerly. She was very lucky in Emily. Some of her friends' daughters had turned just impossible, but Emily was wonderful. George made the introductions.

"Enjoying Princeton, Taylor?"

"It's wicked, sir. Especially calculus." Taylor Walker smiled, an attractive easy flash of teeth. "No head for figures, I'm afraid. Professor Boyden is just out of control."

"Hughes Boyden?" C'Lanth asked.

"Yes, sir," Taylor said. "Do you know him?"

"Slightly. I did a lot of reading at Princeton when I first came here. Some of the professors were very helpful. In fact, I was up to Princeton this year for Bicker and Sign-ins."

Taylor and Emily grinned at each other: some private joke. Emily said, "Totally paralytic. I didn't get to bed until seven A.M."

Mabel Calucci looked at her. Her voice went slightly shrill. "I was always glad that my daughter Tammy had the chance to attend Bob Jones University. The moral standards there are very high."

Fury rose in Sarah. The sheer smug *stupidity* . . . Emily, who was Dean's List and honor committee . . . this horrible stupid woman. . . .

But all she said was, "Can I get anyone a drink? Taylor? Emily?"

"No, thanks, we're off," Taylor said. "We'll be at the club, Mrs. Atkinson. Nice to have met you, Mr. C'Lanth."

"Pleased, I'm sure," Mabel Calucci said coldly. Taylor and Emily left.

"I liked the young people Hughes Boyden introduced me to at Princeton," C'Lanth said, almost musingly. "There was about them a sort of . . . playful ease."

Calucci said brusquely, "Not supposed to be easy, is it? Toney school like that. Probably has real high admission standards. Now, George, I really think we got to get down to business. I'm sure the ladies will excuse us."

Sarah didn't glance at Mabel Calucci. Nonetheless, she knew that the woman was staring at Brandy, now curled in the wing chair on top of the *Forbes* and *Smithsonians*, half of which had tumbled to the floor. She knew that Mabel Calucci was surreptitiously tugging at her red satin neckline, which had slipped even lower. She even knew that in a moment Mabel Calucci would say something conciliatory, bright and sweet and cheerful, from lips still pursed like lemons. "I'll come and listen," Sarah said.

George looked relieved. Calucci looked annoyed. C'Lanth smiled. "Glad to have you," the alien said.

When George came back from the short drive to the station, Sarah was already in bed. She sat up against the pillows and watched George undress. George said nothing until he had flung his coat on a chair, loosened his tie, kicked off his shoes. Finally it burst out.

"That C'Lanth is a cutthroat."

"Oh, I don't know, I thought he was rather amusing."

"*Amusing?*"

"I thought of seeing if he'd come down the weekend of the third, when we have the Talcotts and the Hendersons."

George turned slowly towards her.

"You know how John Talcott is always complaining that no one he meets can ever give him a really good tennis game. And Louise so enjoys talking to people who actually know something about art. Really, George, don't look at me like that—it's not such a bizarre idea."

"Sarah—he's an *alien*. And you heard how the business talk went, the part of it you stayed for anyway—where the devil did you go? Mabel Calucci complained in the car that you never came back to the living room. C'Lanth is going to ruin me if we don't get this deal moving."

"Well, wouldn't a chance to get to know him better help that?" Sarah said reasonably. George went on staring at her; after a moment she looked away. He was a dear, but he got so worked up. Unnecessarily, really. After all, they had her money, which was much more than the firm brought in. And when George wrinkled his face like that, he *did* look like the hardware store man.

"It would be more useful to get to know Buddy Calucci

better," George said heavily. "He's the one holding the real clout here. Although C'Lanth might—"

"Oh, really, darling, do come to bed. It's late, and I don't want to argue. You haven't signed any papers yet, after all. Anything could happen."

George didn't answer. He finished undressing, climbed into bed, turned out the light. Sarah waited. When a few minutes had passed, she said softly, "You might be a little nicer to me, George. I *did* just spend an evening with you with those two dreadful people."

"I know," George said. She felt him reach for her in the darkness, and she put her head on his shoulder.

"I'm sorry I didn't go back to the living room, darling. Truly I am. But her *smugness*. And that inane chatter. And those little frizzy dyed curls. And him—that eager hard-eyed grin."

"I know," George said again.

"I did try."

"Yes, you did."

"And you'll think about having C'Lanth down on the third?"

"Might be a good idea," George said sleepily.

Sarah snuggled in closer against his shoulder. She was glad George thought she had tried, glad he wasn't angry. Because of course the truth was that she *had* been rude to those terrible Caluccis, rude with a sort of reverse-English rudeness of not having been polite enough, not having picked up the cues, not having tried at all to enter into their territory. But, really, with some people you just couldn't, and it was no good pretending. Everybody knew that, really. With some people, do what you might, the gap was just too wide.

"THE ROSE GARDEN"

Steven Popkes

"The Rose Garden" was purchased by Gardner Dozois, and appeared in the August 1987 issue of IAsfm, with a beautiful illustration by Terry Lee. Popkes is another young writer who seems fascinated by the theme of alien-human relationships, having dealt with it in several stories for the magazine, including 1989's popular novella The Egg. Here he shows us how love can sometimes take seed on even the most barren of ground. . . .

One of the fastest rising young writers in SF, Steven Popkes is a frequent contributor to IAsfm. His well-received first novel, Caliban Landing, appeared in 1987, and he is involved in working on a projected anthology of "Future Boston" stories being put together by the Cambridge Writers' Workshop. He has a master's degree in physiology, and lives in Somerville, Massachusetts.

Antonia did not like the rain.

On days like this, when the summer waters came down gently, fully, inexorably, she longed for winters with their actinic sunlight.

But in the winter the Paedash migrated south near the equator and the plains were covered only by a gray, stubborn tundra. She liked that less than the rain.

So she stood on the chair to see out the dirty window toward the rose garden. The gray fence leaned in and out, crooked as a drunkard's walk, the wet wood as paintless as rock, enclosing the garden's overgrown jumble of thorns and flowers. She could see the old fountain, choked with brambles and half-filled with matted soil washed down by the rain.

Beyond the garden were the Paedash, the real reason she chose this window. If she could not walk between their boles and under their spherical leaves, she could at least watch them from a distance, swaying together as elephants in dance. Antonia had been a literate child and had first seen pictures of earth elephants when she was very young. She had found them in a book, very old and broken with mold and dry rot, in the dim, dusty room her mother referred to as "the library." The library had belonged to Antonia's father, Andrei, and her mother never entered the room. Andrei and Josef, Antonia's brother, were killed in the Mutiny. The library was Antonia's favorite place.

That the Paedash were plants and only resembled elephants in bulk and slight motion did not bother her. Such details were not important.

"Where's Fyodor?" her mother asked behind her. Antonia turned to the voice.

Catherine Brobeck stood behind her, shallowly smoking a cigarette. She wore an ancient dirty white gown torn through at the elbows. "Antonia?" she called, this time confused and quavering.

"Here, mama." Antonia did not move towards her, wary. "Mama? Do you hear me?"

Catherine did not answer but watched the ash on the cigarette. The ash had grown nearly an inch long. She stared at it fixedly as the tobacco smoldered towards her fingers. The coal touched the skin and Antonia could smell the hair burn. Antonia trembled. Catherine made no sound. The ash fell suddenly.

"Ha!" Catherine cried. "Damn near two inches that time." She looked at her finger. "Hurts," she said vaguely.

Antonia relaxed, came to her and took her other hand. "Mama?" she said softly.

"Yes, baby. What is it?" Her mother smiled at her.

Antonia led Catherine down the hall towards the kitchen. "You called me?"

"Call you? You were by the window. I was remembering when Andrei and I were married here." Her eyes became dreamy. "The house was so bright. The Paedash were holding the lights over the garden. The roses were in bloom . . ." She paused, looking blank. Her face grew wild. She took Antonia and shoved her against the wall, pinning her shoulders. "What were you looking at outside? What? Tell me!" Her eyes burned fever bright.

"The rose garden," she said, lying. Her shoulders hurt and she could barely speak. "Only the rose garden!"

Her mother stood, looked at her hands, then at Antonia. "Yes, of course." She let Antonia go, hid her hands in the fold of the dress and looked away. "The rose garden. What did you see there?"

"Roses."

"Yes. You would see that." She stared off into the next room, unseeing. Tears came down her cheeks and she looked grief-stricken. "Where's Fyodor?" she asked blankly.

Antonia took her to the kitchen and bandaged her hand.

Every Thursday at two o'clock, her uncle Fyodor brought their week's groceries. He rode his horse, Leo, from the south, following the road religiously from his small house to the old Brobeck mansion and never taking the shorter route through the Paedash forest. Antonia knew this, for when she was a child one afternoon as he rode back, she beat him home by cutting through the forest. She burst out in front of the horse and the big roan shied away from her. He calmed it, laughing nervously, looking at her, then the forest. He insisted on carrying her back to her mother on Leo, taking again the road south to the fork, and back again up towards her house. Antonia thought this silly, but she loved the smell of him, of saddle soap and wool, of the dogs he kept and the herbs of his garden.

The day gradually cleared and by the afternoon the sky was a deep violet blue, the Paedash a rich rust red. Antonia waited for Fyodor on the porch, watching the road and across the road the Paedash. Her world was marked by extremes, her uncle, solid as earth, and her mother, as changeable as weather. The seasons of Georgia, its settled roots deep in the soviet province, mirrored those extremes. The humid, chokingly hot summers would give way to dry, cold winters. Humans lived here in a narrow temperate band north and south of the equator. The Paedash followed the most livable weather. Livable for plants could be defined as the right water, the right light and the right heat to photosynthesize. Antonia lived in North, the country north of the equator. She knew the Paedash, listened to them. At times it was as if they spoke to her, the echo of a voice, the hollow within a shout.

Fyodor rounded the road's curve into view. Not really thinking or watching for him any more, he seemed to ride over the curve in the earth, appearing from South, half a world away. He rode Leo at a walk, preoccupied. When he reached the yard, he dismounted and tied Leo to the rose garden fence. She walked to him and stood before him, expecting to be hugged. "Uncle Fyodor." She smiled.

Instead, he lifted her and held her close. "Antonia," Fyodor murmured.

"What? Did you say something?" she asked, startled. He wasn't the same. He did not laugh or tell her anything new from home.

Fyodor set her down and looked down at her. "You are how old? Twelve?"

"You know how old I am." She laughed nervously. He smiled slightly and she grew frightened. "Thirteen. I am thirteen.'' She backed away from him, stopped when she saw the hurt come into his eyes.

"What do you think of school?'' he asked.

She shook her head. "I don't know. I've never been.''

Fyodor took the saddlebags of food from Leo and they sat on the edge of the porch together. Antonia watched him out of the corner of her eye. She held her hands together.

He fidgeted, brought out his pipe and filled the bowl with tobacco. Flakes spilled onto his pants and he brushed at them irritably. He stopped when he saw her watching him, smiled slowly and took a deep breath, emptied the pipe and put it away. He watched the Paedash. "You were two during the Mutiny. Do you remember any of it?''

"No.'' She looked at her hands. "I don't have a good memory, I guess.''

"At two? No one has a good memory that young. It's all right.'' When he said that, some of the Fyodor she knew came out, the bedrock calm, the kindness. The strange Fyodor, the nervous, indecisive, unknown Fyodor diminished. She relaxed a little.

"We don't speak of it,'' he continued. "What do you know of it?''

She shrugged. "It was a war. Like the old earth wars.''

"Who fought? And why?''

"I don't know, really.'' She stared at her hands, frightened again.

He sighed and lowered his voice. "Please. It's important.''

Antonia wouldn't look at him. "We play a game . . .''

"Who?''

"Me. Leonid from near you. Nikita. Maria. We *used* to play it. It's a kid's game.''

"What's the game?''

"Jack South.''

He didn't speak for a moment, then asked her in a strangled voice: "How is this game played?''

Antonia glanced at him briefly. His eyes were closed. "You get a group together. One of them gets to be Jack South. He sings:

Jack sings from the forest.
From there comes the chorus.
Go crazy and come join us.
All burn down!

"Then, he divides the group into the crazies and the dead."

"The crazies and the dead," repeated Fyodor, his eyes still closed.

Antonia nodded. "Then, the crazies and the dead play war."

"Who wins?"

She shrugged. "Depends on who's Jack South." He didn't respond to her. She rubbed her hands together. "I played it all while I was a little kid. I haven't played it for a couple of years. It made me feel funny. It's a kid's game."

He nodded at last, opened his eyes and looked so sad Antonia forgot to be afraid of him and touched his hand. He took her smaller hand and held it in his two large ones.

"Was the Mutiny like that?" she asked.

"Yes," he said distantly. "Andrei and Josef were killed that way."

Antonia felt confused. "Who were the crazies?"

He looked at her and smiled strangely, though the pain was clear on his face. "Why, we were, of course."

"Then," she asked slowly, "who was Jack South?"

He did not answer, but straightened his back and breathed deeply. Gradually, it seemed to Antonia, his strength flowed back into him, filling him, making him larger. He reached out a bear-like arm and drew her across the leather bags to his side, holding her. She hugged him.

"Antonia," he said after a time, "I have a great deal to discuss with your mother."

"She's inside," Antonia said, trying to be helpful.

He looked down at her, again her Uncle Fyodor. "Good. Will you do me a favor?"

"Yes." She smiled at him.

"Would you leave us alone this afternoon. Come back, say, dinner time. Would you do that for me?"

She nodded. ''I'll go see Nikita.''

''Do that. Tell him hello for me.'' He stood and took the groceries. He looked at the Paedash momentarily and his expression was lost again. He brought himself back and grinned at her. ''Until dinner time.'' He left her and went inside the house.

She stood for a few minutes on the porch, looking inside after him. Then, she jumped into the yard and ran down the road towards Nikita's, nothing in her now but the need to run.

Nikita Perchikoff was sitting outside his family's barn watching the forest. His brother and his aunt had been killed in the Mutiny, leaving only him and his father to run the farm. He idly chewed a twig. He was nearly fifteen, and was already a thin attenuated boy with big eyes and a stiff, formal smile.

''Think they'll mind?'' she called to him.

The hand holding the twig twitched and Antonia knew she had startled him.

''No,'' he said as she sat on the bench beside him. ''They don't feel anything like twigs. The squirrels chew on them, don't they? The Paedash don't feel that.''

''They aren't really squirrels,'' corrected Antonia. ''I've seen real squirrels in books. From earth.''

Nikita shrugged.

''What are you doing?''

''Watching them. What do you think?''

Antonia waited for him to explain. In a collection of bright if unschooled children, Nikita shone with brilliance. He did not seem aware of the impact he had on Antonia, which made Antonia put him in a class with her Uncle Fyodor.

''I was thinking about what the Paedash bring with them. The squirrels, the wolves, the bushes—all of the forest. When they leave, nothing's left but the tundra.'' Abruptly, he turned to her. ''Hear about the sensitives?''

''Sensitives?''

''Turns out some people can actually *talk* with them.

There's a school for them in Andropov.'' He didn't say anything for a moment. "I'd like to be able to do that."

"Who told you?"

"Leonid. He heard about it from his mother. She wants to send him.'' The disgust was evident in his voice.

"Leonid! He carves his initials in their trunks." To Antonia, there was no greater sin.

"I know it. *He* knows it. He just wants to stay here and raise pigs.'' Nikita shook his head. "*I'm* going to the university in Dansk."

"Why does his mother want him to go?"

He snorted. "Some status thing, I guess. Mrs. Petrovich would saw off both Leonid's feet at the ankles if she could be,'' he imitated Mrs. Petrovich's high, nasal whine "'as big here as the old Brobeck family.'''

Antonia laughed. "Nothing's much left of that. Catherine talks about it sometimes."

"Yeah,'' said Nikita. "I remember it a little."

"Tell me?"

"I don't remember much,'' Nikita confessed. "The house was always lit up bright. And the Paedash underworkers were everywhere, in the fields, around the grounds. One took care of you, I think. That's all."

"I don't remember anything,'' she said, feeling wistful. "It must have been beautiful."

"You were real young.'' They fell silent, one remembering just an impression of time past, the other trying to imagine it.

"I want to play Jack South again,'' said Antonia suddenly.

"That's a kid's game.'' Nikita shifted uneasily.

"No, it's not. You know it's not,'' she heard herself say.

"Sure it is. I haven't played it in years."

"Why not?'' she demanded.

"I don't know,'' he said, looking first at the forest, then back at her. "I just felt strange."

"Me, too. I want to play now. I want to,'' she paused, thinking, "to know why it felt strange."

"We need more kids,'' he said, stalling.

"We do not. We can just play the Jack South part."

"You can do that yourself."

"I can't. I don't want to. It," she looked down, "scares me."

He nodded. "Yeah. It scares me, too."

"Well?"

"Okay," he said reluctantly and stood up.

They walked deep into the Paedash forest. The spherical leaves spilled shadow over them. The forest was hushed, the animals moving quickly over the trees and the ground making no sound. The tundra was thick and springy under them and they could see the fresh turned earth between the newly dropped roots of the trees. Hitchhiker bushes had separated from the trees and were closing slowly over the ground. Though the forest was silent, Antonia could almost hear murmurings, chants, or a low, vibrant hum.

They found a likely looking clearing between three giants, trees fifty or more feet high. Like grandfathers, she thought.

"You want to be Jack South?" Nikita asked lamely.

"Not really," said Antonia, hesitant now, feeling a presence around them.

"You *ought* to. You wanted to come here."

"I will. All right, I will."

She stood away from him and began to sing:

"Jack sings of the forest . . ."

Something moved in her, a touch, a harmony. She sang louder, not remembering the words, humming through the parts she could not recall. She heard Nikita gasp and didn't care. She danced as she sang, and someone danced and sang with her.

Who? she asked herself.

I don't know. Suddenly frightened, she stopped. In front of her was one of the giants, holding itself out of the ground on its mobile roots, quivering, swaying back and forth with her. She backed away from it, her hand over her mouth. Nikita was next to her.

"It just moved over to you. Lifted itself right out of the ground." He sounded awed.

"Oh no," she whispered, "oh no." She grabbed Nikita by the shirt front.

The Paedash eased itself down on its main trunk and its roots slid easily into the earth. They could see now, on its side, a worn plastic case bolted to the trunk.

"An orderbox," breathed Nikita. He pulled away from her and stood in front of it. "That's how they used to run them. Antonia, the ones on your farm had these!"

"It was the one that took care of me, maybe?" she asked no one in particular.

Nikita didn't hear her. He had pulled out his knife and was scraping the overgrown bark from the edge of the orderbox.

"Don't hurt it," she begged.

He stopped and looked at her, pale. "Is it hurting, do you think?"

She looked at the Paedash. "I don't know. I don't think so."

"Good." He traced the thin line of the case with his knife. "They were supposed to remove all of these after the Mutiny."

"Do you remember the Mutiny?" Antonia asked eagerly.

"No," he said shortly.

She reached for his shoulder. "You're lying to me," she said slowly.

"Yes. All right, I remember."

"Tell me."

He turned to her. "I can't. I don't want to."

"Please. I don't know anything."

He turned back to the orderbox. It sprang open. "It's voice controlled, I think." There was a switch inside painted bright yellow. Nikita pulled it down. Two red lights came on inside the orderbox.

Antonia felt panic around her. "I don't think this is a good idea."

Nikita ignored her. "If it's voice controlled . . . Stand up!"

The Paedash rose stiffly, ponderously onto its mobile roots. Antonia felt pain, deep fear and a great sadness. "Nikita," she said.

Nikita smiled, a twisted smile of someone who knows he is doing wrong but stubbornly refuses to admit it. "Waltz," he said.

"*Nikita!*" she screamed as the pain overwhelmed her and she went for his throat. She knocked him down and they rolled over and over in the dirt. Towering over them, the Paedash danced, first on one root, then on another.

"Antonia! I'll stop!" he yelled. "I'll stop!"

She struck him with her fists, filled with maniacal strength. All she could see or hear or feel was the pain of the Paedash, dancing against its will.

Nikita pushed her away, bleeding from his lips and nose. She rolled against one of the other trees and stopped, blinking. Snarling, she picked up a large rock. He scrambled for the orderbox and pushed up the yellow switch as she raised the stone.

The pain died in her, replaced with relief and a vegetative feeling of complacency. The Paedash settled back into the soil. She dropped the rock, seeing Nikita for the first time. "Nikita," she called softly and knelt beside him. He cringed away.

"Not again," he whispered.

She tore her jacket and cleaned his face. He blew his nose and the cloth came away bloody.

"I'll be okay," he said. "You didn't really hurt me."

She sat back ashamed. "I couldn't help it. It hurt."

"The crazies couldn't help it either," Nikita said bitterly. "They dragged people screaming from the houses. Burned them up if they couldn't get them outside." He looked at her. "That was the Mutiny. Half of everybody going crazy and killing the other half. For some damned tree." He struck at the bark of the Paedash. The Paedash did not respond. "All burn down," he muttered.

"I'm one of those sensitives you were talking about."

"We're all sensitives. Who do you think the crazies were?"

"I can talk to them. No, not talk. Feel them? Know them?" She shook her head.

He stared at her. "I thought so as soon as Leonid told me about the school."

"Why didn't you tell me?"

"I didn't want you to go away," he said simply.

"*You're* going away, to Dansk."

"Not for a long time, anyway."

She felt a sinking sensation in her stomach. "That's where Uncle Fyodor wants me to go," she said softly.

"What?"

"Nikita, they're going to send me *away!*" She buried her head in his shoulder and sobbed.

He held her, looking confused. "What are you talking about?"

While she was crying, she told him of her uncle earlier that afternoon.

"What'll I do?"

"I don't know," said Nikita.

It was night when she returned.

The front room had the stiff silence of an aborted argument. Fyodor stood staring at the floor, his unlit pipe in his hand. He had not looked up when Antonia entered. Catherine sat on the couch watching Antonia, holding herself as if she had been struck.

"Baby?" she called softly. "You won't leave, will you? Promise me."

Antonia walked over to her slowly, dizzy with the tensions in the room. Catherine held her.

"Promise me," she crooned in a voice like a drill.

She smelled of cigarette smoke and old, dirty clothing, of the moldering smell of the house. The smell and her voice and the low, undervoiced mutterings between Fyodor and Catherine confused Antonia and made her feel nauseous.

"Answer me," said Catherine, her voice harsh. "You're all I have left."

Antonia brought her gaze to Catherine's face and Catherine looked afraid.

"She knows," Catherine said, her voice climbing. "Where were you this afternoon? Spying? What were you doing?" She raised her hand.

Fyodor grabbed her and held her high. "Catherine!" he roared.

Antonia watched the two of them grapple. She backed out the door onto the front porch, closed the door and turned towards the forest. She closed her eyes.

After a time, she heard Fyodor put Catherine to bed. Soon, he came out onto the porch. The night was warm and close, as clear as crystal.

"I think you had better come home with me, this night." He leaned against the post watching the sky.

"I'll stay here." Her voice was small.

"Antonia," he began, then stopped, began again. "Your mother's not well."

"She's crazy," Antonia said simply. "But she won't send me away. She wants me."

"Who wants to send you away?"

She looked up towards him but his face was in darkness. "You do. You want to send me to that school in Andropov."

"Who told you that?"

"Nobody. I figured it out. I won't go." She drummed her heels against the porch. "I don't want to go."

Fyodor coughed and shifted towards her, stopped when she stared at him. "Your mother gets . . . sicker every year. I'm afraid for you."

"She won't hurt me."

"She might."

"She *hasn't*. She only hurts herself." Antonia felt tears begin to fall. "If I go, nobody'll take care of her when she burns herself, or when she falls down, or breaks something."

"I'll take care of her."

"You won't. You'll send her away like you want to send me away." From the sudden stillness, she knew she spoke truth, and the tears fell faster.

"You don't understand . . ." he said softly.

She did not answer him.

At last, he stood, smaller than she thought. "She'll sleep all right. I gave her a sedative. I'll be back early in the morning."

Antonia shook her head. "We don't need you."

He untied Leo. "Maybe not." With that, he dug his heels into Leo's flank and left her.

Antonia did not know how long she stood on the porch after Fyodor had gone. The moon came out and made the shadows silver, the Paedash branches covered with Christmas ornaments. She left the porch and moved into the yard, watching the forest, the nightbirds. The forest, as always, swayed, making no sound.

"Jack sings from the forest," she sang and began to cry again. She felt something reach for her, drawn by her. She let it come and didn't look through her tears for a long time. When she did, the Paedash she had danced with settled into the ground before her. She felt it, now, as she knew she had felt them all. Nikita was wrong. She could no more speak with them than she could with Leo. No human could. They were too different. What the two of them could do, and this was little enough, was sit next to one another, or dance together, or sense each other's great, block emotions. Neither knew what those emotions, that depth or that dance meant. This was sensitivity.

She heard the porch door swing open.

Catherine stood there, a white ghost in the moonlight, her face a silver blur. She was silent, then went back inside.

Antonia felt uneasy. Catherine was supposed to be sleeping. "Go back," she said to the Paedash. Nothing happened. Had she expected anything different? She tried to feel her way into the Paedash, to tell it to leave. Nothing. Catherine came out again, holding a stick with a wad of cloth on the end. As Antonia watched, she lit it.

Antonia scrambled around the side of the tree, yanked open the orderbox, pulled down the switch. "Go to the forest. Wait for me. *Go!*"

Ponderously, in a mixture of pain and betrayal that nearly blinded Antonia, the Paedash stood and began to walk down to the forest. Catherine followed it.

Antonia stumbled after. Catherine did not see her, her eyes fixed on the forest, a little smile on her lips. Her face was as bloodless as death. Antonia reached up and grabbed the torch, pulled it down to the ground and stamped on it until it was out.

Catherine dropped the other end and stared at Antonia. Her eyes were huge caverns, her mouth half open. Her teeth glowed in the light.

"Mama?" said Antonia softly. The sound was swallowed up in silence. She backed away.

Catherine followed her. She matched Antonia step for step, as Antonia backed up the yard. Antonia couldn't stop looking at her. Antonia's right arm brushed against something and she felt of it. It was the gate of the rose garden. She couldn't catch her breath and her stomach hurt. The gate moved and the ancient garden shovel fell between them.

Catherine stopped. Antonia continued backing into the garden. Catherine picked up the shovel slowly, and smiled, and lunged.

Antonia screamed and broke for the rose bushes, Catherine running after her.

The thorns ripped at her clothes and she slowed, then heard Catherine behind her. She looked behind her. Catherine threw the shovel at her and she jumped to one side. The shovel struck the earth like a knife.

Antonia ran between two tall, overgrown hedges, blind in the sudden shadow. At the end, there were only rose bushes. She could hear her mother behind her. She dove under the thorns and crawled over old, broken brambles to the trunk. Catherine hacked at the brambles, stopped, then struck the bush. Antonia sat there and trembled. "Go away," she whispered. "Mama, go away."

Catherine fell silent.

In a little while, Antonia felt as if she could breathe again. "All right," she said. She felt her way through the thorns, biting her tongue so that she might not cry out, to the other

side of the bush. She eased out from under the roses and
looked up.

Catherine was waiting for her, the shovel high in the air.

Antonia pulled back under the bush and the shovel struck
earth where her head had been. The scraping of the shovel
against stone was like metal against bone. Antonia returned
to the trunk of the bush and froze.

Catherine stabbed randomly into the thorns. "I swore
you'd never know," she muttered. "I promised Josef and
Andrei."

The hollow space around the trunk of the rose continued
down the row. As quietly as she could, stifling the pain as
the thorns gashed her knees and ankles, she moved down
the row away from Catherine and pushed out of the brambles. She looked back. Catherine was still striking at the
bush where Antonia had been, her breath coming in angry
sobs.

Antonia moved to where the fence leaned out and climbed
on it.

"*Antonia!*"

"No, mama," she cried and jumped across it. She ran
down the yard and across the road.

"Antonia, come back. Come back," her mother called
over and over. "Andrei, Josef. Come back." Antonia disappeared into the forest.

She found the tree by following its trail of pain and fear.
She turned off the orderbox and sat on the ground next to
the tree, dull. Her hands hurt and she looked at them. They
were ripped and bleeding. As she looked, she gradually felt
the rest of her body. There were great gashes on her arms
and one on her face. She felt aching punctures on her knees
and shins. Her feet were stuck to the inside of her shoes
with blood.

"Are you all right?" came a voice.

She tumbled around the tree and hid.

"It's me. It's Nikita. I heard your mother."

She looked around the tree. Nikita stood in the faint light.

"She was going to kill me," Antonia said as she came around the tree.

"Are you all right? You look a mess."

"No." She shook her head. "She tried to *kill* me."

"You're bloody all over."

"I know."

Nikita turned and looked at her back. "We've got to get you out of here. I'm going to take you to your uncle's."

She did not answer.

"Is that all right?"

Silence.

"Can you walk?"

She nodded. He led her through the forest to Fyodor's farm. Fyodor opened the door and she smiled up at him. "Uncle Fyodor."

"She killed Papa and Josef, didn't she?"

Fyodor had bathed her and dressed the wounds with herbs. She bore the stinging in silence. He picked her up and sat her on the sofa. Nikita helped as best he could.

"What happened?" asked Fyodor after she spoke.

"Did she?"

Fyodor nodded slowly. "When Jack South sang, we all heard him. We all heard the Paedash. That was his gift, to bring out what we didn't know we heard. All of the sensitive people. All of the crazies."

"I know about that."

Fyodor was silent a moment. "I shouldn't have left you there."

Antonia shrugged. "Tell me."

Fyodor stared at his hands. "The madness faded after a while. We didn't think. We just—we were animals biting at a cage. A cage not our own. I came to myself watching the Perchikoff house burn, knowing I set the flames."

"You—" began Nikita.

Fyodor stared at Nikita with a cold anger. "Don't think only the Brobecks kill their own. Your father killed Old Man Petrovich and his son. Mrs. Petrovich helped." The anger faded and all that was left was weariness. "I almost went crazy again when I remembered Catherine. Andrei. Josef. You. I rode Leo to the mansion until he stumbled up the yard. You were crying in the library."

"At first, I thought, the house is still standing. It must be all right. But I couldn't find Catherine. I could find no one but you. I looked all through the house and then stood in the window, confused and frightened. I could see into the rose garden, where Catherine was standing. She didn't move, but I could see the knife and the bodies."

The breath came out of him then and made the flames in the fireplace dance. His voice went leaden flat. "I stayed with her all that winter. She wouldn't get out of touching distance from you. She seemed to get better for a while. Then, then she got worse."

Antonia did not speak for a long time. "You had better go see to her. And give me some money. And give me the name of that school."

"The Institute of Human Responsibility," he said automatically. "Antonia—"

"You go see to my mother," she said, smiling. "Or I shall return for you."

Fyodor looked at her and shuddered. He went to the wall and opened the safe, looked at her a moment, then left. She didn't look at him, the smile still on her face.

Antonia turned to Nikita for the first time. "Will your father loan us his cart?"

Nikita nodded slowly. "I suppose."

She took his hand. "Thank you, Nikita. I need you to take me to the train station."

"There aren't any trains running now."

She nodded. "I know. I'll wait. Will you wait with me?"

He took her other hand in his. "I will."

She sat next to the window as the train skirted the edge of the mountains before it began the long descent to Andropov's valley. The lights of the city calmed her. They gleamed like pin-prick stars. She sat up and stared and the city of Andropov was gone. For a short moment, before it had been masked by the trees, she had seen in the lights of the city the face of a woman she did not know, her face of rose petals, her hands of thorns.

"OF SPACE-TIME AND THE RIVER"

Gregory Benford

"Of Space-Time and the River" was purchased by Gardner Dozois, and appeared in the February 1986 issue of IAsfm, *with one of Terry Lee's best covers (his first for us) and a striking interior illustration by Gary Freeman. One of the busiest people in SF, Benford doesn't appear in IAsfm as often as we'd like, but each appearance he does make there is memorable, and this one was no exception. Here, in one of the most powerful stories of that year, he takes us to the shadow of the pyramids for an encounter with a race of enigmatic aliens who are strangely fascinated with Egypt's ancient past. . . .*

Gregory Benford is one of the modern giants of the field. His 1980 novel Timescape *won the Nebula Award, the John W. Campbell Memorial Award, the British Science Fiction Association Award, and the Australian Ditmar Award, and is widely considered to be one of the classic novels of the last two decades. His other novels include* The Stars in Shroud, In the Ocean of Night, Against

Infinity, Artifact, *and* Across the Sea of Suns. *His most recent novels are the bestselling* Great Sky River *and* Tides of Light. *Benford is a professor of physics at the University of California, Irvine.*

Dec. 5, Monday, 2048

We took a limo to Los Angeles for the 9 A.M. flight, LAX to Cairo.

On the boost up we went over 1.4 G, contra-reg, and a lot of passengers complained, especially the poor thins in their clank-shank rigs, the ones that keep you walking even after the hip replacements fail.

Joanna slept through it all, seasoned traveler, and I occupied myself with musing about finally seeing the ancient Egypt I'd dreamed about as a kid, back at the turn of the century.

> If thou be'st born to strange sights,
> Things invisible to see,
> Ride ten thousand days and nights,
> Till age snow white hairs on thee.

I've got the snow powdering at the temples and steadily expanding waistline, so I guess John Donne applies. Good to see I can still summon up lines I first read as a teenager. There are some rewards to being a Prof. of Comp. Lit. at UC Irvine, even if you do have to scrimp to afford a trip like this.

The tour agency said the Quarthex hadn't interfered with tourism at all—in fact, you hardly noticed them, they deliberately blended in so well. How a seven-foot insectoid thing with gleaming russet skin can look like an Egyptian I don't know, but what the hell, Joanna said, let's go anyway.

I hope she's right. I mean, it's been fourteen years since the Quarthex landed, opened the first diplomatic interstellar relations, and then chose Egypt as the only place on Earth where they cared to carry out what they called their "cultural studies." I guess we'll get a look at that, too. The Quarthex keep to themselves, veiling their multi-layered deals behind diplomatic dodges.

As if six hours of travel wasn't numbing enough, including the orbital delay because of an unannounced Chinese launch, we both watched a holoD about one of those new biotech guys, called *Straight from the Hearts*. An unending string of single-entendre jokes. In our stupefied state it was just about right.

As we descended over Cairo it was clear and about 15°C. We stumbled off the plane, sandy-eyed from riding ten thousand days and nights in a whistling aluminum box.

The airport was scruffy, instant third world hubbub, confusion, and filth. One departure lounge was filled exclusively with turbaned men. Heavy security everywhere. No Quarthex around. Maybe they do blend in.

Our bus across Cairo passed a decayed aqueduct, about which milled men in caftans, women in black, animals eating garbage. People, packed into the most unlikely living spots, carrying out peddler's business in dusty spots between buildings, traffic alternately frenetic or frozen.

We crawled across Cairo to Giza, the pyramids abruptly looming out of the twilight. The hotel, Mena House, was the hunting lodge-cum-palace of 19th-century kings. Elegant.

Buffet supper was good. Sleep came like a weight.

Dec. 6

Keeping this journal is fun. Joanna says it's good therapy for me, might even get me back into the habit of writing again. She says every Comp. Lit. type is a frustrated author and I should just spew my bile into this diary. So be it:

> Thou, when thou return'st, wilt tell me
> All strange wonders that befell thee.

World, you have been warned.

Set off south today—to Memphis, the ancient capital lost when its walls were breached in a war and subsequent floods claimed it.

The famous fallen Rameses statue. It looks powerful still, even lying down. Makes you feel like a pigmy tip-toeing around a giant, *a la* Gulliver.

Saqqara, principal necropolis of Memphis, survives three km. away in the desert. First Dynasty tombs, including the first pyramid, made of steps, five levels high. New Kingdom graffiti inside are now history themselves, from our perspective.

On to the Great Pyramid!—by camel! The drivers proved even more harassing than legend warned. We entered the Khefren pyramid, slightly shorter than that of his father, Cheops. All the 80 known pyramids were found stripped. These passages have a constricted vacancy to them, empty now for longer than they were filled. Their silent mass is unnerving.

Professor Alvarez from UC Berkeley tried to find hidden rooms here by placing cosmic ray detectors in the lower known rooms, and looking for slight increases in flux at certain angles, but there seem to be none. There are seismic and even radio measurements of the dry sands in the Giza region, looking for echoes of buried tombs, but no big finds so far. Plenty of echoes from ruins of ordinary houses, etc., though.

No serious jet lag today, but we nod off when we can. Handy, having the hotel a few hundred yards from the pyramids.

I tried to get Joanna to leave her wrist comm at home. Since her breakdown she can't take news of daily disasters very well. (Who can, really?) She's pretty steady now, but this trip should be as calm as possible, her doctor told me.

So of course she turns on the comm and it's full of hysterical stuff about another border clash between the Empire of Israel and the Arab Muhammad Soviet. Smart rockets vs. smart defenses. A draw. Some things never change.

I turned it off immediately. Her hands shook for hours afterward. I brushed it off.

Still, it's different when you're a few hundred miles from the lines. Hope we're safe here.

Dec. 7

Into Cairo itself, the Egyptian museum. The Tut Ankh Amen exhibit—huge treasuries, opulent jewels, a sheer wondrous plentitude. There are endless cases of beautiful alabaster bowls, gold-laminate boxes, testifying to thousands of years of productivity.

I wandered down a musty marble corridor and then, coming out of a gloomy side passage, there was the first Quarthex I'd ever seen. Big, clacking and clicking as it thrust forward in that six-legged gait. It ignored me, of course—they nearly always lurch by humans as though they can't see us. Or else that distant, distracted gaze means they're ruminating over strange, alien ideas. Who knows why they're intensely studying ancient Egyptian ways, and ignoring the rest of us? This one was cradling a stone urn, a meter high at least. It carried the black granite in three akimbo arms, hardly seeming to notice the weight. I caught a whiff of acrid pungency, the fluid that lubricates their joints. Then it was gone.

We left and visited the oldest Coptic church in Egypt, supposedly where Moses hid out when he was on the lam out of town. Looks it. The old section of Cairo is crowded, decayed, people laboring in every nook with minimal tools, much standing around watching as others work. The only sign of really efficient labor was a gang of men and women hauling long, cigar-shaped yellow things on wagons. Something the Quarthex wanted placed outside the city, our guide said.

In the evening we went to the Sound & Light show at the Sphinx—excellent. There is even a version in the Quarthex language, those funny sputtering, barking sounds.

Arabs say, "Man fears time; time fears the pyramids." You get that feeling here.

Afterward, we ate in the hotel's Indian restaurant; quite fine.

Dec. 8

Cairo is a city being trampled to death.

It's grown by a factor of fourteen in population since the revolution in 1952, and shows it. The old Victorian homes which once lined stately streets of willowy trees are now crowded by modern slab concrete apartment houses. The aged buildings are kept going, not from a sense of history, but because no matter how rundown they get, somebody needs them.

The desert's grit invades everywhere. Plants in the court-yards have a weary, resigned look. Civilization hasn't been very good for the old ways.

Maybe that's why the Quarthex seem to dislike anything built since the time of the Romans. I saw one running some kind of machine, a black contraption that floated two meters off the ground. It was laying some kind of cable in the ground, right along the bank of the Nile. Every time it met a building it just slammed through, smashing everything to frags. Guess the Quarthex have squared all this with the Egyptian gov't, because there were police all around, making sure nobody got in the way. Odd.

But not unpredictable, when you think about it. The Quarthex have those levitation devices which everybody would love to get the secret of. (Ending sentence with preposition! Horrors! But this is vacation, dammit.) They've been playing coy for years, letting out a trickle of technology, with the Egyptians holding the patents. That must be what's holding the Egyptian economy together, in the face of their unrelenting population crunch. The Quarthex started out as guests here, studying the ruins and so on, but now it's obvious that they have free run of the place. They *own* it.

Still, the Quarthex haven't given away the crucial devices which would enable us to find out how they do it—or so my colleagues in the physics department tell me. It vexes them that this alien race can master space-time so completely, manipulating gravity itself, and we can't get the knack of it.

We visited the famous alabaster mosque. It perches on a

hill called The Citadel. Elegant, cool, aloofly dominating the city. The Old Bazaar nearby is a warren, so much like the movie sets one's seen that it has an unreal, Arabian Nights quality. We bought spices. The calls to worship from the mosques reach you everywhere, even in the most secluded back rooms where Joanna was haggling over jewelry.

It's impossible to get anything really ancient, the swarthy little merchants said. The Quarthex have bought them up, trading gold for anything that might be from the time of the Pharaohs. There have been a lot of fakes over the last few centuries, some really good ones, so the Quarthex have just bought anything that might be real. No wonder the Egyptians like them, let them chew up their houses if they want. Gold speaks louder than the past.

We boarded our cruise ship, the venerable *Nile Concorde*. Lunch was excellent; Italian. We explored Cairo in mid-afternoon, through markets of incredible dirt and disarray. Calf brains displayed without a hint of refrigeration or protection, flies swarming, etc. Fun, especially if you can keep from breathing for five minutes or more.

We stopped in the Shepheard Hotel, the site of many Brit spy novels (Maugham especially). It has an excellent bar—Nubians, Saudis, etc., putting away decidedly non-Islamic gins and beers. A Quarthex was sitting in a special chair at the back, talking through a voicebox to a Saudi. I couldn't tell what they were saying, but the Saudi had a gleam in his eye. Driving a bargain, I'd say.

Great atmosphere in the bar, though. A cloth banner over the bar proclaims,

> *Unborn tomorrow and dead yesterday,*
> *why fret about them if today be sweet.*

Indeed, yes, ummm—bartender!

Dec. 9, Friday, Moslem holy day

We left Cairo at 11 P.M. last night, the city gliding past our stateroom windows, lovelier in misty radiance than in dusty day. We cruised all day. Buffet breakfast & lunch, solid Eastern and Mediterranean stuff, passable red wine.

A hundred meters away, the past presses at us, going about its business as if the pharaohs were still calling the tune. Primitive pumping irrigation, donkeys doing the work, women cleaning gray clothes in the Nile. Desert ramparts to the east, at spots sending sand fingers—no longer swept away by the annual flood—across the fields to the shore itself. Moslem tombs of stone and mud brick coast by as we lounge on the top deck, peering at the madly waving children through our binoculars, across a chasm of time.

There are about fifty aboard a ship with capacity of a hundred, so there is plenty of room and service as we sweep serenely on, music flooding the deck, cutting between slabs of antiquity; not quite decadent, just intelligently sybaritic. (Why so few tourists? Guide says people are maybe afraid of the Quarthex. Joanna gets jittery around them, but I don't know whether that's her old fears surfacing again.)

The spindly, ethereal minarets are often the only grace note in the mud-brick villages, like a lovely idea trying to rise out of brown, mottled chaos. Animal power is used everywhere possible. Still, the villages are quiet at night.

The flip side of this peacefulness must be boredom. That explains a lot of history and its rabid faiths, unfortunately.

Dec. 10

Civilization thins steadily as we steam upriver. The mud-brick villages typically have no electricity; there is ample power from Aswan, but the power lines and stations are too expensive. One would think that, with the Quarthex gold, they could do better now.

Our guide says the Quarthex have been very hard-nosed— no pun intended—about such improvements. They will not let the earnings from their patents be used to modernize Egypt. Feeding the poor, cleaning the Nile, rebuilding monuments—all fine (in fact, they pay handsomely for restoring projects). But better electricity—no. A flat no.

We landed at a scruffy town and took a bus into the western desert. Only a kilometer from the flat floodplain,

the Sahara is utterly barren and forbidding. We visited a
Ptolemaic city of the dead. One tomb has a mummy of a
girl who drowned trying to cross the Nile and see her lover,
the hieroglyphs say. Nearby are catacombs of mummified
baboons and ibises, symbols of wisdom.

A tunnel begins here, pointing SE toward Akhenaton's
capital city. The German discoverers in the last century
followed it for 40 kilometers—all cut through limestone, a
gigantic task—before turning back because of bad air.

What was it for? Nobody knows. Dry, spooky atmosphere. Urns of dessicated mummies, undisturbed. To duck
down a side corridor is to step into mystery.

I left the tour group and ambled over a low hill—to take
a leak, actually. To the west was sand, sand, sand. I was
standing there, doing my bit to hold off the dryness, when
I saw one of those big black contraptions come slipping
over the far horizon. Chuffing, chugging, and laying what
looked like pipe—a funny kind of pipe, all silvery, with
blue facets running through it. The glittering shifted, changing to yellows and reds while I watched.

A Quarthex riding atop it, of course. It ran due south,
roughly parallel to the Nile. When I got back and told Joanna
about it she looked at the map and we couldn't figure what
would be out there of interest to anybody, even a Quarthex.
No ruins around, nothing. Funny.

Dec. 11

Beni Hassan, a nearly deserted site near the Nile. A steep
walk up the escarpment of the eastern desert, after crossing
the rich flood plain by donkey. The rock tombs have fine
drawings and some statues—still left because they were cut
directly from the mountain, and have thick wedges securing
them to it. Guess the ancients would steal anything not
nailed down. One thing about the Quarthex, the guide
says—they take nothing. They seem genuinely interested
in restoring, not in carting artifacts back home to their neck
of the galactic spiral arm.

Upriver, we landfall beside a vast dust plain, which we
crossed in a cart pulled by a tractor. The mud brick palaces

of Akhenaton have vanished, except for a bit of Nefertiti's palace, where the famous bust of her was found. The royal tombs in the mountain above are defaced—big chunks pulled out of the walls by the priests who undercut his monotheist revolution, after his death.

The wall carvings are very realistic and warm; the women even have nipples. The tunnel from yesterday probably runs under here, perhaps connecting with the passageways we see deep in the king's grave shafts. Again, nobody's explored them thoroughly. There are narrow sections, possibly warrens for snakes or scorpions, maybe even traps.

While Joanna and I are ambling around, taking a few snaps of the carvings, I hear a rustle. Joanna has the flashlight and we peer over a ledge, down a straight shaft. At the bottom something is moving, something damned big.

It takes a minute to see that the reddish shell isn't a sarcophagus at all, but the back of a Quarthex. It's planting sucker-like things to the walls, threading cables through them. I can see more of the stuff further back in the shadows.

The Quarthex looks up, into our flashlight beam, and scuttles away. Exploring the tunnels? But why did it move away so fast? What's to hide?

Dec. 12

Cruise all day and watch the shore slide by.

Joanna is right; I needed this vacation a great deal. I can see that, rereading this journal—it gets looser as I go along.

As do I. When I consider how my life is spent, ere half my days, in this dark world and wide . . .

The pell-mell of university life dulls my sense of wonder, of simple pleasures simply taken. The Nile has a flowing, infinite quality, free of time. I can *feel* what it was like to live here, part of a great celestial clock that brought the perpetually turning sun and moon, the perennial rhythm of the flood. Aswan has interrupted the ebb and flow of the waters, but the steady force of the Nile rolls on.

> Heaven smiles, and faiths and empires gleam,
> Like wrecks of a dissolving dream.

The peacefulness permeates everything. Last night, making love to Joanna, was the best ever. Magnifique!

(And I know you're reading this, Joanna—I saw you sneak it out of the suitcase yesterday! Well, it *was* the best— quite a tribute, after all these years. And there's tomorrow and tomorrow . . .)

> He who bends to himself a joy
> Does the winged life destroy;
> But he who kisses the joy as it flies
> Lives in eternity's sunrise.

Perhaps next term I shall request the Romantic Poets course. Or even write some of my own . . .

Three Quarthex flew overhead today, carrying what look like ancient rams-head statues. The guide says statues were moved around a lot by the Arabs, and of course the archeologists. The Quarthex have negotiated permission to take many of them back to their rightful places, if known.

Dec. 13

Landfall at Abydos—a limestone temple miraculously preserved, with its thick roof intact. Clusters of scruffy mud huts surround it, but do not diminish its obdurate rectangular severity.

The famous list of pharaohs, chiseled in a side corridor, is impressive in its sweep of time. Each little entry was a lordly pharaoh, and there are a whole wall jammed full. Egypt lasted longer than any comparable society, and the mass of names on that wall is even more impressive since the temple builders did not even give it the importance of a central location.

The list omits Hatchepsut, a mere woman, and Akhenaton the scandalous monotheist. Rameses II had all carvings here cut deeply, particularly on the immense columns, to forestall defacement— a possibility he was much aware of, since he was busily doing it to his ancestors' temples. He chiseled away earlier work, adding his own cartouches, apparently thinking he could fool the gods themselves into believing he had built them all himself. Ah, immortality.

Had an earthquake today. Shades of California!

We were on the ship, Joanna was dutifully padding back and forth on the main deck to work off the opulent lunch. We saw the palms waving ashore, and damned if there wasn't a small shock wave in the water, going east to west, and then a kind of low grumbling from the east. Guide says he's never seen anything like it.

And tonight, sheets of ruby light rising up from both east and west. Looked like an aurora, only the wrong directions. The rippling aura changed colors as it rose, then met overhead, burst into gold, and died. I'd swear I heard a high, keening note sound as the burnt-gold line flared and faded, flared and faded, spanning the sky.

Not many people on deck, though, so it didn't cause much comment. Joanna's theory is, it was a rocket exhaust.

An engineer says it looks like something to do with magnetic fields. I'm no scientist, but it seems to me whatever the Quarthex want to do, they can. Lords of space/time, they called themselves in the diplomatic ceremonies. The United Nations representatives wrote that off as hyperbole, but the Quarthex may mean it.

Dec. 14

Dendera. A vast temple, much less well known than Karnak, but quite as impressive. Quarthex there, digging at the foundations. Guide says they're looking for some secret passageways, maybe. The Egyptian gov't is letting them do what they damn well please.

On the way back to the ship, we pass a whole mass of people, hundreds, all dressed in costumes. I thought it was some sort of pageant or tourist foolery, but the guide frowned, saying he didn't know what to make of it. The mob was chanting something even the guide couldn't make out. He said the rough-cut cloth was typical of the old ways, made on crude spinning wheels. The procession was ragged, but seemed headed for the temple. They looked drunk to me.

The guide tells me that the ancients had a theology based on the Nile. This country is essentially ten kilometers wide and seven hundred kilometers long, a narrow band of livable earth pressed between two deadly deserts. So they believed the gods must have intended that, and the Nile was the center of the whole damned world.

The sun came from the east, meaning that's where things began. Ending—dying—happened in the west, where the sun went. Thus they buried their dead on the west side of the Nile, even 7000 years ago. At night, the sun swung below and lit the underworld, where everybody went finally. Kind of comforting, thinking of the sun doing duty like that for the dead. Only the virtuous dead, though. If you didn't follow the rules . . .

> Some are born to sweet delight,
> Some are born to endless night.

Their world was neatly bisected by the great river, and they loved clean divisions. They invented the 24 hour day but, loving symmetry, split it in half. Each of the 12 daylight hours was longer in summer than in winter—and, for night, vice versa. They built an entire nation-state, an immortal hand or eye, framing such fearful symmetry.

On to Karnak itself, mooring at Luxor. The middle and late pharaohs couldn't afford the labor investment for pyramids, so they contented themselves with additions to the huge sprawl at Karnak.

I wonder how long it will be before someone rich notices that for a few million or so he could build a tomb bigger than the Great Pyramid. It would only take a million or so limestone blocks—or much better, granite—and could be better isolated and protected. If you can't conquer a continent or scribble a symphony, then pile up a great stack of stones.

*L'eternité,
ne fut jamais perdue.*

The light show this night at Karnak was spooky at times, and beautiful, with booming voices coming right out of the stones. Saw a Quarthex in the crowd. It stared straight ahead, not noticing anybody but not bumping into any humans, either.

It looked enthralled. The beady eyes, all four, scanned the shifting blues and burnt-oranges that played along the rising columns, the tumbled great statues. Its lubricating fluids made shiny reflections as it articulated forward, clacking in the dry night air. Somehow it was almost reverential. Rearing above the crowd, unmoving for long moments, it seemed more like the giant frozen figures in stone than like the mere mortals who swarmed around it, keeping a respectful distance, muttering to themselves.

Unnerving, somehow, to see

. . . a subtler Sphinx renew
Riddles of death Thebes never knew.

Dec. 15

A big day. The Valley of the Queens, the Nobles, and finally of the Kings. Whew!

All are dry washes (wadis), obviously easy to guard and isolate. Nonetheless, all of the 62 known tombs except Tut's were rifled, probably within a few centuries of burial.

It must've been an inside job.

There is speculation that the robbing became a needed part of the economy, recycling the wealth, and providing gaudy displays for the next pharaoh to show off at *his* funeral, all the better to keep impressing the peasants. Just another part of the socio-economic machine, folks.

Later priests collected the pharaoh mummies and hid them in a cave nearby, realizing they couldn't protect the tombs. Preservation of Tuthmosis III is excellent. His hook-nosed mummy has been returned to its tomb—a big, deep thing, larger than our apartment, several floors in all, connected by ramps, with side treasuries, galleries, etc. The inscription above reads *You shall live again forever*.

All picked clean, of course, except for the sarcophagus, too heavy to carry away. The pyramids had portcullises, deadfalls, pitfalls, and rolling stones to crush the unwary robber, but there are few here. Still, it's a little creepy to think of all those ancient engineers, planning to commit murder in the future, long after they themselves are gone, all to protect the past.

Death, be not proud.

An afternoon of shopping in the bazaar. The old Victorian hotel on the river is atmospheric, but has few guests. Food continues good. No dysentery, either. We both took the EZ-Di bacteria before we left, so it's living down in our tracts, festering away, lying in wait for any ugly foreign bug. Comforting.

Dec. 16

Cruise on. We stop at Kom Ombo, a temple to the croc-odile god, Sebek, built to placate the crocs who swarmed in the river nearby. (The Nile is cleared of them now, unfortunately; they would've added some zest to the cruise . . .) A small room contains 98 mummified crocs, stacked like cordwood.

Cruised some more. A few km. south, there were gangs of Egyptians working beside the river. Hauling blocks of granite down to the water, rolling them on logs. I stood on the deck, trying to figure out why they were using ropes and simple pulleys, and no powered machinery.

Then I saw a Quarthex near the top of the rise, where the blocks were being sawed out of the rock face. It reared up over the men, gesturing with those jerky arms, eyes glittering. It called out something in a halfway human voice, only in a language I didn't know. The guide came over, frowning, but he couldn't understand it, either.

The laborers were pulling ropes across ruts in the stone, feeding sand and water into the gap, cutting out blocks by sheer brute abrasion. It must take weeks to extract one at that rate! Further along, others drove wooden planks down into the deep grooves, hammering them with crude wooden mallets. Then they poured water over the planks, and we could hear the stone pop open as the wood expanded, far down in the cut.

That's the way the ancients did it, the guide said kind of quietly. The Quarthex towered above the human teams, that jangling, harsh voice booming out over the water, each syllable lingering until the next joined it, blending in the dry air, hollow and ringing and remorseless.

note added later

Stopped at Edfu, a well-preserved temple, buried 100 feet deep by Moslem garbage until the late 19th century. The best aspect of river cruising is pulling along a site, viewing it from the angles the river affords, and then stepping from your stateroom directly into antiquity, with nothing to intervene and break the mood.

Trouble is, this time a man in front of us goes off a way to photograph the ships, and suddenly something is rushing at him out of the weeds and the crew is yelling—it's a crocodile! The guy drops his camera and bolts.

The croc looks at all of us, snorts, and waddles back into the Nile. The guide is upset, maybe even more than the fellow who almost got turned into a free lunch. Who would reintroduce crocs into the Nile?

Dec. 17

Aswan. A clean, delightful town. The big dam just south of town is impressive, with its monument to Soviet excellence, etc. A hollow joke, considering how poor the USSR is today. They could use a loan from Egypt!

The unforeseen side effects, though—rising water table bringing more insects, rotting away the carvings in the temples, rapid silting up inside the dam itself, etc.—are getting important. They plan to dig a canal and drain a lot of the incoming new silt into the desert, make a huge farming valley with it, but I don't see how they can drain enough water to carry the dirt, and still leave much behind in the original dam.

The guide says they're having trouble with it.

We then fly south, to Abu Sembel. Lake Nasser, which claimed the original site of the huge monuments, is hundreds of miles long. They enlarged it again in 2008.

In the times of the pharaohs, the land below these waters had villages, great quarries for the construction of monuments, trade routes south to the Nubian kingdoms. Now it's all underwater.

They did save the enormous temples to Rameses II— built to impress aggressive Nubians with his might and majesty—and to his queen, Nefertari. The colossal statues of Rameses II seem personifications of his egomania. Inside, carvings show him performing *all* the valiant tasks in the great battle with the Hittites—slaying, taking prisoners, then presenting them to himself, who is in turn advised by the gods—which include himself! All this, for a battle which was in fact an iffy draw. Both temples have been lifted about a hundred feet and set back inside a wholly artificial hill, supported inside by the largest concrete dome in the world. Amazing.

"Look upon my works, ye Mighty, and despair!"

Except that when Shelley wrote *Ozymandias*, he'd never seen Rameses II's image so well preserved.

Leaving the site, eating the sand blown into our faces by a sudden gust of wind, I caught sight of a Quarthex. It was burrowing into the sand, using a silvery tool that spat ruby-colored light. Beside it, floating on a platform, were some of those funny pipe-like things I'd seen days before. Only this time men and women were helping it, lugging stuff around to put into the holes the Quarthex dug.

The people looked dazed, like they were sleep-walking or something. I waved a greeting, but nobody even looked up. Except the Quarthex. They're expressionless, of course. Still, those glittering popeyes peered at me for a long moment, with the little feelers near its mouth twitching with a kind of anxious energy.

I looked away. I couldn't help but feel a little spooked by it. I mean, it wasn't looking at us in a friendly way. Maybe it didn't want me yelling at its work gang. .

Then we flew back to Aswan, above the impossibly narrow ribbon of green that snakes through absolute bitter desolation.

Dec. 18

I'm writing this at twilight, before the light gives out. We got up this morning and were walking into town when the whole damn ground started to rock. Mud huts slamming down, waves on the Nile, everything.

Got back to the ship but nobody knew what was going on. Not much on that radio. Cairo came in clear, saying there'd been a quake all right, all along the Nile.

Funny thing was, the captain couldn't raise any other radio station. Just Cairo. Nothing else in the whole Middle East.

Some other passengers think there's a war on. Maybe so, but the Egyptian army doesn't know about it. They're standing around, all along the quay, fondling their AK 47s, looking just as puzzled as we are.

More rumblings and shakings in the afternoon. And now that the light's about gone, I can see big sheets of light in the sky. Only it seems to me the constellations aren't right.

Joanna took some of her pills. She's trying to fend off the jitters and I do what I can. I hate the empty, hollow look that comes into her eyes.

We've got to get the hell out of here.

Dec. 19

I might as well write this down, there's nothing else to do.

When we got up this morning the sun was there all right, but the moon hadn't gone down. And it didn't, all day.

Sure, they can both be in the sky at the same time. But all day? Joanna is worried, not because of the moon, but because all the airline flights have been cancelled. We were supposed to go back to Cairo today.

More earthquakes. Really bad this time.

At noon, all of a sudden, there were Quarthex everywhere. In the air, swarming in from the east and west. Some splashed down in the Nile—and didn't come up. Others zoomed overhead, heading south toward the dam.

Nobody's been brave enough to leave the ship—including me. Hell, I just want to go home. Joanna's staying in the cabin.

About an hour later, a swarthy man in a ragged gray suit comes running along the quay and says the dam's gone. Just *gone*. The Quarthex formed little knots above it, and there was a lot of purple flashing light and big crackling noises, and then the dam just disappeared.

But the water hasn't come pouring down on us here. The man says it ran *back the other way*. South.

I looked over the rail. The Nile was flowing north.

Late this afternoon, five of the crew went into town. By this time there were fingers of orange and gold zapping across the sky all the time, making weird designs. The clouds would come rolling in from the north, and these radiant beams would hit them, and they'd *split* the clouds, just like that. With a spray of ivory light.

And Quarthex, buzzing everywhere. There's a kind of high sheen, up above the clouds, like a metal boundary or something, but you can see through it.

Quarthex keep zipping up to it, sometimes coming right up out of the Nile itself, just splashing out, then zooming up until they're little dwindling dots. They spin around up there, as if they're inspecting it, and then they drop like bricks, and splash down in the Nile again. Like frantic bees, Joanna said, and her voice trembled.

A technical type on board, an engineer from Rockwell, says *he* thinks the Quarthex are putting on one hell of a light show. Just a weird alien stunt, he thinks.

While I was writing this, the five crewmen returned from Aswan. They'd gone to the big hotels there, and then to police headquarters. They heard the TV from Cairo went out two days ago. All air flights have been grounded because of the Quarthex buzzing around and the odd lights and so on.

Or at least, that's the official line. The Captain says his cousin told him that several flights *did* take off two days back, and they hit something up there. Maybe that blue metallic sheen?

Anyway, one crashed. The others landed, even though damaged.

The authorities are keeping it quiet. They're not just keeping us tourists in the dark—they're playing mum with everybody.

I hope the engineer is right. Joanna is fretting and we hardly ate anything for dinner, just picked at the cold lamb. Maybe tomorrow will settle things.

Dec. 20

It did. When we woke, we went up on deck and watched the Earth rise.

It was coming up from the western mountains, blue-white clouds and patches of green and brown, but mostly tawny desert. We're looking west, across the Sahara. I'm writing this while everybody else is running around like a chicken with his head cut off. I'm sitting on deck, listening to shouts and wild traffic and even some gunshots coming from ashore.

I can see further east now—either we're turning, or we're rising fast and can see with a better perspective.

Where central Egypt was, there's a big, raw, dark hole.

The black must be the limestone underlying the desert. They've scraped off a rim of sandy margin enclosing the Nile valley, including us—and left the rest. And somehow, they're lifting it free of Earth.

No Quarthex flying around now. Nothing visible except that metallic blue smear of light high up in the air.

And beyond it—Earth, rising.

Dec. 22

I skipped a day.

There was no time to even think yesterday. After I wrote

the last entry, a crowd of Egyptians came down the quay, shuffling silently along, like the ones we saw back at Abu Simbel. Only there were thousands.

And leading them was a Quarthex. It carried a big disc thing that made a humming sound. When the Quarthex lifted it, the pitch changed.

It made my eyes water, my skull ache. Like a hand squeezing my head, blurring the air.

Around me, everybody was writhing on the deck, moaning. Joanna, too.

By the time the Quarthex reached our ship I was the only one standing. Those yellow-shot, jittery eyes peered at me, giving nothing away. Then the angular head turned and went on. Pied piper, leading long trains of Egyptians.

Some of our friends from the ship joined at the end of the lines. Rigid, glassy-eyed faces. I shouted but nobody, not a single person in that procession, even looked up.

Joanna struggled to go with them. I threw her down and held her until the damned eerie parade was long past.

Now the ship's deserted. We've stayed aboard, out of pure fear.

Whatever the Quarthex did affects all but a few percent of those within range. A few crew stayed aboard, dazed but okay. Scared, hard to talk to.

Fewer at dinner.

The next morning, nobody.

We had to scavenge for food. The crew must've taken what was left aboard. I ventured into the market street nearby, but everything was closed up. Deserted. Only a few days ago we were buying caftans and alabaster sphinxes and beaten-bronze trinkets in the gaudy shops, and now it was stone cold dead. Not a sound, not a stray cat.

I went around to the back of what I remembered was a filthy corner cafe. I'd turned up my nose at it while we were shopping, certain there was a sure case of dysentery waiting inside . . . but now I was glad to find some days-old fruits and vegetables in a cabinet.

Coming back, I nearly ran into a bunch of Egyptian men who were marching through the streets. Spooks.

They had the look of police, but were dressed up like Mardi Gras—loincloths, big leather belts, bangles and beads, hair stiffened with wax. They carried sharp spears.

Good thing I was jumpy, or they'd have run right into me. I heard them coming and ducked into a grubby alley. They were systematically combing the area, searching the miserable apartments above the market. The honcho barked orders in a language I didn't understand—harsh, guttural, not like Egyptian.

I slipped away. Barely.

We kept out of sight after that. Stayed below deck and waited for nightfall.

Not that the darkness made us feel any better. There were fires ashore. Not in Aswan itself—the town was utterly black. Instead, orange dots sprinkled the distant hillsides. They were all over the scrub desert, just before the ramparts of the real desert that stretches—or did stretch—to east and west.

Now, I guess, there's only a few dozen miles of desert, before you reach—what?

I can't discuss this with Joanna. She has that haunted expression, from the time before her breakdown. She is drawn and silent. Stays in the room.

We ate our goddamn vegetables. Now we go to bed.

Dec. 23

There were more of those patrols of Mardi Gras spooks today. They came along the quay, looking at the tour ships moored there, but for some reason they didn't come aboard.

We're alone on the ship. All the crew, the other tourists— all gone.

But that's not the big news. Around noon, when we were getting really hungry and I was mustering my courage to go back to the market street, I heard a roaring.

Understand, I hadn't heard an airplane in days. And those were jets. This buzzing, I suddenly realized, is a rocket or something, and it's in trouble.

I go out on the deck, checking first to see if the patrols are lurking around, and the roaring is louder. It's a plane with stubby little wings, coming along low over the water, burping and hacking and finally going dead quiet.

It nosed over and came in for a big splash. I thought the pilot was a goner, but the thing rode steady in the water for a while and the cockpit folded back and out jumps a man.

I yelled at him and he waved and swam for the ship. The plane sank.

He caught a line below and climbed up. An American, no less. But what he had to say was even more surprising.

He wasn't just some sky jockey from Cairo. He was an astronaut.

He was part of a rescue mission, sent up to try to stop the Quarthex. The others he'd lost contact with, although it looked like they'd all been drawn down toward the floating island that Egypt has become.

We're suspended about two Earth radii out, in a slowly widening orbit. There's a shield over us, keeping the air in and everything—cosmic rays, communications, space-ships—out.

The Quarthex somehow ripped off a layer of Egypt and are lifting it free of Earth, escaping with it. Nobody had ever guessed they had such power. Nobody Earthside knows what to do about it. The Quarthex who were outside Egypt at the time just lifted off in their ships and rendezvoused with this floating platform.

Ralph Blanchard is his name, and his mission was to fly under the slab of Egypt, in a fast orbital craft. He was supposed to see how they'd ripped the land free. A lot of it had fallen away.

There was an array of silvery pods under the soil, he says, and they must be enormous anti-grav units. The same kind that make the Quarthex ships fly, and that we've been trying to get the secret of.

The pods are about a mile apart, making a grid. But between them, there are lots of Quarthex. They're building stuff, tilling soil and so on—upside down! The gravity works opposite on the underside. That must be the way the whole thing is kept together—compressing it with artificial gravity from both sides. God knows what makes the shield above.

But the really strange thing is the Nile. There's one on the underside, too.

It starts at the underside of Alexandria, where *our* Nile meets—met—the Mediterranean. It then flows back, all the way along the underside, running through a Nile valley of its own. Then it turns up and around the edge of the slab, and comes over the lip of it a few hundred miles upstream of here.

The Quarthex have drained the region beyond the Aswan dam. Now the Nile flows in its old course. The big temples of Rameses II are perched on a hill high above the river, and Ralph was sure he saw Quarthex working on the site, taking it apart.

He thinks they're going to put it back where it was, before the dam was built in the 1960s.

Ralph was supposed to return to Orbital City with his data. He came in close for a final pass and hit the shield they have, the one that keeps the air in. His ship was damaged.

He'd been issued a suborbital craft, able to do reentries, in case he could penetrate the airspace. That saved him. There were other guys who hit the shield and cracked through, guys with conventional deep-space shuttle tugs and the like, and they fell like bricks.

We've talked all this over but no one has a good theory of what is going on. The best we can do is stay away from the patrols.

Meanwhile, Joanna scavenged through obscure bins of the ship, and turned up an entire case of Skivaa, a cheap Egyptian beer. So after I finish this ritual entry—who knows, this might be in a history book someday, and as a good academic I should keep it up—I'll go share it out in one grand bust with Ralph and Joanna. It'll do her good. She's been rocky. As well,

> Malt does more than Milton can
> To justify God's ways to man.

Dec. 24

This little diary was all I managed to take with us when the spooks came. I had it in my pocket.

I keep going over what happened. There was nothing I could do, I'm sure of that, and yet . . .

We stayed below decks, getting damned hungry again but afraid to go out. There was chanting from the distance. Getting louder. Then footsteps aboard. We retreated to the small cabins aft, third class.

The sounds got nearer. Ralph thought we should stand and fight but I'd seen those spears and hell, I'm a middle-aged man, no match for those maniacs.

Joanna got scared. It was like her breakdown. No, worse. The jitters built until her whole body seemed to vibrate, fingers digging into her hair like claws, eyes squeezed tight, face compressed as if to shut out the world.

There was nothing I could do with her, she wouldn't keep quiet. She ran out of the cabin we were hiding in, just rushed down the corridor screaming at them.

Ralph said we should use her diversion to get away and I said I'd stay, help her, but then I saw them grab her and hold her, not rough. It didn't seem as if they were going to do anything, just take her away.

My fear got the better of me then. It's hard to write this. Part of me says I should've stayed, defended her—but it was hopeless. You can't live up to your ideal self. The world of literature shows people summoning up courage, but there's a thin line between that and stupidity. Or so I tell myself.

The spooks hadn't seen us yet, so we slipped overboard, keeping quiet.

We went off the loading ramp on the river side, away from shore. Ralph paddled around to see the quay and came back looking worried. There were spooks swarming all over.

We had to move. The only way to go was across the river.

This shaky handwriting is from sheer, flat-out fatigue. I swam what seemed like forever. The water wasn't bad, pretty warm, but the current kept pushing us off course. Lucky thing the Nile is pretty narrow there, and there are rocky little stubs sticking out. I grabbed onto those and rested.

Nobody saw us, or at least they didn't do anything about it.

We got ashore looking like drowned rats. There's a big hill there, covered with ancient rock-cut tombs. I thought of taking shelter in one of them and started up the hill, my legs wobbly under me, and then we saw a mob up there.

And a Quarthex, a big one with a shiny shell. It wore something over its head, too. Supposedly Quarthex don't wear clothes, but this one had a funny rig on. A big bird head, with a long narrow beak and flinty black eyes.

There was madness all around us. Long lines of people carrying burdens, chanting. Quarthex riding on those lifter units of theirs. All beneath the piercing, biting sun.

We hid for a while. I found that this diary, in its zippered leather case, made it through the river without a leak. I started writing this entry. Joanna said once that I'd retreated into books as a defense, in adolescence. She was full of psychoanalytical explanations—it was a hobby. She kept thinking that if she could figure herself out, then things would be all right. Well, maybe I did use words and books and a quiet, orderly life as a place to hide. So what? It was better than this "real" world around me right now.

I thought of Joanna and what might be happening to her. The Quarthex can—

New Entry

I was writing when the Quarthex came closer. I thought we were finished, but they didn't see us. Those huge heads turned all the time, the glittering black eyes scanning. Then they moved away. The chanting was a relentless, singsong drone that gradually faded.

We got away from there, fast.

I'm writing this during a short break. Then we'll move on.

No place to go but the goddamn desert.

Dec. 25

Christmas.

I keep thinking about fat turkey stuffed with spicy dressing, crisp cranberries, a dry white wine, thick gravy—

No point in that. We found some food today in an abandoned construction site, bread at least a week old and some dried-up fruit. That was all.

Ralph kept pushing me on west. He wants to see over the edge, how they hold this thing together.

I'm not that damn interested, but I don't know where else to go. Just running on blind fear. My professorial instincts— like keeping this journal. It helps keep me sane. Assuming I still am.

Ralph says putting this down might have scientific value. If I can ever get it to anybody outside. So I keep on. Words, words, words. Much cleaner than this gritty, surreal world.

We saw people marching in the distance, dressed in loincloths again. It suddenly struck me that I'd seen that clothing before—in those marvelous wall paintings, in the tombs of the Valley of Kings. It's ancient dress.

Ralph thinks he understands what's happening. There was an all-frequencies broadcast from the Quarthex when they tore off this wedge we're on. Nobody understood much— it was in that odd semi-speech of theirs, all the words blurred and placed wrong, scrambled up. Something about their mission or destiny or whatever being to enhance the best in each world. About how they'd made a deal with the Egyptians to bring forth the unrealized promise of their majestic past and so on. And that meant isolation, so the fruit of ages could flower.

Ha. The world's great age begins anew, maybe—but Percy Bysshe Shelley never meant it like this.

Not that I care a lot about motivations right now. I spent the day thinking of Joanna, still feeling guilty. And hiking west in the heat and dust, hiding from gangs of glassy-eyed workers when we had to.

We reached the edge at sunset. It hadn't occurred to me, but it's obvious—for there to be days and nights at all means they're spinning the slab we're on.

Compressing it, holding in the air, adding just the right rotation. Masters—of space/time and the river, yes.

The ground started to slope away. Not like going downhill, because there was nothing pulling you down the face of it. I mean, we *felt* like we were walking on level ground. But overhead the sky moved as we walked.

We caught up with the sunset. The sun dropped for a while in late afternoon, then it started rising again. Pretty soon it was right overhead, high noon.

And we could see Earth, too, farther away than yesterday. Looking cool and blue.

We came to a wall of glistening metal tubes, silvery and rippling with a frosty blue glow. I started to get woozy as we approached. Something happened to gravity—it pulled your stomach as if you were spinning around. Finally we couldn't get any closer. I stopped, nauseated. Ralph kept on. I watched him try to walk toward the metal barrier, which by then looked like luminous icebergs suspended above barren desert.

He tried to walk a straight line, he said later. I could see him veer, his legs rubbery, and it looked as though he rippled and distended, stretching horizontally while some force compressed him vertically, an egg man, a plastic body swaying in tides of gravity.

Then he started stumbling, falling. He cried out—a horrible, warped sound, like paper tearing for a long, long time. He fled. The sand clawed at him as he ran, strands grasping at his feet, trailing long streamers of glittering, luminous sand—but it couldn't hold him. Ralph staggered away, gasping, his eyes huge and white and terrified.

We turned back.

But coming away, I saw a band of men and women marching woodenly along toward the wall. They were old, most of them, and diseased. Some had been hurt—you could see the wounds.

They were heading straight for the lip. Silent, inexorable.

Ralph and I followed them for a while. As they approached, they started walking up off the sand—right into the air.

And over the tubes.

Just flying.

We decided to head south. Maybe the lip is different there. Ralph says the plan he'd heard, after the generals had studied the fast survey mission results, was to try to open the shield at the ground, where the Nile spills over. Then they'd get people out by boating them along the river.

Could they be doing that, now? We hear roaring sounds in the sky sometimes. Explosions. Ralph is ironic about it all, says he wonders when the Quarthex will get tired of intruders and go back to the source—*all* the way back.

I don't know. I'm tired and worn down.

Could there be a way out? Sounds impossible, but it's all we've got.

Head south, to the Nile's edge.

We're hiding in a cave tonight. It's bitterly cold out here in the desert, and a sunburn is no help.

I'm hungry as hell. Some Christmas.

We were supposed to be back in Laguna Beach by now. God knows where Joanna is.

Dec. 26

I got away. Barely.

The Quarthex work in teams now. They've gridded off the desert and work across it systematically in those floating platforms. There are big tubes like cannon mounted on each end and a Quarthex scans it over the sands.

Ralph and I crept up to the mouth of the cave we were in and watched them comb the area. They worked out from the Nile. When a muzzle turned toward us I felt an impact like a warm, moist wave smacking into my face, for all the world like being in the ocean. It drove me to my knees. I reeled away. Threw myself further back into the cramped cave.

It all dropped away then, as if the wave had pinned me to the ocean floor and filled my lungs with a sluggish liquid.

And in an instant was gone. I rolled over, gasping, and saw Ralph staggering into the sunlight, heading for the Quarthex platform. The projector was leveled at him so that it no longer struck the cave mouth. So I'd been released from its grip.

I watched them lower a rope ladder. Ralph dutifully climbed up. I wanted to shout to him, try to break the hold that thing had over him, but once again the better part of valor and all that—I just watched. They carried him away.

I waited until twilight to move. Not having anybody to talk to makes it harder to control my fear.

God, I'm hungry. Couldn't find a scrap to eat.

When I took out this diary I looked at the leather case and remembered stories of people getting so starved they'd eat their shoes. Suitably boiled and salted, of course, with a tangy sauce.

Another day or two and the idea might not seem so funny.

I've got to keep moving.

Dec. 27

Hard to write.

They got me this morning.

It grabs your mind. Like before. Squeezing in your head.

But after a while it is better. Feels good. But a buzzing all the time, you can't think.

Picked me up while I was crossing an arroyo. Didn't have any idea they were around. A platform.

Took me to some others. All Egyptians. Been caught like me.

Marched us to the Nile.

Plenty to eat.

Rested at noon.

Brought Joanna to me. She is all right. Lovely in the long draping dress the Quarthex gave her.

All around are the bird-headed ones. Ibis, I remember, the bird of the Nile. And dog-headed ones. Lion-headed ones.

Gods of the old times. The Quarthex are the gods of the old time. Of the great empire.

We are the people.

Sometimes I can think, like now. They sent me away from the work gang on an errand. I am old, not strong. They are kind—give me easy jobs.

So I came to here. Where I hid this diary. Before they took my old uncomfortable clothes I put this little book into a crevice in the rock. Pen too.

Now writing helps. Mind clears some.

I saw Ralph, then lost track of him. I worked hard after the noontime. Sun felt good. I lifted pots, carried them where the foreman said.

The Quarthex-god with ibis head is building a fresh temple. Made from the stones of Aswan. It will be cool and deep, many pillars.

They took my dirty clothes. Gave me fresh loincloth, headband, sandals. Good ones. Better than my old clothes.

It is hard to remember how things were before I came here. Before I knew the river. Its flow. How it divides the world.

I will rest before I try to read what I have written in here before. The words are hard.

days later

I come back but can read only a little.

Joanna says You should not. The ibis will not like if I do.

I remember I liked these words on paper, in my days before. I earned my food with them. Now they are empty. Must not have been true.

I do not need them any more.

Ralph and his science. It was all words too.

later

Days since I find this again. I do the good work, I eat, Joanna is there in the night. Many things. I do not want to do this reading.

But today another thing howled overhead. It passed over the desert like a screaming black bird, the falcon, and then fell, flames, big roar.

I remembered Ralph.

This book I remembered, came for it.

The ibis-god speaks to us each sunset. Of how the glory of our lives is here again. We are one people once more again yes after a long long time of being lost.

What the red sunset means. The place where the dead are buried in the western desert. To be taken in death close to the edge, so the dead will walk their last steps in this world, to the lip and over, to the netherworld.

There the lion-god will preserve them. Make them live again.

The Quarthex-gods have discovered how to revive the dead of any beings. They spread this among the stars.

But only to those who understand. Who deserve. Who bow to the great symmetry of life.

One face light, one face dark.

The sun lights the netherworld when for us it is night. There the dead feast and mate and laugh and live forever.

Ralph saw that. The happy land below. It shares the sun.

I saw Ralph today. He came to the river to see the falcon thing cry from the clouds. We all did.

It fell into the river and was swallowed and will be taken to the netherworld where it flows over the edge of the world.

Ralph was sorry when the falcon fell. He said it was a mistake to send it to bother us. That someone from the old dead time had sent it.

Ralph works in the quarry. Carving the limestone. He looks good, the sun has lain on him and made him strong and brown.

I started to talk of the time we met but he frowned.

That was before we understood, he says. Shook his head. So I should not speak of it I know.

The gods know of time and the river. They know.

I tire now.

again

Joanna sick. I try help but no way to stop the bleeding from her.

In old time I would try to stop the stuff of life from leaving her. I would feel sorrow.

I do not now. I am calm.

Ibis-god prepares her. Works hard and good over her.

She will journey tonight. Walk the last trek. Over the edge of the sky and to the netherland.

It is what the temple carving says. She will live again forever.

Forever waits.

I come here to find this book to enter this. I remember sometimes how it was.

I did not know joy then. Joanna did not.

We lived but to no point. Just come-go-come-again.

Now I know what comes. The western death. The rising life.

The Quarthex-gods are right. I should forget that life. To hold on is to die. To flow forward is to life.

Today I saw the pharaoh. He came in radiant chariot, black horses before, bronze sword in hand. The sun was high above him. No shadow he cast.

Big and with red skin the pharaoh rode down the avenue of the kings. We the one people cheered.

His great head was mighty in the sun and his many arms waved in salute to his one people. He is so great the horses groan and sweat to pull him. His hard gleaming body is all armor for he will always be on guard against our enemies.

Like those who fall from the sky. Every day now more come down, dying fireballs to smash in the desert. All fools. Black rotting bodies. None will rise to walk west. They are only burned prey of the pharaoh.

hhaoh rodethree times on the avenue. We threw ourselves down to attract a glance. His huge glaring eyes regarded us and we cried out, our faces wet with joy.

He will speak for us in the netherworld. Sing to the undergods.

Make our westward walking path smooth.

I fall before him.

I bury this now. No more write in it.

This kind of writing is not for the world now. It comes from the old dead time when I knew nothing and thought everything.

I go to my eternity on the river.

Cross Indiana Jones with Captain Kirk—
for a swashbuckling hero whose
exploits span the stars!

Dr. Bones™

series!

His name is Dr. Bones. His adventures take him across the galaxy in search of lost cities, secret empires, and vanished species. And sometimes into exploits less peaceful than that, when his background makes him the only man for a dangerous job...

__BOOK 4: THE DRAGONS OF KOMAKO
John Gregory Betancourt 0-441-15671-1/$3.50
__BOOK 5: NIGHTMARE WORLD David Stern
0-441-15669-X/$3.50
__BOOK 6: JOURNEY TO RILLA Thomas Wylde
0-441-15678-9/$3.50

© Byron Preiss Visual Publications, Inc.